Praise for *Open Visa*

"This is a very moving and readable book detailing with the hassles, trials and successes of real people. I expect that new as well as prospective immigrants, especially care givers, will find it informative and valuable because of its many themes: separation from family and loved ones, adjusting to a new culture, difficult employers, coping with loneliness and temptation, unscrupulous lovers, infidelity, the value of wise counsel, integrity, hard work, and support of family, caring friends and church fellowship."

ARLEIGH PORTE
Ph. D. Registered Psychologist

"As an immigration lawyer I see the paperwork and the problem with Immigration Canada. This book completes the whole picture. Romeo gives you an intimate look into the daily lives of new immigrants and foreign workers. A must-read if you are coming to Canada."

IRMA ROBERTS

"This book has really captivated my heart because it depicts typical stories, struggles and successes of caregivers like me. I recommend this book because the stories are great, very inspiring and full of courage."

JASMIN REMOQUILLO
Filipino-Canadian Princess of Songs (Alberta)

"It is actually very inspiring book depicting the lives, challenges and successes of Overseas Filipino Workers around the world. As a caregiver for many years before and, coming from a third world country, one wouldn't recognize that we are a valuable member of society wherever we are in the world until you read this book. These people are the heroes of today."

MYRA MORILLO
Registered Nurse

"An intriguing story with many twists and turns about what Filipino citizens, especially women, face when leaving their homeland in order to seek to provide for their families. Ultimately, it points to Jesus as the answer. Be braced to learn about cultural views and adaptations with a surprise ending!"

H. WILSON NELSON, D. MIN.

OPEN Visa

A Novel

Dear Dixon,

Your support to the Philippines
is very much appreciated.

Bless your heart!

Romeo Honorio

ISBN: 978-1-77069-269-5

Printed in Canada

Word Alive Press
131 Cordite Road, Winnipeg, MB R3W 1S1
www.wordalivepress.ca

Library and Archives Canada Cataloguing in Publication

Honorio, Romeo
    Open visa / Romeo Honorio.

ISBN 978-1-77069-269-5

    I. Title.

PS8615.O502O64 2011   C813'.6   C2011-901687-7

Dedication

This book is heartily dedicated to countless overseas foreign workers and caregivers scattered around the world. In their pursuit of a better life abroad, no amount of discouragement and ill will can stop them from moving on. The amount of service, sacrifice and care they afford to others is immeasurable. They deserve commendation, recognition, and appreciation. They are, indeed, the new heroes of today's fast-paced world and care-deficient society.

Caregiver. Nanny? Whatever!

Feeling so great, options out there are many
Leaving the school to the world of reality
Oh yes, here I come, observe, watch, and see
My passion and role, a noble responsibility

Countless kids of wealthy families, alone and crying
Seniors' and retirees' hands on the wheelchair gripping
Handicapped and disabled waiting for support and care
Where to turn to? Seems no one's available out there

> I'm your caregiver, nanny, or whatever
> Hands ready to support, nurture, and care
> Who else but me looking for your welfare
> My passion, skills, and talents to offer

Diapers just wet, baby food in your face—yucky!
After years of caring, no longer a bubbling teeny tiny
Your mom's away and dad's working overtime
I'm always on your side, don't you ever worry

Walking cane needs adjustment, bed sheets need laundry
Here's your eyeglass, Granny, our bingo time is at three
Oh yes, sir, that arthritis and pain in your ankle and knee
Pop those pills down, just do it my friend, do you hear me?

Chapter 1

"Assembly time is 8:00. We have to be there by 7:45," Lily said while adjusting her shawl and gown. "How do I look?"

"I can't believe it. You look so pretty in that gown," replied Nora.

The gym was two blocks away from their three-story dormitory. The morning rush was so frantic—tricycles, jeeps, and even those nasty, smoke-belching Baliwag Transit buses were cluttering the narrow Del Pilar Street. A block away, east of the dormitory, was the Provincial Capital. As usual, both the front and back alleys of the building smelled of brewed coffee and the faces of zombie-like bureaucrats were everywhere, coming in and out of the edifice.

It was a special day for Lily and Nora. Tomorrow they would be graduating from the Philippine's Wesleyan University. Nora's dreams of becoming a social worker were finally coming to fruition.

What a noble way of helping street people, Lily thought. As for herself, her passion came from her mother's experience of giving birth to her. After years of sweat and toil, today was the moment she'd been waiting for. She would be one of those heroine midwifes so highly respected by the expectant moms visiting their village's delivery room.

The gym was packed with people from all over the province. The scent of flowers dominated the hall. Parents were excited to witness their sons and daughters marching toward their assigned rows of chairs. While that heartbreaking graduation march played, Lily's mind had nowhere to settle. The little village clinic in her hometown was on her mind, and she was visualizing the role she played there as the savior of all birthing mothers.

"Wake up, Lily," said another graduate to her left. "Your name was called. Get up and receive your diploma."

From the stage, she clearly recognized her mom and dad in the audience way at the back of the auditorium, waving and wiping their teary eyes.

"Thank God I made it," were the only words uttered while she headed back to her assigned chair after taking the diploma.

—

"So where are you going to work?" inquired Nora as they mingled around in the midst of the zoo-like gym.

"I'm not quite sure yet," Lily replied. "Mike is urging me to work with him in the Middle East, so we can be together."

It had been three years since Mike had started working in Jeddah, Saudi Arabia. Their short-lived high school romance had been made even shorter when Mike's need to work abroad became apparent. His family was dependent on the money he would earn, and supporting a family of nine was a big task for him. He was the eldest of the seven kids.

"I suppose a month-long rest is enough time for me to settle down and focus on what to do next," Lily said with a sigh.

"A friend of mine was telling me of a job opportunity working with kids in Mindanao," Nora said. "These kids have been orphaned by the never-ending struggle between the Muslim separatists and the government. I suppose this is my big break."

Nora's family couldn't do anything about her decision. They had no choice but to allow Nora to hit the road. Her family depended on farming. Their three hectares of rice paddy was not enough to pay for her education. Opportunities were out there, but she had to be swift in claiming them.

As they entered the Bake Shoppe along Paco Roman Street, one of the city's best restaurants, tables were ready and waiters were on hand to take their orders. Coming from a religious family, Ka Oscar, Lily's dad, said grace over the food and everyone around the table started excitedly talking about everything under the sun.

Only the arrival of the food was enough to slow down the conversation.

"Mike sent me an open-dated ticket to Jeddah," Lily said as her mom took a sip of iced tea. "When I'm ready, I can fly to Saudi Arabia to be with him anytime. He told me about an opportunity there to work in a hospital near his workplace. I applied for the job."

"He's from a good family," her mom said in a persuasive voice. "Your *tatay* and I have no objection to your plan to work together abroad. However, wouldn't it be nice if Mike could take a holiday here before setting your wedding date?"

"I'll call him tonight and discuss the matter," Lily commented.

"So what part of Mindanao are you going to, Nora?" Lily's dad said as all their eyes shifted to the other graduate. Lily was very much aware that this was just her *tatay's* way of changing the subject.

"Cagayan de Oro, po," she replied.

The spaghetti was salty and not particularly good, but the thin-sliced sausages and clumsy red beans were delicious. The place was packed with hungry people of all sizes, shapes, and smells.

It was just about 2:30 in the afternoon when the tip was handed to the server and the group headed out to the graduates' dormitory. A regular thirty-minute walk turned into a forty-minute ride on a tricycle, due to heavy traffic.

Their bags were packed, their bills were paid, and the place was relatively clean for the next year's students. For years, through thick and thin, Lily and Nora had established a sense of unique identity in the building. At their age, it was uncommon to still be serious, courageous, and dedicated to something they were passionate about. Being away from home had molded and developed their characters. Now, they resolved to prove themselves in the real world. Their focus to survive, strength to succeed, and hope to live at peace with the community was evident in the way they dealt with others.

Their education had been just a tool to fully understand and appreciate life in its reality and entirety. Now that they were on their own—both showing a degree of excitement, and sometimes anxiety—Nora's trip to Mindanao would be like an experiment in osmosis, a salt particle plunging into a tub of uncertainty. This was the vision Lily had of her friend's upcoming trip to head south the following month.

Lily's own planned trip to return home consisted of a three-hour drive from Cabanatuan City to Cuyapo. Ford Fiera jeeps had been servicing the outlying towns of the province for more than ten years and there had been no sign of any improvement in the quality of the ride; the drivers were more concerned with squeezing in as many passengers as possible than making the ride a comfortable one.

They stepped off the jeep to the sight of a hundred pairs of eyes excitedly awaiting their arrival. They were treated like movie stars. It was a village-wide celebration. The *lechon* (roasted pig) was crispy outside and tender inside. The day was set aside to celebrate Lily's graduation with her relatives, friends, neighbours, and bystanders. *Puto* (rice cakes) were really tasty both with *sopas* (congee) and *dinuguan* (chocolate pork stew). People had to wait and stand behind the group feasting on the food at the table. It took almost three hours for every soul present to feel good, thankful and expectant of the next celebration in the village.

As they settled in for a coffee, Ka Oscar, Lily's dad, a well-known and respected elder, stood up before the crowd. Out of respect, and most likely due to the calming effect of the food consumed, all ears were tuned to him as he spoke.

"For your support and prayers for my family, and for my daughter in particular, I would like to thank you all. Also, thank you for coming and sharing with us this joyous day." This was the only audible sentence to those listening. Black coffee kept the people's minds alert but unready to hear more. Nonetheless, he continued, "Now I would like to call on a friend wishing to congratulate Lily."

It was unusual for this kind of gathering to have anyone speak who was outside the family circle. From behind the Acacia tree fifteen meters away, a man came out in a Ray Ban ball cap. He was heavily bearded and almost unrecognizable. It took about ten seconds before Lily's heart pumped to its fullest throttle. It was Mike! The blood rushed to her head and her heart thumped as if she was experiencing indigestion.

"*Siya ba and boyfriend ni Lily?*" was the question floating through the crowd as Mike and Lily shared a kiss. People were astounded by the sweetness of their kiss and the joy in their teary eyes.

"You surprised me," she whispered to Mike. "You didn't mention you were coming home the last time we talked."

"I just wanted to make sure you had the most unforgettable celebration of your life," he said, his fingers combing the back of Lily's hair.

Everybody stood still and waited for another scoop. The spark of their meeting was so intense that they forgot people were watching them. It took a while before Mike composed himself.

"There are three things I would like to say to Lily," he said loudly enough for everyone to hear. "First, congratulations. Second, I wish you the best tomorrow. Third, I love you. Will you marry me?"

It had turned out to be more than a graduation celebration for Lily; now she also had to make a very important decision. Her smile and tears were enough to convince Mike of her answer.

—

A week after the celebration, Mike flew back to Saudi Arabia, leaving Lily with a hope that someday they would be together for good—if not in the Philippines, then elsewhere abroad.

For Lily, the reality of her life after graduation was unfamiliar territory. Her first week at work was uneventful. The birth of her cousin's fifth child, weighing nine and a half pounds, was the only remarkable and outstanding event. The community was happy and proud to see one of their own delivering babies for all moms, young and old alike. A sense of satisfaction and fulfillment was evident on Lily's face when she delivered the child.

However, that satisfaction was short-lived. Her need for a companion, and the surge of her biological functions, was growing intense. She had Mike in her heart, but he was too far away for them to truly be together. Mike's monthly letters were not enough to quench her longing for him.

"I have to find a way to be with him," she told the head midwife at the village's delivery room. The woman was both her workplace supervisor and her closest confidante. To gain insight, Lily brought to her the issues of her life.

"What about applying to one of the hospitals in the Middle East?" the head midwife responded.

Lily's application had been forwarded to the Overseas Employment Centre in Manila. Mike, on the other hand, was busy looking for a job opening for Lily in the Middle East. Besides, the open-dated ticket was still securely tucked away in one of her purses. She could use it any time opportunity knocked.

In the last two years, fifteen boys and twenty-five girls had been delivered by Lily's caring hands. Half of the baby girls had been named after her. The rest had been named using her suggestions to the moms. The appreciation and trust of the moms was so profound that most of them requested Lily be their child's godmother, or at least one of the sponsors to their christening. Her name's fragrance spilled over to other villages, towns, and even neighbouring provinces. People seldom heard of more extraordinary service and care provided to expectant mothers. She was the best. Referrals were flying left, right, and from all directions.

It took a long time before she received a response to her application from the hospital in the Middle East where Mike wanted her to work. The application process was a little bit strict and confusing. The moment she gave focus and attention to the process, the harder she found it to detach herself from her work and passion for the local mothers who needed her. The honor and respect accorded to her by the community was not only a motivation to stay, it was a passion to sustain. Though her income was not as high as she wanted it to be, the comfort, flexibility, and peace she had been experiencing was somewhat hard to ignore.

Also interesting was that Mike's contact with her via letter, and even phone calls, was becoming few and far between. The usual thirty-minute talks they had started out with were now only three to five phrases in length. With the sparks gone, traveling to be with him was a big decision.

The decision to leave her comfortable rural life for an unknown, restricted, and culture-shocking environment was a perplexing and complicated one. Haphazard assessments of the situation could do her more harm than good in the long run.

Marieta, one of her client moms who operated one of the bakeries south of the village, was very cautious and open in sharing her wisdom with respect to Lily's plan of moving to Jeddah. It was a well-known fact that Marieta's bakery business was the fruit of her ten-year labor in Kuwait. She told Lily that her future rested upon how well she and Mike fared with their work and career in the Middle East. Finally, after her last sip of iced tea, Lily's mind was clear. Moving to Saudi Arabia was just the first stepping stone to the brighter and more challenging life ahead.

She would go.

—

People plowing the field, women doing their laundry in a river-bank, and school children were not able to attend her send-off party. Most of the moms in the village were present and happily sharing with each other their most unforgettable labor experiences, and whatever anecdotes came to their minds with respect to motherhood.

Lily's farewell speech revolved around her village life. The community was her life, passion, and inspiration for living. The community was where she had found the purpose and reason to pursue a higher and nobler calling. However, it was also in this community where she had realized that a person's destiny was neither given nor accepted. She was fully convinced that her future was at hand.

With a sad note, she inspired the group by promising to leave a legacy to them—a legacy that the moms would never forget and that young people would always appreciate. If she could achieve success later in life, her visits back to the village would become a regular thing, footprints of something significant that could be built in their village.

Lily had to move on. She packed two traveling bags almost as big as she was and a carry-on bag with all the paraphernalia she would need to relocate to the Middle East. Her departure was a very emotional moment for her family, friends, coworkers, and scores of mothers.

The flight was less interesting. Aside from the tourists, who were comfortably tucked away in the plane's business class section, the cabin was occupied by Pinoys—other Filipinos. So much excitement and anxiety were painted in the faces around her. For those who were returning from their holidays, the trip was just an ordinary affair. The food served was more of an exception than the norm; Lily was having difficulty remembering the names of the items on the menu. All that remained in her head was the smell of curry-based chicken served with sticky buns.

It was late in the afternoon when the plane landed, six hours after it had taken off from Manila. The horizon was lit brightly with neon lights. Jeddah's airport was bigger than Manila's. The forecast upon arrival was sunny and a sweltering twenty-nine degrees. As she had never left the Philippines before, it was too hot for her. The cleanliness of the airport was obvious, though. All the people around her were waiting with great anticipation for their arriving love ones.

It took Lily ten minutes to make her way from the tarmac to the baggage claim. Mike was nowhere in her sight. She had confirmed with him her flight number and arrival time twice. Her grumbling stomach was becoming louder, begging for something to eat—anything, as long as it was substantial. With her carry-on bag in one hand, it was going to be impossible for her to haul her other two large bags, which were coming out of the chute.

"Where in the world is Mike?" she murmured.

When she grabbed the brown luggage with her name printed on the side, a hand from behind snatched it away from her. Her surprise was replaced with a smile when Mike's face appeared inches away from her own. She sensed Mike was tempted to kiss her, but he held himself back, given the strict laws governing how men and women behaved around each other in public. Talk was kept to a minimum. Though it was hard, they managed to act as if they were both newcomers to the city. Mike just whispered to call her later. Tears and a nod were Lily's only responses.

Her shuttle bus was waiting outside. Minutes later, she left airport without fanfare. Traffic was not as crazy as it had been in Manila. After her shuttle was on its way, Mike headed back to his company's headquarters.

The name of her housing unit was Rawalah, a women-only compound nestled inside the King Fahad National Guard Hospital campus. While waiting in line, she learned from one of the welcoming receptionists that Filipino foreign workers accounted for more than sixty percent of the women living there.

After registering her name at the reception booth, she was directed to proceed to a room where all the other medical recruits were gathered. The orientation meeting lasted two hours and in no time they were dismissed to their assigned rooms.

The day following orientation was Friday, a free day, a time dedicated to getting unpacked and settling in.

"Now, what am I going to eat?" she asked in response to her hungry stomach. She remembered Mike had given her a bag of food items during their meeting in the airport.

"He's so thoughtful. He knows what I need," she whispered with a sigh. She searched for more items that he might have stuck into her bags. Everything was cleared and accounted for—there was no more food to satisfy her hunger.

Because she was still suffering from jetlag, she needed an extra hour of sleep. Her eyelids were getting heavier with each passing moment. Her tired legs led her to the edge of the bed. The temptation to sleep was strong. The pillow and blanket were warm and inviting. Her only option left was to say yes. In less than five minutes, her eyes closed.

The alarm clock was set to go off at 6:45 in the morning.

Time and discipline were two important allies she had relied on for many years. Up she went to the kitchen and figured out what to eat. She decided on a meat loaf and scrambled eggs for breakfast. Once she was fed, she could think about unpacking.

After putting away her things, she decided to familiarize herself with her surroundings.

Before she could get going, her cell phone rang.

"How was your night?" Mike's voice asked from the other end of the line. "Did you get a good night's sleep or are you still adjusting?" He promised to buy her enough groceries to last her two weeks.

Their conversation was interrupted by a loud knock at Lily's door. Mike said goodbye as Lily stood, walked to the door, and opened it. A young lady with a big smile stood waiting for her. Her teeth were white and her dimples were deep. Lily reciprocated the smile and gestured for her to come in and sit down. Without hesitation, they both went straight to the dining table where the remnants of Lily's breakfast were scattered around.

The woman's name was Mary, and she had been a midwife at the hospital for five years. When she had found out that another Filipina midwife was arriving, her excitement was intense. No wonder she hadn't been able to wait to see Lily, taking fifteen minutes of her break to do it. Mary was staying in one of the housing units, Medical City, situated north of the hospital. Their talked revolved around how Lily could adjust better and faster to her workload and new environment.

It became apparent that Mary was to be her mentor for the day. That fifteen-minute break was so fruitful for Lily, and not only for gathering work-related information; Mary hinted at the many things in the compound which were to be avoided—like being friends with the wrong kind of people, the kind of people who were just looking for flings. These types of women didn't seem to care about fidelity. Whether single or married, they liked to hang around with other guys into the wee hours of the night. In a number of cases, other nurses snuck in and out of the men's quarters. Not only was their work perform-ance affected, but also their families back home.

The hospital compound was vast and well-kept. As the newest recruit, Lily was trying to figure out the configuration and locations of all the buildings. She was assigned to a unit located at the east end of Rawalah. Her room was spacious, but the aura of the previous occupant, which could be traced by scent, was still there. Curry, indeed! A small outdoor deck overlooked the north entrance of the hospital; it was a good spot to unwind and find solace. All in all, it was definitely a more convenient place to live than her old digs in the Philip-pines. However, the suite was just her temporary home, she was told. She would soon be moving to another room with three other Filipinas. She thought this arrangement would be better than the one she was in. She longed for a warm body to talk to. Staying alone in that room was not the best situation for her.

After days of being alone, the matron finally handed her the key to her new place. She knew better now what to do in terms of moving, packing, and unpacking her things. Lily had to do the moving swiftly to avoid noise and embarrassment during the process.

She carefully opened the door, trying not to disturb the occupants of the other rooms. Disturbing them so early in the afternoon, naptime, on a Saturday would not get their friend-ships off to a good start. In no time, Lily was able to carry out her belongings into the corridor. She looked at the key for her new place—the room number was etched into it.

She was able to slickly move all her stuff to her assigned room, which was only five doors down the hall. It was bit easier this time, but she wondered why there wasn't any noise from people waking up coming out of any of the other rooms. It took Lily half an hour to arrange her new room and again unpack her belongings. When everything was in its place, she once again made the decision to explore. She put on her slippers and slowly went outside her room.

The names Karen, Kay, and Elvie were hanging along the mirror at the right side of the closet, just meters away from her door. In the absence of any noise, she concluded that the three women were either out already or somewhere in the hospital working. In the living room, a huge mirror hung on the wall, which was painted pink. The thirty-two inch television was so inviting.

She was surprised when she opened the refrigerator. It was full to the brim. On top of the range were two pots—the smaller one had rice in it, and the other *adobo*. She wondered why the foods had not even been touched.

At the far left corner of the hall was a room with no name attached to the door. She opened the door. "Not bad!" she said with a sigh. Their pantry was full of enough food to last for at least a week.

As usual, the washroom was full of ladies' paraphernalia. Ladies' shavers were scattered in one corner. The opposite corner was cluttered with different kinds of gel, oil, ointment, and whatever else it took for a woman to feel and look good. When she looked at herself in the mirror, she found specks not from her face. The mirror needed thorough washing. It was splattered with toothpaste.

She was coming out of the washroom when the front door opened. As expected, three women entered the room with wide smile on their faces.

"So, you must be Lily?" Karen asked.

"How was your trip?" added Kay.

"Was the orientation long and boring?" Elvie said, interjecting herself into the conversation.

Take it easy, ladies, thought Lily.

The pots on top of the range, plus the package of food that the three had bought from the hospital restaurant, served as a welcome dinner for the newest member of the group. They were not in a hurry to finish dinner. Everyone was aware that tomorrow was Sunday. This was the best time for them to welcome Lily and establish friendships with her.

Her first weekend consisted of familiarizing herself with her new environment. It was also a time for getting to know her new friends' personalities. These three women were like a newfound family to her.

Karen had grown up in the small town of Bukidnon, in the Philippines. After graduating from college, she had moved to Hong Kong and worked in one of the well-known clinics there for children. Life in the British colony in the early 90s was not pleasant, especially for foreign workers like her. Emotional, physical, and sexual harassment was rampant. Ocean Park was one of the places where she could find refuge and forget the bad experiences of the past week. It was a place of freedom. Karen, just like any other ordinary workers, had been a fixture in and around the sidewalk of the park. It was a common occurrence to see literally hundreds of young women hanging around and killing time with friends. Some brought game boards, others simply sat around gossiping, while others were hoping their dream guy was just around the corner. Once Disneyland Asia, another entertainment destination, was in full swing, the number of Filipinas slumbering in the park dwindled.

Karen had not deemed life worthwhile if she just spent it working for some strange family and during the weekend drowning in an aimless sea of people. Her application to work in Saudi Arabia was accepted shortly after. This was now her third year working with the palliative care unit. She was well-paid and enjoyed the professional environment.

If Hong Kong had its Ocean Park, Singapore was proud to have Sentosa, a place where foreign workers could spend their weekends. Just a few blocks away was Lucky Plaza. As a nanny, Kay's regular visits to this place had become a habit. Her family back home badly needed her financial support. She had a disabled dad and a bedridden mom who had put all their hopes in her. Still, the family was fortunate that Kay had finished her Med Tech degree from the University of St. Tomas before the tragedy that crippled her dad. The university had been founded in the Philippines by a missionary Catholic priest in the late 1800s.

Kay's life was of great interest to Lily. Kay had recently returned to the Philippines for a holiday. While there, she found out the husband she had met and married only two years before was in fact now married to another woman. Without her knowing, the guy was supporting two young children in a private school in Cabanatuan City. Distance, boredom, and biological needs were the most compelling reasons why he had done it.

Lily wondered what would happen to her if this work arrangement with the hospital went on for many years. Though she had been talking to Mike on the phone, the opportunity for them to be together was very slim, even now that she had come to Saudi Arabia. Mike's work was far from normal. He was constantly moving around the country, looking after the operations of the company he worked for.

One Saturday afternoon, Lily's contemplation of events was disrupted when Kay entered the room with tears in her eyes.

"This is it. I'm giving up on this relationship!" Kay said in a trembling voice, talking about her husband in the Philippines. "I can't put up with this guy."

Lily stood, wrapped her arms around Kay's shoulder, and handed her a box of tissues. The sobbing subsided after Lily uttered whispers of assurances.

"I'm sorry to hear that," Lily said. "How can I help you?" Less than thirty minutes later, once Kay was settling down and had told her sad story, Lily found out that Kay's husband was pressuring her to increase the support she was sending to his kids in the Philippines. Lily kept her silence.

The last thing Lily heard from Kay was, "If he can have an affair, then I can, too!"

Lily and Kay were surprised when Elvie appeared at the door just then. She was staring at the two sitting on the couch.

"Is there something wrong?" Elvie asked.

"As expected, my intuition was correct," Kay said with teary eyes. "My husband is married to another woman, and she is five months pregnant. He lost his job and is pressuring me to increase my financial support to him. Bastard!"

"I'm very sorry to hear that. Actually, we included you in our prayer session just a short time ago," Elvie said. She was secretly meeting with other women in one of the rooms in the building for fellowship and prayer. Lily motioned for Elvie to come and sit with them so Kay could feel their comfort and care in her time of distress. Their presence was more than enough to assure Kay of their help and concern for her.

More encouragement followed the conversation. They forgot the time. The most important concern was the time they spent together in this moment of compassion. The night was getting late and the three decided, over a cup of hot tea, to retire to their respective rooms for the night.

The morning was so nice and inviting. Sleeping in was common for them. The earliest to get up was Elvie, and the last one was Kay.

They packed a lunch for their picnic in the park. Their destination was the famous Al Shallal theme park, which was twenty minutes away from the hospital. The park was not only good for hanging around, but also a safe place for them to talk about the challenges and intimate issues of life. Mike came with them.

At the park, Lily took out her cell phone and dialed Mike's number, even though he was just three meters away from her. Their eyes were in constant contact while their fingers moved over the buttons of their respective cell phones. Texting, they called it. Many others in the park were doing the same thing, as if there was a competition underway to see who could text the fastest. Mike and Lily had to be proficient texters in order to avoid wasting valuable time and money.

"I miss u so much"

"Me 2"

"How was ur wk"

"ok"

"Karen & Kay got problem with their husbands"

"Cheating?"

"Yup"

"2 bad"

"wat r u eating"

"veggie stew"

"u?"

"bbq"

"lol"

"yes, lol"

"gtg, ladies go to bathroom"

"ok, cu"

"luv u"

"luv u2"

"txt me later"

"I will"

Once the food was prepared, the group decided to eat quickly so they would have more time to go around and meet new friends.

Their time in the park lasted three hours. Just like everyone else, when the park closed they packed up their stuff and went home.

Once back in their quarters late in the afternoon, Lily, after reading letters from home, looked off at the horizon. She had been in Saudi Arabia almost six months, and so many human dramas had unfolded before her very eyes—the infidelity issue of Kay's husband; Karen's reserved personality, which made her life a secret onto itself; Elvie's obsession with spiritual matters; her own relationship with Mike; the concerns coming from her parents in the Philippines… Together, these were the spices that molded her life in this part of the world.

She was doing well with her job. The pay was good enough for her to create some savings and send some support home. She was earning a living, but not making a life for herself, since having a relationship with Mike was extremely difficult in the strict Middle Eastern environment. What other options were out there?

The idea came into her mind to find a place where she and Mike could be free to talk, walk, and even hold hands together, a place where she could work freely and independently. She had heard of many people who moved and worked in other places outside the Middle East—such as Europe, North America, and even Australia. She also considered going to a place where she could make new friends who shared her morality and values. Sometimes she missed her life in the Philippines. That small village where she had started her career was very special to her.

Mike shared the same aspirations to her via text. Deciding what the initial steps would be to make such a move was an overriding question for them. How could they ever do it? They needed a plan and enough time to execute it.

Weeks and months passed, and before long she had been with the hospital for more than a year. Her only consolation was her entitlement to a month-long holiday back to the Philippines. Lily counted three more months before she could take her holiday. Her mind was flying ahead of the plane.

Chapter 2

Being part of a big family had its advantages and disadvantages, Dana thought. One of the advantages was the ever-present support system provided to her from all corners of the village. Salt, sugar, and even cooking oil were available over the *bakod* (fence) from other family members.

It took a community to raise a child, but knowing and memorizing all the names of Dana's family tree was a challenge. Her generosity always attracted people during Christmas, birthdays, and other special occasions. She had to have deep pockets to satisfy everyone in her circle.

Dana's mom, the oldest of ten, had been blessed with seven kids. One thing that impressed her about her family was their excellent reputation when it came to cooking. On Barrio fiesta, christenings, birthdays, and weddings, the presence of either Dana's mom or aunt cooking in the background was notable. Her family had always been known for its skill in the kitchen. Their passion for preparing food was part of their DNA.

It took Dana four years to complete her Bachelor of Science in Home Economics from Central Luzon State University in Munoz, Nueva Ecija. From the experiences she learned from her family and the education in culinary theory she got from school, Dana became effective enough to cultivate her heart's desire for cooking and food preparation. Right after graduation, she was fortunate to get a job teaching in one of the newest private schools in her town, San Matthew High School. She was just an ordinary teacher instructing young people about how to prepare healthy and economical menus for themselves. Teaching was fun!

In her high school, her students, as young as they were, showered her with sincere affection and adoration. The nobility of this career gave her greater self-esteem and self-respect.

However, the challenges of teaching and developing new menus and other styles of food preparation also took time away from some of her other important goals in life. Her biological clock was ticking. Rudy, her boyfriend, was a motorcycle-riding fraternity boy at the university campus. Their desire to be together and start a family had become a priority, but settling down as a couple and sustaining two souls under one roof were two entirely different matters. For one thing, Dana had to look for a better paying job. For Rudy, driving to a nearby town for work was not a problem. He worked for one of the rural banks in the province, east of Munoz, which was very helpful. The couple's savings were growing and they knit their plans together perfectly. The only thing that was missing was her getting a better paying job.

"Congratulations!" Dr. Miquel said to Dana after an hour-long interview. As the hiring executive for the Central Luzon State University Marketing Cooperative, Dana was given the position of manager, almost three months after submitting her application. It was unbelievable. With Rudy's persistence, their plan to settle down or get married was moved ahead many months. Dana had been working for four years as manager and had two beautiful kids—the second child came after just twelve months! What else could she have asked for? Life was moving along smoother than expected.

The challenges and pressures one faces are different in every stage of life. Inflation, the high cost of living, and other socio-economic imbalances in the third world were the reasons why Dana's family's situation changed so drastically. The unpredictability of the Philippines' financial situation and the uncertain economy caused many people to lose their jobs, including Rudy. Again, due to motherly instinct this time, Dana set her vision outside the country. If her family was to prosper, she had to move on.

In the mid-1980s, her application to Saudi Arabia was approved. A wealthy family in Riyadh was looking for a person to take care of their young children, and Dana was perfect for the job. She was an excellent cook, and because of her experience raising her own kids, she would make sure they were given healthy, balanced meals. Her education and experiences made her the perfect candidate for the job.

That same year, Rudy finally got a job with the Bureau of Natural Resources. As part of the job, he was frequently sent to neighbouring provinces. Dana's job, being physically away from home, required them to make immeasurable sacrifices on behalf of their two children—Maria and Len. Fortunately, because of their large extended family, they were given the flexibility and understanding to continue to live the lifestyle they had become accustomed to. Dana's oldest sister Ita was more than happy to help take care of the kids when Dana and Rudy were both away on business.

It was good to know that their kids' needs were being met, both in school and at home. Dana missed her kids while she was in Riyadh. Maria was a blossoming young lady in her elementary school. She was full of promise and had great expectations of life. Len, on the other hand, was a bubbling lad with interest in the arts. Their report cards, letters, and phone calls gave Dana the strength to move forward.

Rudy's travels, however, were a big limiting factor in terms of his ability to be a father to them. However, once back home on the weekends his time with the kids was fully appreciated. It was a thing of beauty to imagine him playing the guitar and singing with the children. They were just an ordinary family in an extraordinary situation, trying to make ends meet.

Dana was having good time with her employer. The kids under her care, Lisa and Kuto, were growing fast and were even learning how to speak some of Filipino words. Funny! She was sometimes given the opportunity to tag along with her employer's family on trips to Europe and the United States, which was a dream come true. The Eiffel Tower was a terrific place to visit. Disney World in Florida was beautiful and enchanting. London's Big Ben tower was accurate with respect to time. Because the English pound was more valuable than the American dollar, Dana saved more during her stays in the United Kingdom. One of the fringe benefits of traveling was getting to collect souvenirs from the hotels and airplanes she visited. She knew many Pinoys who had been known to enjoy this particular hobby.

In 1990, Dana's sister Aida and her family were preparing to immigrate to Canada. The bond between Len and Aida's son, Rolly, was growing strong at the time.

One warm April night, Maria phoned to inform Dana about Aida's plan to leave the Philippines in a matter of months. With a word of caution and great assurances, Dana was told that a mad dog had bitten Len; dog bites in the community were common occurrences. Canines were everywhere, competing with kids for the attention of adults who would give them food.

Hours after Len was bitten, he was rushed to the university clinic for observation. The cut was not deep and the anti-rabies vaccine was deemed unnecessary. The consensus was to just bring Len to the quack doctor (*albularyo*). Ka Ipe, the quack doctor, was known to locals for treating various kinds of diseases and bites like this one. Rudy, as much as he didn't want to take any chances, was swayed to go along with the treatment plan concocted by some of the old folks in the community—to apply herbal leaves to the wound. In a few days' time, the wound was healed and Len was back into action.

Months passed and Dana was happy to witness the kids under her care continue to grow up and develop their skills. Lisa and Kuto were now at an age where they could be on their own—feed themselves, wash themselves, and prepare their own packs for school. It was part of the family's plan for her to switch roles from taking care of the kids to taking care of the kitchen, which was a nice change of pace! The family really liked *saluyot*, which Dana found surprising; the *saluyot* vegetable leaf was common in the Philippines, but she had never before seen it prepared in the Middle East. They enjoyed Dana's cooking, all modesty aside.

As a favor for her excellent performance, the family hired Dana's brother, Ezra, to work as their family driver. This provided just the emotional and physical support Dana needed. His job performance was outstanding and the family was really happy having him around.

As for cooking, the family didn't care to eat the extremities of a dressed chicken, so Dana and her friend Anita—a maid in the house—feasted on *adobo* (marinated chicken feet), *sinigang* (vinegar-based chicken feet soup), and barbequed chicken feet almost every other day of the week. The family was ignorant of what they were doing with the parts of the chicken they didn't want.

One evening, Dana was in a mood to make a long distance call to her oldest sister Ita, who was still taking care of Dana's children. Rudy was in good shape, networking with friends to find extra work. Maria was moving on to her junior years in school and Len was exhibiting general uneasiness—but otherwise he was fine. Dana had to end the call. Their phone bill had jacked up again. Besides, it had been a long day for Dana.

The next morning went the same as the day before. There were no unusual happenings in and around the house. Ezra picked her up at 10:00 to buy their weekly groceries. Dana was busy working with the *saluyot* when the phone rang. It was Ita, whom she had just talked to the previous night, informing her that they'd had to rush Len to the hospital. Dana's heart began to pound heavily. She was frozen, shocked, and her breathing was restless.

"His jaws are stiff and he can't eat," Ita told Dana. "He's not feeling well. He has a fever, he's sweating, and he's very uneasy."

Tears fell from Dana's eyes. "Oh my God!" she said as her body trembled with fear. It had been seven weeks since the dog-biting incident. On their way to the hospital, Ita had made a short stop to the house of Aida, their other sister. Young as he was, Len was able to say goodbye to them and Rolly, his buddy cousin. Dana's brother-in-law's prayer to spare Len from harm and for healing was not answered positively. Len's remaining breaths were taken less than three hours later in the hospital with Ita at his side.

According to local myths, a person can die from rabies after seven days, seven weeks, seven months, or even seven years. Ka Ipe had not been such a good doctor after all. Dana' family was not the only one to learn that lesson. The awareness of the whole community with respect to dog bites was raised. Ka Ipe's mantra turned out to be no match for the reality of rabies. As a result of this tragedy, all people who had been in contact with Len were given a shot of anti-rabies—even Aida, who was going to immigrate to Canada the following month. Thousands of pesos were spent out of fear and ignorance of the situation. Dana's family became the talk of the town.

With her eyes swollen for many days, Dana finally managed to fly back home. It was a five-hour drive from the airport to their little community. When she arrived, it was the second day of her family's wake for Len. It would not make things right if she blamed anybody for the tragedy. She thought to herself that God had His way of showing how much He was in control. It was hard to comprehend that Len was not hers, but God's. As a family, they were united again in a way that nobody fully understood. Rudy, Maria, and Dana were devastated. Dana gathered together enough savings to pay for Len's funeral. Life had to move on.

She decided to stay with Ita for four weeks of mourning, but that plan was cut short when Dana's employer phoned. She was reminded of their trip to Europe the following month, which she was expected to join them for. She had to fly back to Riyadh. Three days before Dana's flight, she talked with Aida, who was flying to Canada shortly. Her hope was that someday they could live together in North America. That hope stuck in Dana's mind.

Dana's energy, enthusiasm, and drive to work waned in the first few weeks back with the family in Riyadh. Her son's death haunted her wherever she went. If only she had listened to Ita's initial admonition to bring Len to a doctor for an anti-rabies shot, he might not have died. But the wheel of life had to roll on. Indeed, time heals and distance dims imagination.

In the first week of July 2001, Dana flew to Europe with her employer for the family's annual holiday break. It was there where she learned that Aida's family had safely landed in Winnipeg. However, there was a recession going on in Canada and Aida and her husband, Rony, had a hard time finding work there. Two weeks later, Rony moved to Calgary, where he landed a job as a data entry clerk for an oil and gas service company. Three months later, Aida and Rolly moved to Calgary to join him.

More than three years after settling in Calgary, Aida's plan for her family came to fruition. Her year-and-a-half-old daughter, Dina, needed a nanny; Aida herself had to go back to work to help the family pay the rent, and other bills.

She took advantage of the Foreign Live-in Caregiver program, which was sponsored by the federal government. Their application to hire Dana as Dina's nanny was approved by Canadian Immigration. Aida advised Dana to return to the Philippines for a holiday so that the processing of her application would be easier. Dana's employer in Saudi Arabia was generous to grant her this holiday. Moreover, he was in favor of her plan to move to Canada. Their kids were now grown up and they were able to find a replacement for her in the kitchen. However, they assured Dana of their willingness to welcome her back if her plan didn't work out. Ezra was not happy knowing that sooner or later he would be left alone in the Middle East.

Dana took the month-long holiday and returned to the Philippines. She stayed with Nery, another of her sisters, who was living in Sampaloc, a part of Manila. The traffic along the nearby Maharlika Highway was heavy during the Sunday afternoon drive, heading toward downtown Manila. Because of the traffic, the transit bus was running late.

It was about 10:00 in the evening when Rudy and Dana stepped up to Nery's door. Over a sumptuous dinner, they were able to map out their plans for the next day.

"What is your first stop tomorrow?" Nery asked.

"My scheduled appointment with the Canadian embassy in Makati is at 9:30," Dana replied.

Exactly three months after submitting her application and medical examination, Dana found herself standing in front of a small numbered window—#3—with a smiling woman behind it. She handed Dana a working visa with gusto.

"Congratulations!" she said. "You don't need an interview."

Dana found herself in the same predicament as before. She had to leave, while Rudy and Maria had to stay behind in the Philippines. Maria was going to continue her studies and Rudy had to keep job-hunting—again. He had lost his last job. He soon landed a job with his former boss in a fish pond business as a technician and caretaker. Maria, on the other hand, was having fun with her studies. At school, a stare from her crush was enough to produce goose bumps. She was in the midst of a teenage fantasy.

Dana's Air Canada flight landed at Calgary International Airport five minutes behind schedule. It was a windy and chilly night. Aida was right to have told her that the weather would be cold. The baggage claim area was surrounded by people of different looks and they were all tired but excited to pull their bags from the moving conveyor belt. It was not hard to identify Dana's baggage; she had wrapped a string around the outside of the box to make it unique, just like all the other Filipinos arriving from the Philippines. Her previous travels with her Arabian employer had prepared her for this trip.

From a distance of fifteen meters, she recognized Aida, Rony, Rolly, and Dina. Their eyes were on the door where passengers were coming out. Coming from behind, Dana surprised them with a loud, "*Hoy, andito na ako!*" People around them were staring. Who was this tanned lady? For sure, Dana's complexion was far darker than the rest of people in the airport—except for one other family fresh from the Philippines.

Who cares? she said to herself. *What's important is my arrival in this great country.*

They loaded Dana's three items of luggage into Rony's van and drove to their place. The road, Barlow Trail, was clear and the weather was very inviting for hikers and joggers alike.

Laughter and crying, balanced as they were, made Dana's first night in Canada very long. It lasted almost until the following morning. Jetlag kept her awake at nighttime and sleepy during the daytime for almost two weeks.

Dana's job was easy. All she had to do was prepare food and take care of Dina. Aida went back to work while Dina and Dana worked hard to get acquainted with each other. Dina had no choice in the matter, since her mom and dad worked the whole day and Dana was the only one around the house. Rolly was enjoying his newfound friends in his nearby elementary school.

Dana and Aida decided to place Dina into a daycare once Dana got a job from another employer who could pay her a full-time salary.

One Monday morning, the phone rang. The woman at the other end of the line wanted Dana to report for a job interview somewhere around the Spring Bank area. Dana remembered having faxed her resume to several prospective employers during her first two weeks in Calgary. Now responses were coming back. The upcoming weekend was the best time to schedule an interview.

It took them forty-five minutes to locate the house where the interview was taking place. Both of the interviewers were practicing medical doctors with offices in downtown Calgary. The house was really big; it even had an indoor swimming pool. Aida and Rony were impressed. However, Dana told them that the house was nothing compared to the house of her employer in the Middle East!

The interview lasted an hour. Dana's main problem was the distance it would put between her and her sister's family. She could stay with this family on weekdays, but there was no bus going from their house back to downtown Calgary. It was possible to take a taxi, but the fare would be a half-day's pay. Besides, when the couple found out Dana was new to Canada, having only been there four months, they were not sure they can entrust their kids and house to her care. She had no regrets over not getting the job. She knew there would always be another family that needed her services. Dana mailed out five resumes the following week to prospective employers around the city.

Life went back to normal at her sister's place. Dina was getting heavier and talkative. Though she couldn't yet speak in their Filipino dialect, her comprehension and understanding of it was fantastic.

While preparing the menu for dinner one day, Dana heard the mailman deliver envelopes into the mailbox. One of her tasks was to get the letters and many flyers that were forcefully stuffed into the metal mailbox. Aida told her that in Canada this was called "junk mail." The main objective of junk mail was to entice households, especially women, to buy more goods perceived to be needs of the family. Most often, junk mail ended up in the garbage, but if one was smart enough, lots of savings could be realized from them.

Goose bumps surfaced on Dana's arms when a larger than ordinary envelope arrived with her name written on it. She had been in Calgary for only a few weeks and here in her hand was a notice from Rider's Digest saying that she had won a million-dollar lottery! Thrilled and excited, she phoned Rony to come home and help her out in deciding what to do with her winnings. He responded that she had not really won anything; the notice was just a way for the magazine to take on new subscribers. Dana insisted that in the notice it said, "Congratulations, you won a million dollars!" To appease her from being too excited, Rony drove home. He showed her the catch of the notice. Indeed, Rony was right. Dana was eligible to win that prize once she put in her order for their products. Oh well… it was just one more new experience of this new society.

The Canadian winter was really bad for her health. Dana's body told her to accumulate more fat to cope with the cold weather. She gained about four pounds. One way to shed that extra weight was exercise. Shoveling the front walkway was a good start, but in the minus twenty-degree temperatures, it was very cold. Dana heard on the radio that it only took a couple of minutes for a person's exposed skin to burn in those cold conditions. This was called "frostbite." January and February were the most brutal months. She had to cover everything except her eyes. It was a good thing she had small eyes. In fact, her friends often told her that she looked Chinese!

Her complexion was lightening up, too. Everyday she was covered with a sweater indoors and a winter coat outdoors, so her skin became pale and dry. Another thing that was confusing to her was this thing they called "wind chill." The temperature outside had two different readings. One was the actual temperature, and then there was a second temperature which took into account wind chill. Usually the wind chill made the actual outdoor temperature feel much colder than it was.

One Tuesday morning, while Dana was going out to shovel snow, she saw footprints in the snow leading from the front of the house to the backyard. The community was well-known for break-ins, so she said to herself, *Vigilance is needed!*

True to her expectations, almost a month later there was a man walking in the backyard. She was not sure whether to call 911 or the police, so she called Rony to tell him about the guy in the yard. Sensing her fear and shock, Rony drove home in ten minutes—it usually took him fifteen or twenty! Before long, he was at the door. The guy was gone and his footprints passed just below the electric meter on the side of the house. He explained to her that the man had been a meter reader from the electric company. Another mystery solved. Dana was learning, indeed. It was a good thing he had come on his lunch break. Before heading back to the office, he enjoyed the *pakbet* she had cooked for lunch.

Her adjustment integrating with a group of Filipinos attending Aida's church was smooth and easy—especially when they found out about her cooking! Dana established friendships with them through a series of potlucks where they were able to sample her specialties. As they say, a person's stomach is the fastest way to their heart. Dana was the newest in the group, so to make them happy she accepted their challenge to be the person in charge of the kitchen for most of the group's fellowship potlucks. This was a great opportunity for her to hone her skills in cooking North American foods.

One day, she noticed a lump on her right wrist that was getting bigger. The discomfort she was feeling was enough that she couldn't ignore it. Dana requested that her brother-in-law to drive her to a medical appointment somewhere in the southwest corner of the city.

A week later, she was sitting on a bed at Rocky View Hospital, groggy and unstable. The operation to remove the lump took only thirty minutes, but the effect of the anesthetic remained. The procedure had been free. *Incredible*, she said to herself. Aida told her that the medical insurance premium Dana paid every month covered this kind of operation. This was one of the good aspects of living in Canada; there was a universal health care plan for everyone. In the Philippines, or even in the United States, a person's savings could be eaten away by the kind of treatment Dana received! It only took her a week before she was fully capable of going back to everyday chores at home.

After many months, a divorcee from the northwest part of the city called Dana for an interview. The woman was in need of nanny to take care of her two young kids and the house. Her name was Lita, and Dana's interview with her was short and very interesting. As a live-in caregiver, Dana would have to live with them from Monday morning through Friday afternoon. If Aida and Rony were in a mood for a leisurely drive, her weekend commute would be free. She decided to take the job.

Dina was sad about Dana's moving out. However, it only took her a few days to fully adjust and enjoy her days at a daycare in the neighbourhood. Weeks later, Dana moved in with her new employer. The arrangement was perfect for Aida, Rony, and Rolly.

She had her own room downstairs and the whole house and its upkeep and cleanliness was her domain. The kids, both in grade school, were attending school four blocks away. The walk to and from school was exactly the kind of fitness program Dana needed—walking for ten to fifteen minutes, twice a day. Certainly, the house was far bigger and better than Aida's.

But this also meant she had to spend more time cleaning and scrubbing.

As a divorcee with two growing kids, Lita's life was a puzzle to Dana. Lita's ex-husband was working as a broadcaster in the entertainment industry. The guy had left the family when the kids were still in their early years. Between Lita's work—managing a hotel—and her wealthy parents, the family was able to sustain a comfortable lifestyle.

Lita may have been financially stable, but sexually she and Dana were in the same boat—barren.

One morning, Dana was given quite a shock. When everyone was gone to their respective destinations, she was compelled to clean and arrange Lita's closet. Folding up her stuff was not a problem, but then she reached the inner portion of the closet where a sex toy was hidden. She blushed for almost thirty minutes. In the Philippines, this kind of thing was treated very confidentially and secretly. Dana came to realize that this was just a normal part of life for some people. To her amazement, a number of her friends were encountering similar experience with their employers.

Lita's need for a companion and fatherly figure in the home caused her to entertain James. James, a corporate lawyer, was a heavy smoker. He was separated from his wife and had moved into Lita's place with his teenage daughter. A wedding was nowhere in the future for James and Lita. Dana was not sure if marriage was a thing of the past for these people. The affair changed the dynamic of Dana's work and interaction with the family. Washing a man's underwear, for instance, was an annoyance. Her only consolation sometimes was the extra cash this brought her.

The new kid in the corral was becoming a nuisance to Lita's kids. New opinions and pressures around were not healthy for them. This was one of the realities Dana faced while working for a mixed family. These arrangements were very common in Canada. Sometimes it was shocking. Certainly it was entirely different from the kinds of families that were common in the Philippines.

Dana wasn't a divorcee, but she could fully identify with Lita's feelings and emotions about being physically separated from her spouse. Dana's hardship stemmed not only from being away from Rudy, but also from not knowing how long their separation would last. Even Maria was three hours away from her dad most of the time. The only times dad and daughter saw each other was on special family occasions. But that only happened once or twice a year, over a cup of hot chocolate and toasted bun.

In one more year, Dana would apply for her open visa and include Rudy and Maria in the application. This demanded that she spend more time working and put more savings in the bank.

In the course of staying with Aida every weekend, Dana found out that one of her best friends from the Middle East, Anita, was also applying to move to Canada. Their correspondence was frequent and full of hope and encouragement. She learned from her that Ezra was doing well. He was still working for Dana's former employer. Anita's husband was also friends with Ezra.

In a matter of months, Anita was fortunate to find work in Calgary as a nanny. Her employers, a doctor and a lawyer, had two school-age boys. Their house in the McKenzie Lake area was big and Anita couldn't cope with the cleaning and upkeep of it. She needed the help of a part-time cleaner. Dana made an arrangement with Lita so that she can find time to help her best friend.

This working arrangement worked perfectly for over a year. Distance became a problem after a while, however, so

Dana had to terminate this part-time job. She was wasting too much time commuting between the two houses. The only consolation she got from this was the chance to close her eyes and rest them for a while. She was so tired, she couldn't even read a paper or a book. Sometimes her mind was overwhelmed with tasks she needed to finish off at home. The full loads of dirty laundry that were waiting for her, finding the time to iron them … it was too much. Dana was feeling anxiety over not being able to finish her other work—such as cooking.

Back home, Maria was taking a course to become a physical therapist, and she was nearing her final years. Her education was getting to be expensive, and her dad's support was no longer enough to cover it. The only way she could keep going was for her mother to send her money. She had so many things to pay for—an internship, books, allowances, and boyfriend-related expenses. Cleaning Anita's employer's house was not enough to make up the difference, though. Dana needed a job that was nearer her employer and a bit higher in terms of salary.

The Southern Alberta Institute of Technology (SAIT) had an opening for someone in their cafeteria. Taking into account Dana's background and experience, she reported to SAIT on a part-time basis a week after the interview. She was able to conveniently work out her schedule with Lita. Tada! SAIT welcomed its new pizza lady. The job was not hard. There were eight other people in the kitchen, all of them coming from different backgrounds and cultures, which created challenges in the crew which they had to face head-on. The advantage of being the oldest in the pack was that they viewed Dana with respect and let her do things her own way.

She came to have all kinds of different life experiences. Among her coworkers were all sorts of hidden realities—abusive relationships, separations, divorce, and even couples who were merely living together, a common cohabitation arrangement in North America. It took her quite a while to fully understand this new culture of relationships.

Months later, her daughter's application to move to Canada was approved. Maria picked up her visa and flew in from Manila a few weeks later. What a reunion! Their eyes swelled for five hours as they cried tears of happiness. Their plan was to continue working to satisfy the requirements of Dana's open visa application; she wanted to bring her entire family to Canada. Her daughter was only the first step.

Ultimately, after a year of staying in Canada, Maria had to fly back to the Philippines to finish her massage therapy course. Time flew by so fast. Before the opening of another school year, Maria flew back to Manila. It was a lonely chapter of Dana's life as she once again found herself without family.

After months of studying her situation, she decided to rent a new place together with Anita and another friend of theirs, Annie, who was a chemist. Though Aida's house was open to them, they decided to do what was expected and get their own place, which was just a block away from Aida's house and just a stone's throw away from the church they were attending.

Having trusted friends in a foreign land was one of the most important things that happened to Dana. It was impossible to express how important it was to have people to talk to in the midst of her struggles. Their prayer, love, and care for her were amazing. Her small group walked the talk of their faith. This reaffirmed Dana's belief in God. Even when she had been in the Philippines, she believed that having a personal relationship with God through His son Jesus Christ caused goodness to flow out of a person's life to others. It occurred to her that if only others knew this secret, they could avoid lives of despair and helplessness amidst material plenty and prosperity. Many families, and even single people, had the same needs, but everybody had a different way of coping with the realities of life. Some people simply resorted to various forms of escape. The most common routes available were religion, membership to various associations or clubs, and other social undertakings.

Rudy's application to immigrate to Canada was finally submitted. It took years to be processed due to some technical and health issues. Nevertheless, they were eventually notified of the good news that he could come. It was a ray of sunlight at the end of a long, dark tunnel. Two years before his expected coming, Maria flew back to Calgary with her massage therapy diploma. With Aida's prompting, Dana decided to buy her own place for her and Maria to share. By this time, Anita and Annie had gone their separate ways—Anita was renting a house within the vicinity and Annie had gotten married to an email pal after months of courtship.

More often than not, Maria and Dana disagreed on what to do with all the junk they had stored in the nooks and crannies of their old place. Now that they were in a new house, Maria wanted to get rid of the junk. Motherly as Dana was, she told her daughter of the sentimental value of that junk, citing that "we might need it later on." They were in a material world and material things would always be part of their lives.

"But not this much," Maria argued. Dana thought her opinion made sense, so she gave away or trashed a third of the accumulated junk.

It didn't take long before they established a routine of daily chores and activities. Once they were accustomed to getting up at 5:30 in the morning, they no longer needed an alarm clock, especially since they had no option but to take public transit to get to work. Dana's roles and responsibilities at Lita's place had changed over the years. She was no longer responsible for taking care of the kids; the job now revolved around cooking and cleaning.

Many of Dana's close friends wanted to know more about her family, specifically when her husband would be arriving. They were having a hard time believing that she had waited seven full years for Rudy. It was surreal when they found out that Rudy was finally coming.

Months later, Rudy arrived. The family was happy and complete.

Rudy's life had been uncertain until the day he landed a job in SMED (Surety Mechanical and Enterprise Development). Woodworking was not his forte. Cabinet-making forced him to sharpen his concentration and focus on details. Back home, his hands and fingers were used to bring healing to aching backs and sore muscles. It ran in his family. His dad had been a local massage therapist in the community.

With Calgary's booming economy, the demand for cabinets and office furniture had increased dramatically. This resulted in Rudy increasing his net pay. Correspondingly, though, his time with the family was cut back considerably

One Monday morning, during Dana's usual walk to the bus shelter, a man approached her wanting to know what time it was. As he inched closer to her, she just told him it was 5:45 and then quickly walked away to the bus, which was pulling up to the curb. It was a good thing the guy was pulling a cart. That was the first time it happened, but the same occurred again three times the following week. The area, according to a number of media reports, was known for harboring community outcasts. News of sexual assaults, extortions, and other social ills were common occurrences. Dana and Rudy didn't waste any time consulting with Rony, her brother-in-law. He recommended that she report the matter to the police. She didn't want to go to the police, but if that guy persisted in bugging her, she would have no recourse but to report him.

Dana was ready and prepared the next morning as the same guy approached and asked the same question. She told herself not to be intimidated.

"So what exactly are you doing out so early in the morning?" she asked.

"Can't you see?" he said. "I'm making a living!" He was a newspaper deliveryman. He had to wake up early to deliver papers. Her anxiety settled down.

Having too much overtime strained the fibers of her family's relationships. Family pep talks were reduced to three minutes or less. Maria's work had been eating time away from the family. Her afternoons were spent at her full-time job, and yet she still found time to take on new massage clients. More than two dozen warm bodies experienced her amazing touch. She had to reschedule people all the time to accommodate all her appointments. Her monthly cell phone bill was so high that a four-month bill was equivalent to a round-trip visit to the Philippines. The high bills were a result of making long-distance calls to her boyfriend and some other friends around Calgary. Letter writing became a thing of the past. Even texting was no longer part of her lingo. She preferred the ease and personal touch of a phone call.

It was not long after when the course of fate caught the family unprepared. Maria had become a licensed massage therapist and was doing well with her business, Gracious Care Massage. Maria and her boyfriend, months after getting married, moved to the southwest corner of the city. It was most unexpected when Dana became pregnant again. At the age of 42, Dana conceived her third child, a menopause baby.

Chapter 3

"While you were out this morning, Dr. Stuart informed me that we can only stay in the hospital for two days. You have to take Wednesday off," Dana told Rudy while Junior, their two-day-old son, slept soundly at her side.

"I think we can manage," Rudy replied. "We have everything prepared. Junior's crib is ready and his stuff is waiting for him."

Winter was three months away. The weather in Calgary was unpredictable. Even in the midst of winter, you would feel warm air coming from the west. Mounds of ice could melt in a couple of hours. Those bouts of warm weather were called Chinook winds, a mass of warm air coming from the Pacific Ocean. In a matter of hours, the temperature could rise as much as fifteen degrees. That morning was no different. The morning breeze was cold, but the temperature went up late in the afternoon. Dana and Rudy had to do what was told of them. They checked out in the afternoon.

Rudy had been with SMED for almost two years when he moved to another job. His next job was at a company called Bantrel, where he was assigned to a unit in charge of maintaining the electrical equipment of corporate offices throughout the city. He was the assistant to a guy in charge of making sure all the equipment was properly maintained and calibrated for optimum performance.

Dana was promoted to a higher position with better pay. Her part-time cleaning job added extra working hours. They needed the money from this cleaning job to deal with the mounting pressure of paying the mortgage and other bills. But who would look after the baby? A year of parental leave was good, but they needed to work so as not to disrupt the challenges and demands of their chosen lifestyle. After conducting a thorough review of their budget and a series of consultations with trusted friends, they came up with a plan that would not only benefit them, but also their daughter Maria. In five more months, Maria would be a mother herself!

Hiring a nanny from the city would greatly affect their budget. They were made aware that bringing over a nanny from the Philippines would be the most economical option. The couple took advantage of the government's Foreign Live-in Caregiver program. A nanny for Junior was badly needed before Old Man Winter arrived.

"My brother-in-law in Saudi Arabia has a girlfriend who's looking for work," Anita said to Dana over the phone one day. "Her name is Lily and she's a midwife. She's looking for work outside the country. She and her boyfriend seldom see each other and need at least a marriage certificate before they can talk or walk together in public. The pay she's making isn't bad, but she has to work overtime, and even weekends. Both of them are eyeing a move to the United States or Canada. I'll call them this weekend and introduce you. From there, you can contact them and lay down your plan." Anita's voice was filled with urgency.

"Thank you very much, my friend," replied Dana.

The September breeze was getting colder. Their timeline for getting Lily was still manageable. The basement suite was ready for occupancy, according to the specifications set out in the government program. They purchased a seventeen-inch television and black telephone from Value Village. They bought a bed during a final summer sale event. It took Rudy five days to install a portable shower in the basement wash-room. The room was painted green. The only other thing they needed was a portable heater for winter.

"Anita gave me this number for Lily," Dana said casually to Rudy later that day when Rudy got home from work. "After dinner, we'll call and find out if she's interested."

"Sounds good to me," Rudy responded with a hungry look in his eyes.

Junior and Dana were busy doing their evening routine. Junior was becoming too demanding, which was exactly why the couple needed somebody to help them with their daily chores. The demand for his supervision and care was growing larger. Both parents were becoming exhausted.

"What's for dinner?" Rudy asked.

"*Pakbet*," Dana answered. "It's just warming in the micro-wave."

He proceeded to sit in from of the tube, where a hockey game was about to begin. Alberta's two professional hockey teams were playing in what had been dubbed "The Battle of Alberta." Though hockey was usually not a popular game among immigrants coming from the tropics, there was still a lot of excitement and suspense in the game, and Rudy was hooked.

In less than twenty minutes, the food was gone and the game was underway. The street outside was quite. People everywhere were stuck in front of the television.

In the midst of a power play for Edmonton, the phone rang. At first Rudy was hesitant to pick up the phone. It was too late in the evening for Dana to have a long conversation with one of her friends. Most often, these calls were just about gossip. Junior, just like any other six-month-old, crawled toward the phone. Rudy was excited to pick up the phone with Junior's small fist on top of it.

"Hello!" he answered.

"Hi! Can I speak to Dana?"

"She's busy. Can you call back later?"

"It's Anita. Please tell her to call me. Thanks."

Dana emerged from the washroom wiping her hands. She had, in fact, been waiting for Anita's call. She picked up the phone and called her friend back. From the end of the line, she heard, "*Kumare*, have you called Lily yet?"

"Not yet," Dana said.

"She's waiting for your call any time this week. Maybe even today."

"Thanks, I'll call her right now." Dana put back the phone and headed for the other side of the table where there was a pen and phone book.

Dana was little bit hesitant to call Lily. Time was running out in the game and Calgary was two points ahead of their rivals, the Edmonton Oilers. She looked away anyway and dialed Lily's number.

"Speaking! Who is it?" a woman's voice answered.

"Hi, it's Dana, Anita's best friend from Calgary."

"How's Aunt Anita?

"She's doing fine," Dana said. "Actually, she told me about you."

"About me?"

"I was just wondering if you would be interested in moving to Canada to work as a live-in caregiver."

———

Lily's jaw dropped when she heard Dana's offer. Her heart was pounding. Sweat rolled down her left cheek.

She could hardly believe what she was hearing from the woman at the other end of the line. If this was a dream, she didn't want to wake up for a while. The impact of the offer was immense. She had been waiting a long time for this opportunity.

Details were discussed. The offer sounded good. However, Lily was finally learning to love her work in the hospital. She would be receiving a raise and an additional two-day holiday the next month. Perks and other fringe benefits were piling up. Savings weren't a problem anymore. The support flowing to the Philippines had been a blessing for her family.

"I will send you a form and some instructions in the mail. If you are interested with the arrangement and conditions, in few months' time you'll be playing with Junior." These were Dana's parting words.

"I'm very interested," Lily assured her. "Thank you very much. Goodbye!"

Lily's eyes were glowing with happiness. Mike needed to be told about this development. She wrote and sent a letter to Mike and followed it up with a phone call. One week after getting the offer from Dana, Lily and Mike decided to give it a try. Lily would go to Canada first, then send for Mike after.

Lily had enough savings, so her papers were submitted to the nearest Canadian embassy. Lily's employer was generous enough to grant her a month-long holiday in November. So far, it was a perfect plan! Her holiday in the Philippines coincided with her interview at the Canadian embassy in Makati. The time she spent with her family, after almost four years of being away from home, was so sweet and refreshing.

She was in her mid-twenties, and she was ready to explore the next chapter of her life in the West. The only thing that made leaving hard were the friendships she had made in the Middle East, and also her relationship with Mike. But this was the opportunity they had been waiting for. If not now, when would they make the next move? It was time to bite the bullet.

She was scheduled to report for an interview at the Canadian embassy during the second week of November. Very early in the morning, she found herself third in the line waiting for the opening of the embassy in Makati.

"Number three!" the office receptionist called. Lily stood and handed her ticket to the next available wicket. "Enter the door to your left and proceed to Room 12."

Nervous and sweating, Lily knocked and entered Room 12. Behind the table facing the window was a woman in her mid-fifties. Her large eyeglasses were fitting for the wide shape of her face. It was a small office, and there was not much in it. The pictures on the desk were dusty and possibly had not been touched or arranged for many months. Plastic flowers were tucked in an old vase. The windows were certainly begging for a thorough washing. The hum of the air conditioning was louder than the dilapidated old cars outside. *Just ignore the dusty chair,* her subconscious mind pleaded.

"Have a seat," the woman said. According to the small wooden nameplate at the end of the in-and-out tray, her name was Ms. Walters. She was spreading out Lily's papers on the table. "We'll talk about your plan and suitability to work in Canada."

Lily's throat was getting dry, but she was able to answer all the questions. The interview was more of a tell-me-about-yourself type of conversation. Lily dabbed her forehead with a tissue to dry the sweat. The shaking of her legs, though not obvious, was getting less intense. Lily wondered what Ms. Walters was busy writing on the yellow pad in front of her. Lily was tempted to crane her neck to peek, but she knew it was not a good idea. It was best to remain polite.

In less than an hour, she came out of the room with her head held high, sweating profusely. Those who were sitting in the reception room noticed her giggle. As she passed the waiting area, the other applicants curiously following her with their eyes. At the last row of chairs were two women trying to give her a thumbs-up. Their smiles were reciprocated with a whisper of thanks from Lily.

"She's very lucky!" said one of the women. She was wearing a red blouse.

"I wonder what kind of questions and information they'll want to know from us," added the other one while fixing her makeup. Her blouse was pink. She was wearing a polka-dotted headband which stuck out on the left side of her thinning hair.

"One thing they want to know is how well we can speak English," Lily said.

"English! It's easy," the red-bloused woman commented. A nod with an envious look was the only non-verbal cue that came out of the other lady. "What is your destination? Is it Hong Kong?"

"Canada!" Lily answered.

"Where in Canada?" asked the other lady sitting in the far corner of the room.

"Calgary, Alberta."

"Where is that?" snapped the one with overdone makeup and a mid-forties look. "Most caregivers seem to be heading for Toronto or Winnipeg."

"The interviewer told me that Alberta is the province between Saskatchewan and British Columbia," Lily said politely. "It's in the western part of the country."

"When are you leaving?" said the woman in the pink blouse. She was staring openly. It was a normal tendency for people to stare at those coming from one of the cubicles along the hallways of the embassy's thirteenth floor. If there was no spark in their eyes, the chance of them getting a visa was low. The opposite was also true.

"I'm hoping next month."

It was a beautiful day outside. Jeepneys were snaking around Buendia Avenue. After a sweaty and bumpy twenty-minute ride, Lily stepped off the passenger car in front of a shopping center. People were crowding along the sidewalks. Everyone was in a hurry to catch his or her ride home. Lily was also in a hurry to catch the next bus.

Halfway into her drive along the Maharlika Highway, the bus stopped for twenty minutes at a roadside strip mall. It was 7:00 in the evening, and the driver had to stop and eat something. Passengers got off the bus and proceeded to the different shops. Lily didn't bother getting off the bus. Instead, she stood up and stretched her arms and legs. The excitement on her face was still visible. She couldn't believe that in just a matter of a few months, her dream of going abroad would come true. She opened her bag and for the third time read the papers that had been given to her by the embassy.

Her mind started to work, but her body was stressed out and tired. After slipping the paper back into a neatly kept envelope, Lily looked up at the stars and said a prayer of thanksgiving. She closed her eyes and didn't even feel it as the bus started moving again.

Chapter 4

D ana, Anita, Rudy, and Junior were five minutes ahead of Flight 510's scheduled arrival. The December wind was still a cold one. The forecast was not too bad, all things considered; the high was one degree. The arrivals area was packed with people coming and going. Calgary, as one of Canada's booming cities, was a magnet for people both within the country and abroad. Oil and gas was the province's engine of growth, and the city had developed a character that was inviting, challenging, and full of opportunities. Even the airport reflected the strength, power, leisure, and confidence brought about by the province's economic might.

As people emerged from the exit door, the baggage claim conveyor belt started to move.

"Look for Lily," Rudy said. "I'll grab a cart for her luggage."

The people coming through the door were of all different sizes, colours, and scents; it was impossible to miss the distinctive scent of Manila. A slim, shivering woman in a black sweater and tight Levi's jeans emerged from the door. Her dark complexion vividly enhanced her smiling cheeks. She had short hair with conservative earrings that caught their attention. Anita was holding Lily's picture, which they had printed out from an email. Anita looked from the woman back to the picture and recognized the Filipina woman right away. It had to be Lily.

"*Kabayan!*" Anita greeted, already three steps ahead of Dana and Rudy.

"Is that you, Lily?" Dana asked.

Lily smiled. "Yes, *ako nga!*" While the three ladies exchanged greetings, Rudy slipped out to the baggage claim. A few minutes later, he returned pushing the cart with two boxes loaded onto it.

"How do you know that's my baggage?" Lily inquired from Rudy.

Those two boxes had been the only ones with string tied around them. Pinoys were well-known for this.

The group went out the terminal crying. It was quite a nice first day for Lily in Canada.

Stipulated in her contract and the regulations of the live-in caregiver program, the downstairs room they had prepared for Lily was completely furnished with a table, bed, phone, and drawers. Her work would start at 7:30 in the morning and last until 5:00 in the evening. Anything beyond that depended on the agreement—it would be treated as overtime or be paid back as extra holiday hours later. She had the weekends off to go anywhere.

For other arrangements, though, other caregivers pooled their resources and rented rooms to stay during the weekends. This afforded them the opportunity to do whatever they wanted to with their time and money. Lily had to stay with Dana's family for at least two years, as stipulated in the program.

There were three bedrooms upstairs, one guest room on the main floor, and Lily's suite was downstairs. This was typical for a North American dwelling. There were two and a half bathrooms containing all the stuff they needed.

Her first few days were light, though full of challenges and expectations. After three days of doing the same things, day in and day out, Lily became comfortable with the routine. Her household chores were far different from the chores she had been responsible for in Saudi Arabia. She told herself secretly that Junior even accepted the fact that Lily was like his second mom. Junior was gaining so much weight.

Dana was preparing to go back to work in a week's time. Rudy, as usual, was working too much overtime. Their house was three blocks east of Mackenzie Town, along Deerfoot Trail.

It was the third house Dana had lived in since moving to Calgary, and it was further away from Dana's sister Aida, who lived in the Forest Lawn area. In Calgary, seldom did you see a house with only one car parked out front. A van or SUV and a small car were a common combination. Lily did not ever see the family talk with their neighbours.

Every day at 7:30 in the morning, Lily waved her hand to an old lady walking with a plastic bag in her left hand and a leashed dog in her right. Her curiosity about the plastic was satisfied when, one morning, the lady used it to pick up after her dog's poo.

The second week after her arrival, Dana, Lily, and Junior headed downtown. Their priority was getting Lily a social insurance number and Alberta health insurance card. There was a long line of people waiting at the door to the passport office. In fact, the building was packed with people who were either confused or simply enjoying the cozy and warm atmosphere inside the building.

"The American government requires all persons coming from Canada to produce a passport before crossing the border for a visit or for business dealings. The events of September 11 have made the Americans wary," Dana explained.

"What about that room over there?" Lily asked as they passed the Human Resources office.

"That's where unemployed people go who are looking for job openings. Once you get your social insurance number, you'll be able to access the job bank."

"Is that where you found your first job?" Lily asked.

Dana shook her head. "I found mine in the newspaper, but I came here twice before I landed my present job."

"What about Rudy?"

"It's just like in our country. Sometimes it's more about *who* know you than *what* you know."

"Really? I thought that was only true in third-world countries. I didn't expect that practice to be rampant here, too."

"Oh yeah. It's everywhere."

Their talk branched out to other issues related to employment as they inched their way to the line of people submitting documents to the lady in the window.

"Another sad part of an immigrant's working experience is that if your qualifications are better than your supervisor, you can be in big trouble," Dana said. "It's very hard to get a promotion, unless of course you're good at sucking up and bribing people."

Lily handed her documents to the lady at the back of the glass window. After a few minutes of examining the papers and payment, a $10 receipt was handed back to her.

It was Lily's first visit to a big government office in Canada. The three-story building was not very big compared to the buildings back home in Makati, though.

As they left the room, Junior needed his diaper changed. Dana pointed Lily to where she could take Junior. It was a family change room. The room was big and, yes, it was large enough for an entire family to occupy all at once. Junior ran to the side of the room and pulled down the diaper-changing board. Lily picked him up and laid him down. His diaper was soaking wet.

Coming from that room, Lily said to Dana, "I'm impressed. They have this board in there so you can change a baby's diaper."

"This country is very rich. The government has all the resources to meet the needs of everyone. Washrooms are not only for men or women; they're built, like just that one, for family."

When they were done, they proceeded along the belly of the city's business district.

"The Middle East is truly different from Canada in terms of the relationships between men and women," Lily gasped. She witnessed not only a man and woman holding hands in the street, but also goodbye kisses.

"Wait till summer and you will see lots of skin around," said Dana. "But there are also many people who are conservative, especially those who came from Asia and the Middle East."

They had parked two blocks away, along Fifth Avenue.

Devonian Garden was a good place to rest, so they sat and enjoyed the indoor garden while eating their lunch, which they ordered from a nearby fast food restaurant.

"When I'm back to work, there are three things I want you to always remember," Dana said. "Junior has scheduled meals and naps. The second thing is to make sure his diaper is always changed and that he gets his playtime. Thirdly, make sure all other chores at home are taken care off. Rudy is happy when he comes home and finds food ready on the table." The rest of Dana's instructions were written in her job description. Dana also made it clear that Saturday and Sunday were Lily's own days off to enjoy. As she lifted Junior into his stroller, she added, "We'll go down later and show you where you can open your bank account and buy your transit pass."

It was 3:00 in the afternoon when they left the concrete jungle of the city. Afternoons like this one were really problematic in terms of traffic. After almost thirty-five minutes of careful driving along Deerfoot Trail, they turned right and crossed over to a Superstore for their weekly groceries. The store, Lily was informed, was the cheapest and most convenient place to buy groceries in that quadrant of the city. Though the area was cluttered with lots of stores, the family's choice was always Superstore.

While Lily was navigating the cart, she became more aware of the poverty of the Philippines, especially in the village where she had grown up. Here people were dying due to *over*eating, while in her village people were dying from starvation. What a tragedy. She wondered if the fully loaded cart was really enough for a week's consumption. In her estimate, the amount of groceries Dana was buying would last a month. She wasn't aware that about one fourth of the stuff they bought ended up in the garbage.

From behind her, she heard Dana talking to someone.

"Lily, this is Bernie," Dana said, introducing her to another woman with an equally loaded-down cart of the same groceries. "She's Junior's best friend."

After five minutes of preliminaries, both Lily and Bernie knew the basics of who each other were. Lily also learned that more Pinoys shopped at this store than the one in the northeast, which was flooded with Vietnamese, Chinese, and many other minorities.

"How do you like your first week here?" Bernie asked.

"I'm missing my friends and families in Saudi Arabia and the Philippines," Lily responded with sadness on her face. "I know that in a few weeks' time, everything will be fine with me." A smile cracked her lips. As Junior was safely tucked in the cart, Lily pushed it towards the fresh vegetables. She missed most of the fresh oriental vegetables and fruits from back home. It took them almost two hours roaming around the store with no specific list, which was very common for an immigrant family. One thing Lily noticed was the closing time of the store.

At 9:40, the women left the store. It was dark outside and their car was literally packed with groceries.

Chapter 5

The community of Monterey was situated north of 32nd Avenue and east of 52nd Street. At the edge of town, the houses were owned mostly by people hailing from the East. Pakistani and Indian people were very common in the streets here, especially during the summer. The breeze carried the aroma of curry at dinnertime, year in and year out. In one of the cul-de-sacs was Lina and Eva's place. They were sisters, and Eva was the older of the two.

A number of cars were parked in front of the house. Laughter was heard as far as two houses away. Saturday afternoon was the best time for fellowship. It was Lina and Eva's turn to host a monthly meeting of their friends. Dana's family had come early. The living room was filled with the happy faces of people enjoying finger foods served atop the center table. After a few greetings and hugs, Dana directed Lily to bring Junior downstairs to where the kids were playing. The ages of the kids ranged from one to thirteen. What a mess it was to mix this group together; it was like a zoo and a marketplace in one.

The meeting started with singing. People were introduced. Lily, being the newest in the group, got the most attention. Unsolicited advice came from all of her eager new friends—how to do this and to do that was the common theme. A third of the adults present had jobs related to caregiving in one way or another. Four of the women present were still nannies.

Twenty-nine-year-old Lina had been a nanny for the last three years. For her, it was torture working for a Caucasian couple with entirely different values. She couldn't even cook food of her own choosing. Cold cuts, chips, and pop were good enough for a meal. Mentioning God and religion at home was not allowed. Money and material objects were the center and focus of the family's conversations. The husband worked with an oil company while the wife was a dancer at a bar in downtown Calgary. It was a common occurrence for the wife to entertain male visitors while the husband was out of town. Two-year-old Kevin, the child under Lina's care, was a pain in the neck. Aside from being spoiled, he had the same attitude as his parents—in other words, he was mean and disrespectful. Many times, Lina was tempted to lock the rascal in the basement for hours at a time.

The only good thing about her stay with the family was the observance of their employment contract. Saturdays and Sundays were hers to enjoy as she wished. If ever she worked during those days, she was paid overtime. Had her goal not been to earn enough money to pass the provincial nursing exam, she would have long since left the family. Now that she had met her goal, she was ready to move on.

It was a well-known fact that the life of a nanny was full of twists and turns. Being a nanny was only the first step to a more satisfying career. Lina was determined to practice her nursing profession in the very near future. She had finally passed the nursing licensing exam. Part of the evening's meeting was the celebration of her new job as a new staff nurse in the city's biggest hospital.

The food was ready and people were lining up along the table when the doorbell rang. Bert, who was thirty years old, was Dana's nephew. From work, he had driven straight to the meeting. Dana politely introduced him to the group. He was a fresh face from Toronto, just assigned to Calgary by his employer, Suncor. A computer wizard, Bert was in charge of fixing computer hardware for various corporations in and out of Calgary. He had a medium build, and this was his first time mingling in this kind of crowd. His aim, though, was first and foremost the food. Friends came second.

Just like any other gathering of Pinoys, karaoke singing was very common after a sumptuous dinner. The ladies tried very hard not to let themselves be outperformed by the gentlemen.

When the conversation shifted from life in general to computers, everyone had their eyes on Bert. As far as his training was concerned, he could tackle most of the common problems computer problem people had. He could fix almost anything. It was then that Lina's face cracked with a smile. She had been hoping that her computer, dead for almost three months now, could be resurrected. Bert agreed to come by her house the following week to diagnose what was wrong with her personal computer.

The last person to leave the house was Bert, at 11:30. It would take him more than forty minutes to drive home from the northeast corner of the city to the southwest side.

After a series of visits, Lina's computer got all the upgrades it needed. Bert mounted eighty gigabytes of new memory, set up a webcam, and installed various other software programs.

Even the keyboard and mouse were replaced. At the end of many visits, two things were fixed—the computer and their friendship. By the time Bert was ready to leave, they made plans for a dinner date.

One Sunday afternoon, Eva and Lily accidentally met at the check-out counter of Wal-Mart and they began talking.

"How are Bert and your sister getting along?" Lily asked. They were still fifteen people behind the front of the line.

"They just met a few months ago, and they're too close already. Tatay and Inang are worried about their frequent dates," responded Eva.

From what she had observed the last time, Lily's intuition was right. It was very uncommon in Filipino culture to have two family weddings within the same year. Eva had just arrived from the Philippines to visit her fiancé and had set their wedding date before the end of the year. She sensed that Bert and Lina's wedding would be coming up in the same year as well.

"That will be $25.75," the cashier said when they got to the front of the line. "Did you find all that you were looking for?" Her eyes turned to Eva.

"Oh, yes!" Eva answered reluctantly. "Nice meeting you again, Lily. Extend my regards to Dana."

"I will."

That was the last time Lily and Eva ever saw each other.

Pressure from Eva and Lina's parents put a wedge between the two sisters. One of them had to give up or adjust the date of their wedding.

Love is one of the strongest attractions in the universe. Lina and Bert's wedding had to go forward, so Eva decided to go back to the Philippines for her scheduled wedding. Their parents were dumbfounded. Balance and understanding should have been accorded to both sisters, since the parents wanted to see both their daughters start their own families.

The Marriott Hotel just across from the Calgary Tower was one of the most popular hotels in the city. The reception hall was so grand. Twenty tables with ten chairs each were decorated with pink tablecloths and rose centerpieces. Three of the ushers were busy greeting the guests while two others guided people to their respective seats. At this kind of formal gathering, it was hard to know who was a nurse, an engineer, a computer operator, or even a nanny. Everyone was in his or her best suit. Lots of skin was exposed. Barong Tagalog, Filipino formal attire, was worn by about a third of the gentlemen present. The atmosphere was enchanting and alive. Guests who had arrived early comfortably at their tables, tapping their fingers to the rhythm of the music.

The master of ceremonies, after adjusting his suit and tie, tested the microphone.

"Testing, one two three! Hello, hello, hello!"

Guests were getting irritable when the sound system didn't cooperate. The high-pitched squeal of feedback flooded through the speakers. Finally, the hotel's technician was able to fix the problem. Everybody settled down and waited for the next segment of the night. Waitresses punctually filled up the glasses on each of the tables, making sure that everybody had enough to drink before the food was served.

Lily's group was directed to table number seven, not so distant from the head table. Ushers were scrambling to locate vacant seats at the back of the hall as more guests entered the hall. Others simply strolled around in and out the reception area.

"Typical Filipinos, always coming late. Don't they have any sense of shame?" murmured one of the senior citizens at a neighbouring table.

After ten minutes of preliminary introductions, everybody was requested to stand. Bert and Lina's march toward the head table was greeted with loud applause by the hungry crowd, as if to say, "Hurry up so we can start digging in!" It was customary at any occasion, but especially at weddings, for someone to say grace over the food.

"That prayer was touching," Lily said after a man said grace. "Who was the guy who said it?"

"Rene," answered Dana.

"Ah, yes. He was the leader of the group that gathered at Eva and Lina's place last time."

Dana nodded. "You are right."

Since Rudy, Dana, and Lily all attended the wedding, Junior had been taken to spend the evening with a family friend. With them around the table were family friends of the bride. The environment was festive. People were enjoying Caucasian foods while others were jokingly demanding for rice and other well-known Filipino dishes. The steak was juicy and cooked just right.

Everybody was excited and curious about the program.

Ting, ting, ting, ting. The echoing sound of cutlery tapping glasses was a cue for Bert to land a kiss on Lina's lips.

The maid of honor and best man shared their thoughts about the couple. The unforgettable experiences and memories they'd had with them were joyfully shared with the crowd.

"Lina was a very soft-spoken and shy lady," the maid of honor said. "Her gentle personality and sweet smile make my day at work endurable. Aside from being thoughtful, her caring character makes life around the office bearable. Now that she has found her dream man, I believe she will have a nice family in the future. For Lina and Bert, I would like to request everybody to offer them, especially to Lina, a toast. Toast to the bride and to the groom!"

Bert's best friend, Scott, was a Caucasian who had flown in from Ontario two days before the wedding. Scott, without any hesitation or reservation, mentioned how intimate his long years of friendship with Bert were. Now that their fates took them in opposite directions, he still treasured their time together.

"It was really hard to get out of the closet and face your life with another person," was Scott's last sentence before he offered a toast to the groom and bride.

"What does he mean by getting out of the closet?" Lily whispered into Dana's ear.

Dana put her arm under the table and tapped Lily's lap, indicating that they would have to discuss this later. Lily was puzzled. With her mouth shut, her eyes just followed the couple to each table for souvenir pictures. These pictures brought out the best smiles from everybody.

Eva was not around, for a very obvious reason.

The celebration lasted almost three hours. Guests and visitors went their own ways satisfied and full of stories to tell their friends in the days to come. Among other things, Lily was struck by how lucky Lina was. She had gone from being an ordinary caregiver to becoming a registered nurse, and now she was wedded to a guy who had a good job and a wonderful past in Ontario.

Months after the wedding, the couple bought a house in Harvest Hill. Life for them was smooth but far from ideal. From time to time, people would ask how they were doing. The last word spreading around was their plan to move to a different part of the city.

Months later, the couple moved to nearby Panorama. It was a big decision, given the upswing pricing trend in the housing market. Their new home, according to their realtor, was worth $550,000 in the market. They now had two kids, so for a young family like theirs, this accomplishment was worth noticing.

Panorama was one of the newest communities northwest of Calgary. Lina's work required a roughly thirty-minute commute. Very few immigrants could afford to relocate to this community. The family was blessed with nice paying jobs. They were the envy of those who had been in the city so much longer than them.

Envy, jealousy, and misunderstanding for quite some time had infected the relationship between the two sisters, Lina and Eva. Moving to another place was not only for the betterment of Lina, but for the family as well.

Eva and her husband, Eddie, also decided to leave the family house and bought another one about a kilometer away, in the community of Corral Spring. A number of ethnic groups called this community "curry spring," because so many of the families living there were from the East. Many people simply ignored the reality of that place. This community became a battleground for the major political parties and specifically politicians coming from the East.

The couple accepted that having children was nowhere on the horizon.

The rift between Eva and Lina was growing bigger. No talk, phone, email, or communication of any kind was exchanged. Even during family occasions, the sisters remained distant from each other.

Chapter 6

During the first two weeks of December, Lily experienced the bitterness of winter for the second time. It was only 5:00 in the afternoon and the light posts were already illuminating the vast parking lot of Foothills Hospital. The cool and mild breeze coming from the west added a chilling effect to the winter night. It was eighteen degrees below zero, and that was cold enough for Lily. A jacket more suitable for temperatures closer to thirty below was tightly wrapped around her.

Five cars away from where Dana had parked the car, they noticed a nearby car with a half-open window. Smoke coming from the car was being carried by the wind straight to their nostrils. It smelled like a cigarette. As they were heading for the entrance of the building, a big bold sign read, "Smoking in the building and parking area is prohibited." Even in the shelter just meters away, between the entrance and the parking lot, a number of people, including patients, were enjoying their smoke.

"It's ridiculous! Are they not enforcing the hospital's no-smoking ordinance?" whispered Lily as they entered the sliding door.

"It's a joke," Dana replied.

Like synchronized swimmers, they unbuttoned their winter jackets as the elevator climbed the floors of the building. Lily, Dana, and another woman they didn't know proceeded to the east wing of the sixth floor. As they strolled carefully down the corridor, their eyes were fixed on the names attached to each door. They were looking for the room which belonged to the woman they had come to see—Melanie.

Thirty-three-year-old Melanie was still new in the city. Five months ago, Melanie had arrived as one of the many nannies under the foreign workers program. Her employers were happy that somebody of her caliber and ability was available to take care of their young boy. The reality of leaving her family in the Philippines—an eleven-year-old son and a husband—had proven almost too much for Melanie to take during her early weeks in Calgary. Hard work and her employers' wonderful treatment of her had sustained her for the last four months. Unfortunately, Melanie had now caught the attention of the entire Filipino community in Calgary and its nearby cities. She had been released by her employer and sent to Foothills Hospital. After weeks and a series of tests, it was confirmed that she had a terminal case of cancer.

"Thanks for the flowers," Melanie said in her wobbly voice. "They're beautiful!" With tears rolling down her cheeks, Melanie was able to relay, in a struggling spirit, her appreciation to her visitors.

"Lily is also new in Calgary," Dana said. "She's taking care of Junior. We heard you are going back home next month, so we decided to visit and wish you and your family the best."

Silence ensued. There were traces of needle marks in both of Melanie's arms. A half-empty bag of dextrose hung over the bed and was attached to her hand via a small IV tube. From the door came her nurse—whose name was Mila, as indicated by the nametag—with all her records and medication on one tray.

"*Kabayan*, it's time for your pills," Mila said with a sweet smile. That smile was also directed to Lily and Dana.

She then left the room after scribbling notes onto Melanie's medical records. Friends and various Pinoy associations in the city covered the bulletin board at the side of her bed with hand-delivered get-well cards. A picture of her husband and only son at the center of the board was her source of inspiration and her reason to live. Letters from the Philippines were also inserted at the top left corner. The top of her bedside table was covered with different kinds of bread and fruit, and an assortment of flowers was tucked into a vase.

In the course of their talk, Melanie told them about two important wishes she wanted to see before she left this life. One was to see and kiss her family this New Year and the second was to celebrate her thirty-fourth birthday in the last week of January. Their casual talk also focused on some of the initiatives of various Filipino groups. Melanie's trip back to Philippines was made possible by a local Filipino group called "Babae." Her picture had been posted in various Filipino businesses, organizations, establishments, and churches. Filipinos working in different plants and manufacturing facilities responded generously to the appeal for financial assistance. Even Filipino communities from distant places like Fort McMurray, Edmonton, and Lethbridge were sending financial support. A website was even developed exclusively to apprise people of her condition and any updates in her situation. Over a period of time, the amount of money collected became more than enough to cover the airfare, ambulance, medication, and other costs associated with the twenty-hour trip from Calgary to Manila.

It was a very touching experience for Lily. Melanie was going back to see her family and to say goodbye for eternity. What a tragedy it was for such a young life to be taken away.

As they left Melanie's room, Lily noticed one of the nurses working in the nursing station.

"Dana, that nurse in the rubber shoes... wasn't she Lina?" Lily's finger pointed to one of the ladies putting away a patient's chart. The table was being cleared out after that patient's dinner break. Other nurses were already having their dinner. On the table were common Filipino delicacies—rice with barbeque chicken, noodles, and other oriental foods. They also noticed that five of the eight nurses were Filipinas.

"Hi, Lina!" shouted Dana as they walked closer to the nurses' station. Other nurses were craning their necks to see who was speaking loudly and approaching their station. The evening patients were trying to get some sleep.

"Hello," Lina said.

"How are your kids doing?"

"They're doing fine."

"So, Bert's the nanny for tonight?"

"He has no choice."

"I thought you were assigned to the emergency unit."

"They need extra hands here." Lina turned to Lily. "How are you, Lily?"

"Good," Lily answered.

"Melanie's story is so sad," Lina said.

Out of curiosity, Lily asked, "Tell me, how many Filipina nurses are working in the hospital?"

"I don't know. However, I do know that most of us were caregivers before."

"We have to go," Dana interrupted. "Junior is probably looking for us now. It was nice meeting you again, Lina."

"Good night, ladies."

Thirty minutes passed and the two women were back in the parking lot. Lily noted the same "No Smoking" sign and still people were smoking. They got in their car and left the hospital after paying the commissioner behind the window of the pay booth, the sill of which was lined with rubber toy ducks of different colours and sizes.

It took them several minutes to recompose and collect their thoughts.

"This is one of the examples of the uncertainties we immigrants face in a foreign land," said Dana with sadness. "Melanie was so fortunate, not only because of our community's support but because the medical system is so good here. If this had happened in our country, even to a rich person, their entire fortune would have been wiped out after one or two chemo treatments."

It was no wonder so many families and immigrants moved to Canada and decided to stay. Others simply disposed of their properties back home and bought one in the city.

Their discussion branched out to other life-related issues—the "what ifs" and "so whats" of life for foreign workers. Life back home was easier and less stressful. Life in North America was relatively secure, although it was also stressful. Going from a happy-go-lucky life to the rat race was a big challenge. Persistence, perseverance, and patience were the virtues that most immigrants and caregivers alike were holding onto.

Staring up at the ceiling that night, Lily's mind wandered. The reality of Melanie's situation really impacted her. "What if" became a recurring question that came to her mind for many days. How many nannies like her faced the same dilemma in life? What was the chance that she would one day be in the same situation as Melanie?

The story of Melanie's life had been circulating for weeks after her trip back home to the Philippines. In malls and grocery stores, Filipinos were moved by her story and talked about her memory, encounters, and experiences.

———

Lerma, a friend of the deceased Melanie, was also a friend to Dana. One Saturday afternoon, in the midst of their shopping together, Melanie's tragedy extended their sharing time to two hours at the food court of Chinook Centre Mall. Though Lily was busy looking after Junior, her ears were attentive enough to pick up the latest news from the Philippines.

This was Lily's first time meeting Lerma and yet they were able to connect well. Hailing from the summer capital of the Philippines, her complexion was distinct. Lerma's first caregiving experience had been to a Chinese employer in Hong Kong five years earlier.

"It was far different from what we have here in Canada," Lerma explained. In Hong Kong, her quarters had been separated from the kitchen by nothing more than a curtain. A folding cot was her only comfort after nine hours of work. It was unbearable, indeed, but this had been her only option to survive. Her talk reflected more suffering and disappointment. Feelings of hatred and bitterness were present in the discussion. The contempt in her character manifested itself in masculine gestures. Her poise was hard as steel and her manners as rough as gravel.

Then, in the midst of her sharing, she mentioned the opportunity that had come to her via a friend in Canada. One of her friends, Letty, had been looking for a caregiver to take care of a three-month-old kid belonging to her employer's friends. The mother was going back to work in five months and so they needed a nanny before winter. Lerma had to do her part if she really wanted to get out of Hong Kong as quickly as possible. She kept the new opportunity from her Chinese employers, and yes, even from her other friends. In secrecy, it took her months to process the application. She had to send seven hundred dollars of her savings to the recruitment agency in Calgary. It was August 1998 when Lerma finally arrived in Canada, just in time for her waiting employer to go back to work.

The reunion between Letty and Lerma brought happiness and security to both of them. They had been friends in Hong Kong where both of them had been attending a small Christian church. Now both were together again in Calgary.

Time was not a factor in making friends. In less than a week, Lerma was friends with many other caregivers like her. With Letty's coaching, their network of friends grew every weekend. One of their activities was visiting big malls in the city.

Halfway through their dessert, Lerma indicated that her outlook and lifestyle would never change. She would be the same in Canada as she had been in Hong Kong.

"Fair enough," said Dana.

At the back of her mind, Lerma subtly admitted that she was a lesbian.

As the afternoon grew shorter, Lily and Junior went for a walk around the mall. When they came back, they headed towards the two women. Dana and Lerma got the cue; they packed up, stood, and headed toward the exit.

"Hopefully we'll be meeting again sometime," said Lerma to Dana and Lily.

"Of course!" answered Dana with her cart full of purchases for the family.

They left the busy parking lot at 5:15. The traffic was crawling very slowly. The road work being done to ease the traffic plaguing the intersection of Glenmore Trail and Macleod Trail was at its peak. Normally, the travel time from the east side of the city to the west via Glenmore took about twenty minutes. Now, with the snail-like pace, commuters had no option but to bury their bodies in the car seats for an extra thirty minutes.

From Glenmore Trail, the car merged onto Deerfoot Trail. To Lily's puzzlement, Lerma was the subject of conversation.

"So what do you think of Lerma?" asked Dana.

"Is she a lesbian?"

"As far as I know, she had a boyfriend last time we met."

"And now?" Lily asked, growing puzzled.

"She got her open visa last year and changed her job from being a caregiver to working for a company that does accounting. I forget what company she's with now."

"Yes, she mentioned that her course was in accounting," Lily said.

"Well, there's another thing, both good and bad..."

Lily was getting curious. "What do you mean?"

"Months ago, she bought a house somewhere in the northwest. That's the good news. Now she's living with another woman. That's the bad news."

"Is there something wrong with that?"

Dana was hesitant to continue. "The woman has a family, but they've been away from her for almost five years now. It's not a healthy situation. There's no indication that her family is being petitioned to move here."

"Are you implying that Lerma is lesbian?" Lily asked.

"Based on what I was hearing, Lerma and the other woman were doing fine with each other. Especially when the Canadian government passed a law allowing same-sex marriage two years ago."

"Really?"

"In fact, Lerma's employer, a medical doctor, was very intrigued with Lerma's relationship with the other woman," Dana finished.

Junior was awakened from his deep sleep when the car drove over a hump on the street in front of their house. It was dark outside.

Melanie's situation was obviously different from Lerma's. However, Lily recalled her grandparents' position on this matter as being both unhealthy and utterly incomprehensible. Were these extreme experiences, or were they just part of what one had to prepare for in a foreign land? Lerma's situation embedded itself in Lily's mind that night.

Chapter 7

It was a crisp Saturday morning in June. The whole family was having their morning brunch. It was very unusual to have this kind of time together as a family. Rudy, thankfully, had been given a break and the whole day was set aside exclusively for his family. There would be no work and their focus was on having a great day with Junior. The bread was toasted medium, which was everyone's preference. Junior's orange juice was ready. Fresh brewed coffee perked up their morning. They consumed their eggplant omelets and smoked sausage with gusto. By 10:30, they drove to the southeastern corner of the city.

The summer months were the best time to roam around and visit newly built houses. Open houses presented craftsmanship and quality that many mothers and kids could only dream of. Others simply went to get ideas they could assign to the man of the house for future projects.

Copperfield, a three-year-old community, offered one of the best residential settings in Calgary. Many affluent families bought second houses here for rental purposes. Investment-wise, Copperfield was the place to be, according to many realtors.

The open houses opened at 11:00 in the morning.

"I'm not sure if we can afford even the lowest prices in this area," Dana said, adjusting her eyeglass to focus on the display wall of a particular home.

"Are you going to buy another house?" Lily asked.

"We're just trying to get an idea for the price of houses in these new communities," she replied. "With the increasing number of people moving into the city, investing in real property is far more sensible than RRSPs."

"What are RRSPs?" This was Lily's first encounter with Registered Retirement Saving Plans.

"Oh, yes. We forgot to tell you about those. Don't worry, it's not too late for you. You can always set it up with your bank."

"How much do I have to contribute every month?"

"As little as fifty dollars."

"Is my savings in the bank not enough?"

"The savings may help, but an RRSP will take care of your retirement years," Dana explained.

"That's still far off!"

"Yes, but it's better to be prepared early than just depending on your savings. Look at Junior, for example. We opened him an RESP—Registered Educational Savings Plan."

"For his university tuition?" Lily asked.

"Yes. And for your information, the provincial government is contributing another five hundred dollars per year for each child born in 2005 onwards."

"Cool!"

The next house was 1500 square-feet and was definitely more pricy than the last one. There was no way they could afford it. Their mortgage would have been roughly two thousand dollars per month! The houses were so big. What was even more ridiculous was the fact that, on the average, only four people occupied these North American homes—the parents and two kids. It seemed like such a waste.

"What about Cranston," Dana suggested, thinking of another nearby community. "Can we still drive over there? We have time before our other appointment this afternoon."

The houses in Cranston were in the same price range as those in Copperfield. They even had the same style, look, and layout—even the same developers. There was a Chinese family ahead of them in one of the open houses. The house was full of immigrant families.

Three families came out of the burgundy bungalow located at the corner lot. The layout of the house was so appealing. There was a display on one of the walls about how Feng Shue had influenced the building of the house.

They parked just a block away and rushed with excitement towards the next house, which was on a corner lot. Once inside, they were surprised to see other families in almost all the rooms.

"I guess this Indian family is new in Canada," said Rudy.

"And the reason being?" snapped Dana.

"Only that guy, their realtor, is speaking English. The kids don't even speak English yet."

From the main floor, they proceeded to the upper rooms of the bungalow.

"Are they Indian or Pakistani?" whispered Lily to Dana as they came face to face with the family halfway up the stairs. "Or Bangladeshi?"

"Why? Does it matter?" Both concealed their smile and headed out to the front of the house.

They left Cranston and headed for Mackenzie Town Centre. Rudy parked the car in front of a Wendy's. There weren't many people in the line inside. They took their orders and settled in at the west corner of the restaurant. The first few minutes of their conversation were about house prices. The reality of the costs really altered their dreams of buying another home. Based on their combined annual income, they could only afford a house in the $250,000 range. It was hard to believe that in ten years the pricing had risen more than twenty-five percent.

Rental and recreational properties were becoming the trend. Many investors were focusing their eyes offshore, like in the Caribbean, Central America, and Mexico. Other affluent Filipino families were still sentimental with respect to investments, however. Pinoys were buying up vacant lots wherever they could find them.

"The very reason we are looking for another house is the fact that many people, especially from our country, are immigrating here," Rudy said, finishing off his chili. "Whether they have independent or working visas, they all need a place to stay."

"One thing's for sure," Dana said. "There will always be renters."

"Another good thing is that the economic boom has enabled lots of people—yes, even some nannies who have been here a long time—to buy their own homes."

"How's that possible?" asked Lily.

"Through courage and having a good strategy for saving money. Two or three nannies can pool their money for the down-payment on a house. If there is a spare room, they can rent it out to a regular weekender, or even a newly arrived family. It's not bad to collect an extra eight hundred to a thousand dollars in rent every month."

Lily's mind was working rapidly, digesting the implications of this news. The prospect of owning her own home seemed too good to be true.

Their talk then branched out to other topics.

In a society that was so affluent, the dominant impression was that only lazy and irresponsible people were left behind. Opportunities were everywhere. However, many noted that those people who frequented Calgary's drop-in center were enabling themselves to become too dependent upon others. A number of them failed to take the extra steps necessary to improve their lot, and many were victims of the economic crisis. The unemployment rate was so low that records were being set in some areas of the province. Calgary was a magnet not only for offshore investments, but for people, both skilled and unskilled. The oil and gas industry was propelling this boom. Even the numbers of recruitment agencies were growing like mushrooms, and many of those recruitment agencies had satellite branches in the Philippines. Even in the Middle East, many recruiters were putting up offices to lure workers who could pay exorbitant recruitment fees.

"Isn't your boyfriend working for an oil and gas company in the Middle East?" asked Dana.

"I talked to him last time about the possibility of moving here," Lily said.

"Now is the right time for him to move," Rudy said. "Encourage him!" He finished off his last gulp of iced tea.

"We'll get in touch again tonight. I'll discuss the matter with him."

Lily's mind was racing. Was it possible for them to get a house in Cranston or Copperfield? Would their bedroom window face the Rockies, bringing tranquility? She imagined owning a BMW, which she parked inside a three-car garage, next to Mike's Hummer. Hardwood flooring in the first level of the house would bring class, while her refrigerator would be full to the rim, offering saturated fats and cholesterol.

At the back of her mind were thoughts of vacationing in Bermuda, or in Hawaii. Knowing how much money people in the oil and gas industry were raking in, she could easily picture Mike and her working hard to enjoy a month-long cruise in the Caribbean. She also wanted to visit the eastern regions of Canada, such as Niagara Falls in Ontario. Included in the list of places to visit were Parliament Hill and the Museum of Civilization in Ottawa. She knew that if they went to Toronto, she wanted to experience the CN Tower. Besides, the city was home to many of Dana and Rudy's friends. It would be an interesting place to visit. She even wanted to walk along Park Avenue in New York one day.

Ouch! What was that? Lily came back to reality when Dana pinched her arm.

"It's only 3:30 in the afternoon and you're already dreaming," said Dana.

"Am I?"

"You've only seen three new houses and they caught your imagination."

"Isn't it normal to aspire for something better?" Lily asked.

"Yes, but you are forgetting about our appointment at Superstore."

"I thought we were going to Wal-Mart today."

"Whatever," Dana said. "I'll go wherever."

It took them another five minutes to get to the grocery store. Junior had his nap while they were driving.

As usual, the street leading to Superstore was not heavy with traffic. There was lots of space to move around. Junior was unleashed and headed to his favorite toys corner. Dana and Lily, on the other hand, took their usual route through the meat section, then to fruits and vegetables and dry or canned products.

The cart was almost half-filled when they saw a group of store employees trying to figure out what was supposed to go on the pet food shelves. They had obviously been reminded of the latest issue about tainted pet food. Certain brands of pet food were being recalled or taken off the shelves. Dozens of pets, primarily cats and dog, had recently been rushed to veterinarians. No less than fifteen had died as a result of liver failure. Based on the study conducted, the culprit was tainted pet food, laced with rat poison. North American pet lovers had been furious over the incident for three weeks now. A class-action lawsuit had been filed in court.

"This is how Caucasians regard their pets," Dana said. "They are like extended members of the family."

"In the Philippines, our pets only eat leftover foods," Lily observed. "What a shock it is to see families here spending so much money on pet food and taking their pets to see the vet."

"Have you heard about pet daycare centers?" Dana asked.

"Really?"

"More than that, there are even a few stores in the city that carry fashion lines for pets."

Lily couldn't believe her ears. "You're kidding me, right?"

"Why would I joke about that? There are more rich families in Calgary than any other city west of Toronto. For some people, pets are the only living beings that understand and comfort them. Some people spend more on their pets than they give to the Mustard Seed Ministry."

"What is the Mustard Seed Ministry?"

"It's a Christian organization that helps street people by giving them food to eat and a place to stay," Dana explained. "They also train people to gain social and employable skills."

"Isn't that the same thing the United Way is doing?"

"United Way is more about funding not-for-profit organizations to run their respective socio-economic programs aimed at disadvantaged sectors of society."

At the mention of socio-economic programs, Lily thought about her friend back in the Philippines, Nora, who had gone on to become a social worker in Mindanao. If only she had come to Canada, too. Her skills and understanding of social work would have been put to good use. Nora had a passion to help the poor and disadvantaged sectors of society. The only problem was that her English was poor, and she only wanted to do things her own way. Also, she needed to upgrade her schooling and pass the exam to make her a licensed social worker. It would take her at least three years before she could come to Canada and practice her profession here.

The check-out line was getting longer. Many tills were closed due to a shortage of tellers. In front of the store, a big sign read, "Hiring for all positions!" Just like a lot of other stores, this one was largely operated by East Indian employees. East Indians were known as all-around hard workers. They were everywhere, whether it was cleaning residential homes, stores, driving commuter buses, or other related services.

Junior was tugging Lily's jeans while they were in line for the teller. A number of people in line were watching for how she would react to Junior's annoying attitude. Lily knew that Dana would simply ignore him and not act irrationally while they were in public. Others could interpret angry gestures as child abuse.

"I wanna pee!" said Junior.

"Okay, accompany him to the washroom over there," Dana said, pointing to the east side of the customer service kiosk. Minutes later, Lily and Junior emerged from the bathroom door smiling.

As they continued waiting for the cashier, they noticed an older Filipina woman standing a few feet in front of them. She reminded them of another woman they both knew about, one whose story had been circulating around the Filipino community, just like Melanie's story had.

"I heard a woman like that one was admitted to the Peter Lougheed Hospital," said Dana, shifting the topic from charitable organizations to an issue closer to their hearts.

Lily nodded. "Yes, she was just visiting her son's family here when she was diagnosed with cancer."

"It's the same thing all over again," Dana murmured.

"What do you mean?"

"It's just like what happened to Melanie. Pinoy groups are soliciting donations and support from the community every time a case like this hits the media."

"Is there something wrong with that?"

"I'm not sure. But the way I see it, these people are being trivialized while their stories are overhyped."

Suddenly, they were at the front of the line and the cashier was ringing through their purchases. "$125.75," the cashier demanded.

Dana handed her a credit card while Lily and Junior put the groceries into plastic bags. Junior opened one of the cookies they had bought. After a few bites, he put the cookie box back into the plastic bag. His curious eyes scanned the area around him.

A few feet away from the sliding exit doors, Lily waved her hand to a lady in the parking lot. It was Bernie. Her cart was full to the rim.

"Hello, hello, hello!" Bernie greeted with a wide smile on her face. "When was the last time we met here?"

"I'm not sure, but I think six months to a year ago," Dana said.

Bernie smiled, then changed the subject. "Have you seen the latest news from Manila?"

"No! What's happening there?"

"There was this daycare center located just east of city hall. A man boarded a school bus with the kids and drove it to city hall. With a hand grenade in one hand, he demanded that the government promise lasting support for the education and future of kids in the Philippines and to stop government corruption at the expense of Filipino people."

The most intriguing part of the story was the fact that the guy who held the kids captive also happened to be the owner of the daycare. This had been his way of protesting government corruption. Though irregularities in the government were rampant, many kept their eyes and ears closed to this kind of social injustice.

"He was instant news. CNN and many other foreign media stations covered the story. An actor turned senator intervened with the guy." Bernie related the story as though they were in Manila, blocks away from the scene of the hostage drama. The news had been big among the local Filipino communities.

"So what happened to the kids?" asked Lily.

"It took about nine hours before the man was convinced to give up."

"Good thing it ended peacefully."

As they reached their respective cars and unloaded their groceries, Bernie's voice continued, "Are you going to visit that woman at the Peter Lougheed Hospital?" People could hear her at a distance of five cars away.

"So you know the rest of the story about her?" asked Dana.

"Of course!"

Once inside the car, Dana and Lily waved goodbye to Bernie. In just one day, Lily had been nearly overwhelmed with information. Tainted pet food. RRSPs. Visiting the old woman in the hospital. The hostage drama in Manila... all this stress was beginning to make her feel anxious.

Chapter 8

The forecast was balmy, way warmer than the normal temperatures for January. It was very uncommon to see people jogging early in the morning along Memorial Drive, across from Prince's Island Park, with their shorts and sweatshirts on. Some temperature records were being broken elsewhere on the prairies. The warm weather was a bonus for people who had just moved to the city.

It was 2007, the same year that Calgary passed a bylaw prohibiting smoking in public places. That same year, the local government required all pet owners to register and license their cats. Animal shelter operators welcomed the move, especially since that winter's freezing temperatures were just around the corner.

Noemi was one of the many pet-loving nannies lined up at the city hall's animal licensing office that day. Like many others, she was taking advantage of the warm weather to license the family cat before the deadline. The number of Filipina women with kids tagging along in the long line was noticeable. Most of these women were caregivers. Hailing from the same country, Noemi and the woman next to her, Vicky, were talking and enjoying their time in line. Both were pushing identical strollers, except for the colour—Noemi's was blue and Vicky's was pink. Noemi's kid was a year older than the other, who was sleeping sweetly.

"How old is the cat?" asked Noemi.

"Not sure," Vicky said. "I was told Cutie is about three years old, but I've only been working for this family the last two years." The two agreed that taking care of pets was not part of their work contract. However, it was understood that pets, being part of the family, deserved attention from the helper of the house; it was a silent and unwritten agreement. With the passing of the licensing bylaw, the creatures were now indispensable extensions of the family even in legal and social aspects.

"Have you heard about Melanie's fate?" asked Vicky.

"Not since she flew back home."

"Her life was really a tragedy."

"Her time had come, I suppose."

"It's really important to visit a doctor for an annual checkup," Vicky said.

"My employer told me to schedule a check-up with our doctor for a pap smear and breast examination next week."

"It's a good thing you can always have your health checked and monitored in this country."

"A person can become too complacent and focused on their work," Noemi said. "You never know what is lurking in your body."

"That's especially true for us!"

"What do you mean?"

Vicky shrugged. "I'm not sure if it is just a myth or a fact, but if a woman's body is not being used properly or regularly—you know what I mean—breast or cervical cancer is more likely to occur." She also added that the truth of this was attested to by midwives and other medical practitioners in the Philippines. The reason was that a woman's body was designed to bear babies, and that produced certain anatomical changes that, if not properly utilized, could result in certain unhealthy anomalies—which sometimes took the form of malignant tumors or the irregular outgrowth of tissues.

"I've heard that before," Noemi said. "But is there a medical study to prove it? Just imagine how many caregivers or nannies around the world fall into the same 'seldom-used category' as we do!"

"So when is your husband coming?" Vicky asked.

"He failed his medical exam. He'll be back for another round next month."

"Is he smoking or alcohol-dependent?"

"Both, and he prefers meat to vegetables."

"Bad, bad, bad!"

"I know," Noemi acknowledged. "What about you? Are you married?"

"Not yet," Vicky said. "I'm planning to be home next year and marry my fiancé."

"Good for you."

At 11:10, a young Filipina clerk behind the glassed window handed Noemi and Vicky their licenses and receipts. "Thanks, *kabayan*," they said as they left.

T.D. Square Mall housed the biggest indoor park in Calgary. Fifteen different downtown walkways converged in this glass-walled building. It took Noemi and Vicky twenty minutes of brisk walking to get there, which gave them enough time for a hot and steamy bowl of wonton soup at the third-floor food court. The food court was like a zoo. People of all different colours and heights were patiently and slowly moving in line to order food. There were all sorts of foods available, including pizza, sub sandwiches, hamburgers, salads, wraps, Vietnamese pho noodles, sushi, curry chicken, cinnamon buns, and quarter-pound chickens

The children in their care were fully satisfied with the food they had brought along—Jell-O, yogurts, carrot sticks, cheese sticks, and bottles of instant formula. Finally, their orders were prepared and they found a quiet corner to sit down. They were not the only caregivers around the food court; in one corner were three Pinoys and their respective babies sleeping comfortably in baby strollers.

Wonton soup could be very helpful in the middle of January, and they enjoyed every bite of it. Vicky and Noemi were not in a hurry to finish. Some tropical ferns and plants were visible nearby. The fish swimming in the ponds were not only golden, they looked rusty, obese, and huge. There was so much to talk about, but they chose to focus on the various gifts their employers had given them for Christmas.

"I got a humidifier for my room and a 3.2-megapixel Sony digital camera," said Noemi.

"Mrs. Hope was so generous," Vicky said. "We went to a Winners clothing store in the northeast side of the city and she let me find something for Christmas. At first I was hesitant, but when she said 'Go for it,' I didn't give it a second thought. I grabbed a nightgown and pink blouse. But there was a big problem. Only yesterday, Mrs. Hope got her credit card notice. She was a victim of credit card fraud!"

"Well, I suppose that's one of the disadvantages of living in a plastic society," Noemi said.

"I know, but what can you do?"

"I prefer cash for all my transactions," Noemi insisted.

"I used my Visa card in Wal-Mart last Christmas, and that was it."

The kids under their care finally became reckless after being tucked into their strollers for more than an hour. The soup was settling inside and their legs were begging for a stretch. Up they moved and went straight to the elevator. The other people waiting for the elevator were very considerate when they saw the two women with children, letting them get on the elevator first. Noemi and Vicky were convinced that Canadians were well-known for being polite. Even when Noemi and Vicky hopped onto the rail transit, many people gave way for them.

The train was full, as usual. Everyone was in a hurry to get back home. Vicky took the other train heading northwest while Noemi took the one going the opposite direction.

When the train, packed with people, stopped at the Anderson station, somebody stood up from an empty chair and Noemi took it. She positioned the stroller in front of her and locked it between her knees. The people around them were busy chatting about all sorts of things. The hot issue of the week was the rule preventing the city's transportation workers from working voluntary overtime hours during weekends. Their contract with the city had not been signed since the previous year, resulting in interruptions to the commuting schedule, which affected many caregivers.

What would happen to their planned activities during the weekends? Their employers were already so hard-pressed driving their own kids around that they didn't have time to worry about also driving the nanny. At minimum, it could take a passenger at least an hour to wait for a taxi.

While some were busy speculating about this, others were focused on the day's news, such as the increase in gasoline prices. It was perhaps one of the reasons why there were more people riding transit in the past few weeks. The contention was that, since Alberta was the energy capital of Canada, Albertans were paying too much at the gas pump.

The train was moving slowly, which made the people's murmuring sound louder. Noemi and the child under her care started to relax. Their eyes slumbered and, minutes later, closed.

When the train stopped at the Chinook station, the drunken old man next to her got off the train, leaving another empty spot. She felt relieved. From behind came a lady with her sunglass still on. Holding Old Navy bags in both hands, she adjusted her position comfortably between Noemi and another woman. As the train inched its way forward, Noemi's eyes met with the new lady sitting beside her. In less than a minute, Noemi recognized her.

"Lily?"

"Yes! Do I know you?"

"I'm Noemi! Have you forgotten me already?" It took about ten seconds before Lily finally recognized her. "We met at last year's group dinner in one of the churches in the northeast."

"Yes, that's right," Lily said. "I was the one who Andrew drove home after the event."

"Andrew. The widower?

"Yes. You spoke with him for almost an hour."

"So what's his score? Will you consider him?"

"He seemed like a nice gentleman, but I don't know," Lily said. "I have a boyfriend in Saudi Arabia."

"Are you sure your boyfriend is faithful to you? Andrew is already here and you wouldn't need to submit an application and pay for him to move here. It would be more practical, and besides, who knows what your boyfriend is doing there, right?"

Lily pressed her lips together. "I'll just leave everything to God."

Lily was tempted to shut off Noemi. In her mind, Noemi was one of those typical people who always gave unsolicited advice to strangers. She just kept silent and held back her temper from spilling out of her lips.

"Thanks for your advice," Lily's replied hesitantly.

"You're welcome," answered Noemi. "By the way, do you still remember Tina and Cory?"

"Were they the ones who sang during the fellowship?" Lily asked.

"Yes, and you know what?"

"What?"

"They invited me to go with them to a ladies nightclub next weekend."

"What do you mean, a ladies nightclub?" Lily asked.

Noemi explained, "They're regulars at this place along Macleod Trail in the southwest. The place is like a bar or lounge where young and old women, married and single, hang around with friends. Young men dance around on stage and these ladies scream and cheer at them."

Lily's face reddened with disbelief. It was her first time hearing of such a place. "You mean…"

"Yes, and I would like to go there with someone just to experience it. How would you like to go with me?"

From the sounds of it, it was a secretive and exclusive place for women who weren't satisfied with their partners. They went there to find happiness with friends, and sometimes— more often than not—with someone who could answer their loneliness. If a woman couldn't find the thrill of adventure in their workplace or at home, it would be worth visiting a place like that.

"Thanks for the invitation, but sorry, Noemi, I don't think I'm interested in that kind of entertainment."

"That's okay!" said Noemi.

Lily was so thankful when the train decelerated to a stop at the Southland station.Noemi unlocked her stroller, pushed it, stepped out of the train, and disappeared from Lily's sight.

Unbelievably, many lonely caregivers did whatever they could to feel good, especially during the winter months. They couldn't have picnics in the park or travel to other provinces, so the only other practical thing to try was going to someplace new. Besides, nobody would know what they were up to or where they spent the night. The freedom to be themselves and to be happy, tempted some caregivers to loosen their grasp on morality and decency. Nobody would ever know. Their lives were their own to live and they would do anything they pleased to stave off boredom. They worked for their freedom and they were entitled to enjoy it.

Out of more than a thousand nannies in Calgary, it sounded like Tina, Cory, and Noemi were already in this habit. How many more nannies were out there doing the same thing? It didn't matter if some of them were married or even single.

The train came to a halt at the last station, Somerset. Lily was not really in a hurry to step out of the train. Her mind was still absorbed with the implications of Noemi's invitation. Even after comfortably sitting in a connecting bus heading out to her employer's place, Lily remained in a state of unbelief. How could Noemi, Tina, and Cory manage to be active both in a church and in a club?

Chapter 9

Alberta in the mid-2000s was the envy of the rest of Canada. Sitting on a large mass of land with endless oil and gas reserves, the province was elevated to a status comparable to the other major economic cities of North America. Calgary welcomed roughly 35,000 new people in 2006 alone. As one of the most dynamic melting pots in the West, Calgary became a metropolitan city of one million people.

The influx of people coming from all over the country and abroad put pressure on the housing industry. The average price of single-family homes rose from $355,000 to $487,000 in just one year. As a result, young families and newcomers were having difficulty owning their own homes.

The value of construction permits in 2006 reached roughly $4 billion, way more than the three competing cites of Toronto, Vancouver, and Montreal. Millions of commercial spaces were added to the city's core.

The Bow, Encana's signature building, captivated the imaginations of businesspeople around the globe. This spectacular fifty-eight-story glass and steel building stood at the heart of downtown Calgary as a testament to the oil patch Cowtown. Dubbed as the tallest building west of Toronto, the Bow was another show of Alberta's power. However, its construction wreaked havoc in the city core. Sixth Street was closed for nine months. Hundreds of thousands of cars were affected by this closure. The resulting traffic jams greatly changed the land-scape of the city's streets.

Economic activity was so hot that eighty-five percent of parents were working, as opposed to those families where only one spouse had a job. Still, the demand for more workers continued in all sectors. Recruitment agencies sprouted like mushrooms around the province. Social services enjoyed large grants from the government and services to various sectors of society were becoming more and more innovative. Young fam-ilies were flocking to the city. The number of students enrolled in all levels of education increased by more than three percent.

Associated with those developments, however, was the increase in the number of some social illnesses. Specifically, young kids were at risk. Caregiving services were badly af-fected. In the early part of 2007, the YMCA decided to trim down their caregiving services in the city core. Parents had to scramble to find a place where they could put their kids.

Alberta Children's Services reported that in spite of more than 25,328 licensed daycare spots and 4,710 approved family day home slots, there was still a waiting list of several hundred kids who were not in a program. Some families had to wait more than three years before they could be assured of a spot for their kids. It was no wonder some pregnant women were booking daycare spots for their children years in advance.

Others simply resorted to placement agencies to attract caregivers from outside the country. More often than not, new nannies were hailing from the Philippines. Known for their excellent caring attitude, many parents preferred Filipina nannies. They were well-versed in the English language, easily adaptable to the environment, and very knowledgeable. It was no wonder that when Lily visited the Bow, she felt right at home. The atrium was packed with nannies and kids. Junior, who was turning three the following month, was busy roaming around the place and playing with other kids his own age.

"*Kabayan*, how are you?" said Lily to a woman holding a nine-month-old boy on her lap.

"I'm good!"

"Where in the Philippines do you come from?"

"From Bacolod. What about you?"

"Nueva Ecija."

The woman pointed to the baby girl. "Her dad is working here."

"I was told this building was new and beautiful," Lily said. "Instead of staying home all day, I decided to bring Junior with me."

"There is another place you could visit," the woman suggested. "It's called the Calgary Centre for Global Community." The 25,000-square-foot center had been conceived and spearheaded by a society of scholars worldwide, including the Parhad Society at the University of Calgary. It had been designed to be a forum for the discussion, debate, and dissemination of world affairs towards the goal of greater global cooperation. Specifically, the center was intended to be a place where immigrants, ethnic groups, and the mainline population could come together to share and celebrate their differences and similarities in the context of tolerance and understanding.

There were so many beautiful and interesting places to visit around the city, Lily thought. She promised herself that before the chilling winds of winter came she would visit those places, including the Calgary Tower and the Glen Bow Museum.

"How far is the Calgary Centre for Global Community from here?" asked Lily.

"It's a fifteen-minute walk." The woman abruptly changed the subject and asked, "How long have you been in Canada?"

Lily answered, "Almost three years now. How about you?"

"Five years in July."

"Is your family here already?"

"My husband is in the Middle East," the woman said. "My two kids, a two-year-old son and a seven-year-old girl, are still with my parents in Bacolod."

"Where in the Middle East is your husband?" Lily asked. "My boyfriend is there, too."

"Kuwait."

"Why is he still there? Does he have no plan of moving here?"

"We're having marital problems."

Lily blushed. "Sorry for asking."

"It's okay, no problem."

Junior, out of nowhere, came running over to her, crying. He tripped and bruised his knee. Lily cuddled him for a minute. Then his desire to explore the vast atrium overwhelmed him and he jumped back out of her lap as if nothing had happened.

"Be careful next time, Junior!" Lily called after him. It didn't seem like he got the message. Junior was heading in the opposite direction. There were more kids in that corner of the lobby. Lily turned back to the woman and noticed that she was staring at another woman across the atrium. "Who is that lady you're staring at?"

"Don't you recognize her?" the woman asked. "She's the nanny from Balzac being investigated for child abuse. See the bandage on the boy's right hand? The neighbour saw her hit the boy, so they reported her to the police. However, there was no evidence or proof that the boy was maltreated by her."

Lily remembered one newspaper article detailing how social scientists were arguing about the appropriateness of parents disciplining their children by slapping them. Some advocated for harsher penalties or fines, while conservatives insisted that without respect to authority, the youth of today would become the tyrants of tomorrow. Slapping was one of the many tools parents applied to break the bad attitude of youngsters. The tenet lingered in Lily's mind that respect for the rules of life was basic to society's survival. She had grown up in a violent environment where many parents slapped their children to discipline and impose obedience. Domestic violence had been one of the issues facing the village where she was raised.

"What about the parents?" Lily asked. "Did they allow her to continue working for them?"

"I think so. If not, why would they be here now?"

"Tell me," Lily said. "You've been here longer than me. Are there any other issues or experiences that nannies like us should know about?"

"Just keep your ears and eyes open and be alert."

People coming from different levels of the building were crowding the atrium. Kids were screaming upon seeing their moms or dads. In a few minutes, the city would be a mess again. Traffic would crawl by at the speed of turtles. Peak hours in downtown Calgary caused most commuters and drivers to lose their patience.

Lily stood up and placed all of Junior's things under the stroller. She found Junior in a corner playing with other kids.

He was pulling apart a plastic toy. It was really fun to watch Junior learning the skills of childplay. She was aware that her time with him was running out. In just a matter of a few months, she would receive her own open visa and she would have to take a leap of faith. She had to focus on starting a new career or upgrading her profession. The time was coming when she would have to leave the family.

After putting on Junior's jacket, mittens, and toque, they stepped onto the escalator with the rest of the people hurrying to beat the traffic.

Their trip to the Bow had been both educational and fascinating. She had learned so much about the life experiences of other nannies like her. Would she be having a pleasant or unpleasant experience as her life progressed? What else was there to discover about being away from home and living alone in this foreign land? Would her fate here be predetermined or would she be able to alter it? What other things were out there to know? What other things were there for her to discover that might impact her life and future?

It took Lily and Junior one hour and fifteen minutes to take the train home.

"How was your day with Junior?" asked Rudy as they entered the living room.

Lily answered, "Not bad. That building was so big. The atrium was full of caregivers like me. It was a nice place to spend time."

"Did you meet any new friends?

"Yes, but I forgot to get her name. She's from Bacolod."

What was bugging her, though, was her encounter with Noemi several days ago.

"The other day while I was on the train, I ran into Noemi. She invited me to go with her to a club exclusive to female patrons," she said, trying to deflect attention from her Bow experience to her encounter with Noemi.

"Do you mean that strip bar along Macleod Trail?" Rudy asked.

"You know the place?"

"My friend's wife often hangs out there with her other friends. If and when her husband travels outside the country, her presence there can be assured."

"Aren't they ashamed of going there?"

"The show usually starts late at night, so people seldom see them go into the bar. Besides, most of the people don't care about who else goes there. It took months before my friend found out his wife was a regular."

"What happened then?"

"If not for our company's employee assistance program, their marriage might have ended."

"What is an employee assistance program?"

"It's a company-sponsored program for employees who are experiencing difficulties in life like divorce, depression, grief, or other problems that affect their performance in the workplace."

After hearing Rudy's explanation, it was clear to Lily that this program was paid for by the company and was a good tool for employees to regain their health, composure, and balance in life.

"In a few minutes, Dana will be here. Give Junior a bath and we'll have our dinner at 7:00."

"Okay," Lily said.

Before long, dinner was simmering in the kitchen. The aroma of herbs was inviting. She put on the water kettle for tea or coffee after dinner. No amount of good food, however, could erase the picture of the strip bar in Lily's head. What in the world were these women getting from it? She had thought that strip clubs were only for men.

Chapter 10

Dear Lily,

Hello. Do you still remember me? How are you doing now? When is your boyfriend moving?

My name is Marilou, from Cagayan. We met last summer in Jasper. Remember our talk about our careers as midwives in the Philippines? Well, for three years Alberta has been waiting for the government to recognize our profession. The wait was too much for me. Last March, my employers, the McCarthys, moved back to Montreal and I had no option but to go with them. Nathan is three years old now and a very naughty boy. A month ago, we found out that Mrs. McCarthy is pregnant again. The couple is hoping for a girl this time. The husband is a computer engineer for one of the biggest service companies in Quebec.

Montreal is an old but dynamic city. It's very multicultural. Blacks and Asians are everywhere. However, I still like Calgary. Though I stayed in Edmonton for two *years, Calgary is still the best. We are staying in the southeast side of Old Montreal. The city is swarming with different kinds of people hailing from all over the world. We have lots of kababayan here. Just recently, I met a friend from your home province of Nueva Ecija. She told me that she knows you, which is why I am sending you this letter.*

Her name is Courtney Delos Reyes. She worked with me in King Faisal Hospital in Saudi Arabia about four years ago. When an offer was made from one of the hospitals in Montreal, she wasted no time leaving there. She remembered that one midwife, fresh from the Philippines, came to her unit one day for direction. Your name stuck in her mind because of your good work ethic. Do you remember her? She's the one who baked cake when they celebrated your first month in the hospital.

Last year, Courtney was able to pass nursing and French language exams. She's with the trauma unit of Montreal General Hospital. She said it was more traumatic in Montreal than in Saudi Arabia. I imagine she's dealing with many kinds of people speaking many different dialects.

We are renting a two-room apartment together, blocks away from her work. As usual, I am staying with my employer. We only see each other during the weekends. The only thing we do on the weekends is watch movies and eat popcorn.

Another reason why I wrote this letter is to inform you of the latest development in Quebec with respect to our profession. The provincial government here is planning to open twenty birthing centers across the province to promote the use of midwives. Aside from the existing eight, the new centers will be opened gradually. Hopefully, I will get my license as a full-fledged midwife before the end of the year.

I have one more problem. I need to go to school and learn how to speak and write the French language. The only thing I know about French is the French fries at McDonald's. Alberta is too slow to recognize this profession.

I wonder why midwives are the preferred means of delivering babies back in our country, while so few people use them here. Only now is the province seeing the benefits of having midwives around. Is Canada backward or advanced?

Just for your information, you might consider someday moving here to practice your profession.

Extend my regards to Dana, Rudy, and Junior.

God bless, Marilou.

Chapter 11

The Philippines claimed to be the only Christian country in the Far East. For more than three hundred years, the Spaniards had colonized the archipelago. Catholicism was one of the marks left by the colonizers. The impact of Catholic belief on the cultural traditions of the Filipinos was pronounced and outstanding. Most of the Catholic missionaries had been from Europe. The Netherlands was also one of the countries that sent priests to sustain the Catholic belief system.

Father Abraham, a Dutch priest stationed in Gapan, Nueva Ecija, was well-loved by his parishioners. He'd been known not only for his height, 6'5", but also for his deep concern and compassion for the people. From christenings, weddings, and funerals, this towering figure was the inspiration and source of hope for many common folk.

He had just returned from a yearlong furlough back to his home country, and every time he came back good news abounded in the community.

It was in the early 1970s when the Netherlands first began to be in high demand for factory workers from the Philippines. One of the good things that happened to this tiny country after the Second World War was the presence of the Americans. For over fifty years, the commerce, education, and legal system was greatly influenced by the Americans. This led to the society working well. English was the second most common language, and it was spoken by nearly three-quarters of the population.

Born out of hardship, Filipinos learned the value of hard work. Diligence, commitment, and their good command of the English language were traits that employers in Europe and Americas were looking for.

Sunday mass ended at about 8:00 in the morning. After mass, Father Abraham made the announcement that a big garment factory in Netherlands was recruiting workers. Young and energetic women were the priority. Three hundred application forms were distributed to potential applicants that morning. Fifteen young women were expected from Father Abraham's region.

As a fresh graduate from high school, Ofelia took home one of those applications, neatly enclosed in a clean envelope. Her dad was very thorough that week in filling out the forms making sure all the information on them was right. To Ofelia's surprise, her whole graduating class was there, too. It was the opportunity of a lifetime. Staying in town was not a good idea. Each of them needed a fresh start to rise above poverty.

Father Abraham was a man of honor. After three months of waiting, fifteen people were invited to his office for interview. Ofelia was one of the lucky fifteen. Weeks later, Father Abraham handed her a contract, working papers, and ticket for a flight to the Netherlands. But she needed more savings.

Her salary would not be high enough at her new job to cover all her expenses.

The following week, she took the opportunity to work in one of the laboratories of the Nueva Ecija Polytechnic College, which was a thirty-minute bus ride south of town. The salary was not that good, but it was higher than what she would be receiving from the factory job. Her mind was focused on that foreign land where she would be starting a new life, a life full of hope and opportunities, a life utterly different from what she was used to in the Philippines.

Her mind raced with possibilities. She dreamed of having a family of her own, with kids and a comparatively better life-style than what was typical in the Philippines. She dreamed of driving a brand new car and living in a well-established neigh-bourhood.

Ofelia's father was so excited while her mother was fright-ened and anxious about her going away from home. Would she be successful there or not?

Her family was excited on the morning of her departure. The flight was scheduled to leave at 5:00 in the afternoon. Due to lack of resources, only her immediate family was able to accompany her to the airport. No relatives or friends came along. The traffic was so light that early in the morning that their rented jeep arrived thirty minutes earlier than expected.

The drive from Gapan to Manila took only three hours. The jeep was parked meters away from the sliding door of the departure building. Her dad and the driver unloaded and car-ried her luggage to the departure gate. Inside the terminal, there were kiosks for different airlines. At the far left corner was the KLM ticketing window. Her mother, sobbing aloud, embraced and kissed Ofelia. Ofelia promised her that some-day they would be together again.

As a military man, her dad held his emotion and just cracked a smile. He hugged her and his teardrops wetted her shoulder. Ofelia was the first child to leave them. It was a very touching moment for everyone.

Her brothers and sisters were interested more about the stuff she would be sending back to them once she was in the Netherlands. Her handkerchief was wet when she entered the sliding door. From her bag, she pulled out her travel documents and walked straight to the woman smiling at her from the other side of a small window. Minutes later, the agent handed Ofelia a boarding pass and ticket. From inside the building, she saw her family still hanging by the side of the glass window separating them. With great determination and direction from the airline attendant, Ofelia headed straight into the smaller sliding door.

There was no turning back.

This was her first time flying on an airplane, her first time being out of the country, and her first time working for a foreigner. She felt anxious.

Her anxiety doubled when the plane landed at Rotterdam International Airport. Upon arrival, all fifteen of the girls were directed to a waiting bus outside the terminal. The jetlag made them all sleepy, even though the bus ride only took one hour. The housing unit where they were staying was well-furnished. Their quarters were more orderly and pleasant-looking than a three-star hotel in Manila.

Most of them felt drowsy the following morning, yet their eyes were full of excitement, hope, and anticipation. At 9:00, the girls took a bus to the factory. They walked inside and proceeded down a long hallway. The third room to the left was the orientation hall. Half of the seats were taken when the session started. Thirty young, energetic, and aspiring workers were all ears as the speaker began talking. His English was not bad at all. He clearly explained three important aspects of the job—the salary, the benefits, and when they could take holiday time to return to the Philippines.

There was no time wasted during the orientation. There was a ten-minute break in the morning, a thirty-minute lunch hour, and another ten-minute break in the afternoon. By the end of the day, they were all like wilted flowers trying to show their joy and enthusiasm with no luck; their eyes were too heavy.

After work, they boarded the same bus, which took the reverse route going back to their accommodations. Everyone was exhausted and some simply dropped their tired bodies into bed—never mind dinner. Ofelia was one of them. However, at the back of her mind were thoughts of the coming day, her first day of on-the-job training.

At exactly 7:45, thirty of the girls, including Ofelia, got off the bus in front of big metal gates, the entrance of the factory. The locker room was located along a dark and musty corridor. Ofelia's locker was near the back door of the room. She noticed that the room accommodated one hundred lockers. The machines in the factory were not running yet. She figured out that the noise she was hearing came from the other side of the locker room. They were voices, the sound of many different languages being spoken at the same time in a confined room by anxious women. It sounded like being in the middle of a marketplace. Excitement and great anticipation lingered and emanated from the mouths of everyone there.

Ofelia fastened the last button of her blue coveralls when the siren sounded, indicating that it was time for them to proceed to the training room. They proceeded to the room adjacent to the washroom at the back of the building. Exactly thirty sewing machines were waiting for them.

After an hour of talk, the instructor directed them, in a Dutch accent, to pick a sewing machine and start their training. After two or three trial runs, the group was confident enough to start with the actual work.

The first few weeks were not boring. Their love for learning was still a great motivator. Ofelia made friends, but arguments also occasionally erupted between workers, causing people's patience to wear thin. The only consolation was that the girls enjoyed their weekends in the parks and malls. They even took a trip to Amsterdam once, which was more than fascinating.

The Netherlands was a real mystery for foreigners. For instance, how was it possible for the land they were on to be below sea level? That was the number one question. Tulips and yellow wooden shoes were among the most notable features one could see in the countryside. Sixty-four souvenir pictures were instantly sold to them when their group dropped by a small bookstand for a quick cup of coffee one day.

Weeks and months passed and they didn't notice it. They enjoyed receiving their salaries and sending money home to their families. They got used to the routine of the job. Almost every day, Ofelia had the opportunity to learn new things about the lives of her coworkers. Most of the time it was all gossip.

During her second year, which occurred during the early 1970s, the company released an internal memo indicating that the girls' services would be terminated after six months. The recession in Europe was great and the textile and fabric industry had to make cuts. It was added in the memo that the company was doing its best to find replacement jobs for them around or even outside the country. Six months later, the group's survival motto was to save and save and be ready for the worst. Mall shopping turned to window shopping. Travel and excursions were no longer viable pastimes.

Winter soon swept Europe. It was a hard reality to live in the midst of winter with no work and being thousands of miles away from home. However, some of Ofelia's friends were smart. Before their jobs ended, a number of them managed to change their surnames. Dutch men were serious about marrying Filipinas. She was tempted to do the same, but she was not prepared to enter that kind of relationship, especially with a white guy.

The following year, the company reached an understanding with another company in Canada. A hundred and fifty of the girls, including the original fifteen, were fortunate enough to be included in the roster of workers heading for Winnipeg. It was a relief, indeed.

It was a five-hour flight from the Netherlands to Toronto, and another twenty hours in an old Greyhound bus, which was like torture.

The land was flat as far as the eye could see. The bus reached the outskirts of Winnipeg early one July morning. Warm air was coming from the south and the green vegetation and manicured lawns were so inviting. The girls were housed along Lombard Street, just ten minutes away from the textile factory. They did not need to be trained this time; they already had the skills and knowledge to jump straight into the action.

After a few months of working, Ofelia's savings were accumulating handsomely. The skills she had learned about saving money while in the Netherlands were paying off. Her take-home pay was a bit higher than what she'd been receiving before. The ease of her stay and the nature of the work was more of a convenience than a burden. The girls didn't have to wear uniforms, there were fewer restrictions, and they had more time for personal activities. The only bad thing was how cold the city was in winter; for half the year, the city was known as "Winterpeg."

Being alone breeds loneliness. Ofelia was just like any other young woman who was out of reach of her own family. Letters from back home took at least four weeks to reach Winnipeg. Her consolation was often a picnic in the park, a trip to a neighbouring town, or spending the day with a fellow contract worker in the mall, especially Polo Park.

The need for more workers in Canada was starting to shape up. More and more of the pioneering immigrants were retiring and others were reaching their senior years. Factory workers were hard to replace. Workers, after getting their landed immigrant status, often shifted to other working opportunities. Caregiving became the fad. Of the original fifteen of Ofelia's friends, almost all of them landed new jobs caring for the elderly and infants. The pay was higher, there was more flexibility, and they had greater opportunities for the future. However, no amount of career change could quench Ofelia's loneliness. She missed her parents, brothers, and sisters. She really wanted to bring them all with her to Canada. She also missed her friends.

The immigration process was much easier back in the 1970s and many young professionals and families were given opportunities to move into the wide open span of land called Canada.

Exchanges of letters and correspondences were initiated from Ofelia's family back home. Her dad was good at processing papers and negotiating business in Manila. His priority was getting his application ready so that he could immigrate to Winnipeg. He had to make countless trips to Manila just to satisfy the requirements of the application process. The other members of her family also had to change their middle names to be consistent with the rest of the family. They had to follow what had been written down in Ofelia's application. The money she sent home was enough to cover most of their expenses.

After less than two years, her parents, a brother, and a sister arrived in 1981. It was a dream come true for her family, and from what she could gather, the whole neighbourhood back home was envious of them.

They rented a two-room apartment along Sherbrook Street. The area was nice and quiet. Ofelia's role expanded from being the breadwinner to becoming director and tour guide for the family in their first few weeks.

Being with family is one thing, and being with someone you love is quite another. In her early thirties, Ofelia was introduced to a friend in the Philippines. Hailing from Pangasinan, Ted was an accomplished painter. House painting was his master skill. After a yearlong exchange of letters and the prodding of his relatives in Winnipeg, their relationship bloomed into a serious matter. Ofelia decided to visit and marry Ted. Everything went well. In fact, as a way of getting closer to her family, he even went to Ofelia's family home in the Philippines and painted it for their wedding. Her brothers commented that he had done a good job. The two were married the following year.

Six months later, Ted descended from the elevator of Winnipeg International airport. The smile of wonderment and excitement was very obvious in his face. Ofelia's heart was pounding. They shared a long kiss, weary eyes, and loud laughter.

At last, they were together!

It only took a month before she and her family found out about the real Ted. They were living together in one room, but not as partners. The intimacy of newly reunited mates was not seen or heard in the house. He began to be rude to her and treat her unpleasantly. Ted's attitude came out into the open without any shame. He even had the stomach to disrespect Ofelia's mom. Socks were scattered around the house. Soiled clothing was a regular fixture at the base of the stairs and corners of their bedroom. Unwashed dishes were piling up in the sink. Ted showed no signs of initiative. It was too much for the family to handle. They could not bear his irresponsible attitude.

It had to stop.

It was Ted's way of telling her family to get lost. It became very clear to everyone that Ted's motives had changed. Coming to Canada had been his ultimate goal, and he had married Ofelia to do it. Now he wanted to bring over his girlfriend from the Philippines.

Once Ted figured out how to make friends and go from one place to another, he landed a job and wasted no time making known his plan to leave the family.

The turbulent relationship lasted only six months.

Ofelia's experience with Ted was heartbreaking, but she accepted the reality of it. She even initiated the process of looking for a place for him to move to. Once arranged, his first day was not hard. He had everything he needed to get by. Utensils and stacks of fresh and canned food were provided.

It was a big blow to Ofelia's family and friends. The separation was kept secret from her other family members back in the Philippines, though. Having this kind of experience was not good news at all. She was not sure what would happen if they knew what was going on. Few of her best friends knew what had happened. Even her work performance was badly affected. Health-wise, she lost five pounds.

She told herself over and over, "By the grace and mercy of God, I will be able to handle this challenge." It was the only consolation she uttered every morning as the months passed. Her family was very supportive.

From their rented apartment, they moved to the southwest side of the city. They made the collective decision to start anew and move on with their lives. The duplex they now lived in was not bad. The neighbourhood was clean and the neighbours were friendly. It took Ofelia only a few minutes to walk to the nearest bus stop. She was getting better by then and her family was adjusting.

The picture of Ted in her mind was vanishing like smoke that had irritated the eyes for a long time. The rest of her family was thankful for their decision to move. Even her younger brother and sister's schooling went back to normal.

In the meantime, Ofelia's mom and dad were busy with their part-time job of taking care of a one-year-old girl who was staying at their place. The child's mother, a single mom, was a friend of the family. The arrangement was keeping Ofelia's mom busy all day long. Her mom had very little difficulty doing this job; she was good at it. She had born seven kids and raised them all perfectly healthy. The only difference was the environment. During the winter, Ofelia's mom had no way of going out, so they had to stay at home and enjoy each other's company.

During the liberation of the Philippines during the Second World War, Ofelia's dad was recruited to join the U.S. Army. Years later, he had to satisfy certain requirements to get his U.S. citizenship. One of those requirements was moving to the United States, so he had to leave his wife to care for the child. He moved to Oakland, California and ended up working in a retirement home there for years.

Ofelia's younger sister struggled for many months working in one of the nursing homes west of the city, until one day she decided to end the struggle. In less than three years, she got her Registered Nursing degree from St. Boniface General Hospital. Hardship and frustration were the stepping stones for future success—that was one of the lessons the family learned in Canada.

Work, family, and church became Ofelia's inspiration to move on. Ted was able to get his fiancée from the Philippines after three years of separation from her. Life was a challenge for them, a couple with no kids and struggling to make ends meet. Ofelia's friends told her about it. They acted like spies for her.

God was good to her. He brought to her a guy who was gentle and meek as a lamb. His name was Don. They met each other in one of the Bible studies conducted by a small Filipino church. The church had been instrumental in the meeting. She saw him, he saw her, and the chemistry was perfect.

It took another five years before Don and Ofelia decided to tie the knot. Four years later, they moved to Calgary for good. They left behind their pain and frustrations in Winnipeg. As couple, her family had no choice but to let them go.

With Don, Ofelia's life was complete. Though his job at the airport was not that great, his attitude in making sure they had everything they needed to survive *was* great. However, they had no children; she supposed that God willed it that they not have a baby.

The one other concern she had for Don, however, was his health. He was older than her, and considering his age, there were lots of ailments creeping into his system. Two years before, while still in Winnipeg, she had rushed him to the hospital. The doctor had informed them that he had bronchitis, and that it was serious. His three days in hospital taught Ofelia one important life lesson—life is lot easier if you have somebody with you for companionship. Especially in the Western world, which was very individualistic, one really needed to have somebody to whom he or she could relate. That was why so many Filipina nannies dated retirees, widowers, and even seniors.

The apartment the couple was renting in downtown Calgary was not bad. It was only a five-minute walk away from Ofelia's work. However, the $850 rent they were paying every month was too much for them, so they had to look for a new place. They found one in the area of Castleridge. They were hoping to stay there for only six months, since they were thinking about buying a house, but their fear was that they were getting too old. They decided to avail the services of a nursing home when the time came. Don's strength was no longer reliable and Ofelia worried about thick snow falling in front of the house. How could an old person like him ever shovel all that snow? There was no way!

"That was my story, Lily," said Ofelia one day on the bus.

It was about noon when the Greyhound bus reached Red Deer for a thirty-minute stopover. Lily and Ofelia were both heading for Edmonton to attend the wedding of their mutual friend.

"What about you?" asked Ofelia. "What is your story?"

Chapter 12

The Smiths, owners and operators of fifteen summer re- treat cabins located just at the edge of the Athabasca River, were one of the most respected retired couples in Jasper. For a summer stay, guests had to book a cabin no later than Febru- ary. Vacationers coming from all directions in Canada enjoyed Smith Retreat's ten-kilometer guided hiking trail along the river. Known for their safety and excellent tour-guided adven- tures, young people came attracted by the water rafting. From July to September, the retreat was a melting pot of people from all over the world. Summer in and summer out, tourists from other countries occupied a quarter of the cabins. The work- force reflected the same ratio.

There was one Filipina on the scene.

Cristy's realm of responsibility was taking sole care of the cabin where the Smiths were staying during the summer sea- son. Her first three months working with the Smiths' was like heaven. The treatment was excellent. She got her own suite at- tached to the north side of the Smiths' place. Preparing North

American food was not a big challenge. Her five years of experience with an American missionary couple in the Philippines was paying off.

Her relationship with the Smiths was smooth sailing until Mrs. Smith became disabled. The freak accident happened during a Caribbean cruise. Confined to her wheelchair, life would have been impossible without Cristy. For a while, the transition was easy. However, as weeks went by, the pressures were building up.

As expected from a retired and disabled woman in her seventies, her demand for attention and care was getting more intense. The couple's insecurity and anxiety over getting older, though they were rich, was exhibited on their faces. They had always loved to travel, so Mrs. Smith's condition was a drastic blow to their lifestyle. As part of the equation, Cristy's life became more complicated and intriguing.

Cristy was afraid of losing her job, since the money she earned helped sustain her family back home in the Philippines. The roots of her passion were in serving the Smiths, and the familiarity she shared with them.

Scott Smith pronounced his longing for more intimacy with his wife, but because of his wife's condition that part of their life had changed forever. With the passage of time, Mrs. Smith became suspicious that her husband was having an affair—with Cristy. Her suspicions proved to be valid, forcing the Smiths to draft separation papers. A year later, they were divorced, and Cristy was served her pink slip.

Cristy stayed with one of her friends, all the while being supported by Scott. Her future in Canada was in jeopardy, and she didn't know what to do next. She needed to connect with warm and trusted friends for emotional support.

Months later, Lily received a letter from Cristy. Mrs. Smith had been hospitalized after the divorce and died three months later due to liver complications. The relationship between Cristy and Scott had not yet been legitimized. It was spring the following year when she finally left her friend and moved in with Scott.

Months later, she gave birth to a healthy baby. They arranged for a wedding right away. Taking a cruise in the Caribbean was next on the list of things to do, as well as getting a new SUV. Life was looking up for Cristy. However, it was kept secret from Scott's two grown children in Toronto that he now had a new baby. One of his children was a lawyer and the other operated a bakery.

Cristy's situation seemed good on the surface, but it was not built upon a strong foundation. Slowly, the family mess was emerging from its long sleep. Cristy discovered that there was more to the family secret than Scott had told her. The truth was that Scott's oldest son, the lawyer, had been conceived in the Bahamas forty-five years ago with a native dancer. While on a business trip to the Bahamas, Scott had taken advantage of the closeness and sweetness of a local escort. She was fluent in English, which made it easier for them to establish an enjoyable and productive relationship. Being in the escort business, this young dancer attracted Scott and gambled that she would end up with him. Scott had great influence in his company and he was very wealthy, so he made the commitment to help out financially with their son's education. After his son graduated from law school, Scott brought him to live in Toronto, three thousand kilometers away from his own life with Mrs. Smith, who was completely ignorant of the affair.

After many years, he wanted to visit Toronto and see his son, but with his stature it would be too easy for him to be noticed. Coming from a very rich and influential family, Mrs. Smith had the wherewithal to know whether her husband was out on business or doing something else. Also, her family hailed from Toronto.

These were the circumstances which led to them hiring Cristy to be a caregiver. The resort business was the only element of their relationship that still held them together. In their retirement years, managing the resort brought them comfort and ease. Having a caregiver responsible for the upkeep and maintenance of the house meant that there was more time left over to spend with each other. Hence, it gave them hope that their relationship would improve.

But life for Scott and his wife became very rough as the years progressed. Even during the first months of Cristy's employment, she sensed that they were pulling apart from each other. Both of them made so many demands and expectations on the other. In his early fifties, given the present predicament of his relationship with his wife, Scott longed for somebody who would listen to him.

Without a doubt, Lily thought that Scott Smith had been a playboy in his younger years. She looked across the table at Cristy, who was telling her the story.

"How did you know all of this?" inquired Lily with a cup of Tim Horton's coffee in her left hand. It was their second meeting and the continuation of Cristy's story. She really wanted to have someone listen to her story.

While rolling up the rim of her cup, Cristy whispered, "I'm his third mistress, and the smartest one!"

"So do you believe everything that he told you?"

"If I'm not part of his will, I probably won't believe him one bit," Cristy said.

"What about Mrs. Smith? Was she aware of the existence of Scott's two children?"

"That's where the problem lies. In her will, worth about $4 million, there was no mention of the kids. All the monies went to charity. Only the resort and the house in Calgary were named to Scott."

"I don't get it," Lily said. "What's the problem?"

"I forgot to mention that when Mrs. Smith passed away, Scott's stocks were invested in Enron and Nortel. Only a fourth of his fortune survived the fall of those companies. Remember that fiasco?"

Lily always thirsted for news about the economy. There was no way to forget what had happened to Enron and Nortel. She had to be aware of it; Mike's work was closely link to the world economic engine—oil and gas. Besides, Lily had a lot of time to read newspapers during her spare time.

"Since he lost his fortune, his only hope came from his share of his ex-wife's will."

Lily frowned. "But I thought everything was given to charity and philanthropic causes around the city."

"Well, not exactly. Here is the irony that makes things even worse. Scott's son in Toronto, the lawyer, was recently charged with malpractice, barred from practicing law. His other son is currently nursing himself from the pain of his own divorce."

"I still don't get it," Lily admitted.

"Scott's age is advancing rapidly. Our little girl… what kind future is awaiting her?" Cristy asked. "If she doesn't get a share in the will, she won't get anything at all."

"More coffee?" asked the waiter, who came by holding a coffeepot.

"No, thanks," Cristy said. "We better go now."

"Thanks for the coffee," said Lily.

"Don't mention it."

Chapter 13

Over a period of time, Lily made two new friends—Ana, a petite and vertically challenged woman from Cavite, and Ellen, a more vocal and outspoken lady from Pampanga.

Prior to coming to Canada, Ellen worked for five years in Hong Kong. The Chinese family she had worked for, according to her, had been merciless and inconsiderate. She hadn't had any freedom to pursue her own interests inside the house, and her movements were always followed by her disabled employer. Her responsibilities had been divided into two categories—the upkeep of the house and taking care of the kids. All of her spare time had been spent emailing friends in the Philippines, Hong Kong, and one in Canada.

She spent the most time with her Canadian friend. Her ultimate goal was to leave the Chinese family and explore her future in Canada. Correspondence after correspondence, she was able to submit all the requirements of her application.

Finally, after months of secretly processing her papers, opportunity knocked at her door. Her move to Calgary was made possible by her nanny friend in Cranston. Her new employers were a young couple with a two-year-old boy. Cleaning the house was just part of the job; her main responsibility was the welfare of the boy.

Ellen's family was still in the Philippines. Though her contact with them was constant, she had the feeling that her husband of fifteen years was cheating on her. Her suspicions were confirmed when, one time, her husband was not at home and her son answered the phone. Her son could not take it anymore. Ellen's husband had been caught with the other woman when they walked out of a newly built hotel together by one of their family friends.

The number one reason Ellen was working so hard and not wasting time with holidays was that she was trying to get her open visa status as soon as possible. Once she had it, she could then petition her five-year-old son and two-year-old daughter to join her in Canada.

"Never mind with that dumbass," she commented about her husband to Lily one day, contempt in her face.

"What is he doing now?" Lily was excited to get another scoop from Ellen. Ellen's husband was the driver of a public utility vehicle. He spent more time with the other woman than his own two kids. He didn't see them very often, knowing that money from Canada was sure to come on the last week of every month.

The situation made Ellen feel stressed and desperate.

—

In her late thirties, Ana's silence concealed a secret. She kept her silence, even though she knew expressing and sharing her experiences could only deepen the bond of friendship between her and Lily. It was on their fourth meeting, on a Saturday afternoon, that Lily discovered Ana's reluctance to talk about her previous life in the Philippines. Before moving to Canada, Ana was dumped by her boyfriend for another girl. That was why Ana worked so hard, to forget the sad story of her relationship with this guy.

A year ago, Ana had met a Caucasian man named Dave in one of the church fellowships she attended. Dave was in his early fifties, which was not old by North American standards. After a couple of dates, Ana fell in love with him.

For over a year now, she had been very much aware that her live-in relationship with Dave went against her religious beliefs. Worrying about what her parents might think was a secondary concern. The more pressing concern was if and when Dave would take her to the altar and marry her officially. Much to her dislike, it took two years and a one-year-old child before they had their wedding at the Glenmore Inn. For their honeymoon, they went on an African cruise.

The first few months of their marriage, as expected, were blissful. Her friends were so happy to see her dream of being an open visa holder settled without much hassle. At least for this one friend, life had a happy ending.

Lily was so intrigued by her friends' accounts of their lives and experiences. For Ellen and Ana, life had to go on. They had to live in the present and let go of the past. If they held on to the past, their chances of moving forward successfully were nonexistent. Lily was very cognizant of this reality.

Lily and Ana spent three hours together, and the time was filled with much emotional wrangling. Relieved after having the chance to vent their frustrations, they parted ways.

As Lily was on her way home, a shadow of doubt and reservation crept slowly into her subconscious mind with respect to Mike's job in Jeddah. Her biological clock was ticking away. If she was going to have a family, she was running out of time. She started to develop a plan. Nobody would do it for her. She was mature enough to face reality.

Her plan called for a drastic and calculated move. Given Ana and Ellen's experiences, she could not afford to wait any longer for Mike to come up with a plan for their future.

She arrived home without even being noticed by Dana and Rudy. She closed her door and went straight to the phone. She glanced at the clock and dialed Mike's number. "Darling, how are you?" Lily said as softly as possible.

"Lily?" Mike answered in a surprised tone. "Is there a problem? I'm sorry for not getting back to you. We have so much work to do here. I was facing a deadline in the field, which is why I couldn't call you for quite some time," he said apologetically.

Lily was upfront and clear with her message. She wanted to hear from Mike if there was a plan for their future. They'd been engaged for four years and yet no plan had been developed with respect to their future.

"Don't be too worried. Give me two more years, then we'll be together," Mike promised.

"I'm applying for my open visa and I'm going to include you as my fiancé," Lily informed him. She spoke to him with precision and urgency. "You haven't told me yet if you are interested in moving here. Alberta is the energy capital of Canada. Oil and gas are the main engines of the economy, and your skill is needed here."

There was a long pause as she waited for Mike to answer. There were two possible meaning for it—either he was covering something or he could not say anything at the moment.

"Hello, are you still there?" she asked.

"I'm here. What did you say?"

"Do you have a plan to move here?"

"I was thinking of my promotion, the scope of my present work contract, and a number of other matters regarding my family in the Philippines. Give me a week. I'll call you and let you know what the plan is."

"Okay, darling!"

"I miss you. Don't forget to send me a picture. I think you are getting prettier there, right? Also, when you write to the Philippines, inform them of our plan and any other concerns so that they will not be surprised later on."

"I love you," Lily said.

"Bye!"

It had become obvious to her that Mike's plan had little to do with moving to Canada. Their conversation stuck long in Lily's mind. Mike's last words ran through her head, leaving some big questions unanswered. But he had not been smart enough to conceal what was important to him. In any relationship, distance was one of the main obstacles for growth and maturity.

Were those the only reasons Mike needed a week to decide? Was there something else that she needed to know? If she only had a friend in Saudi Arabia who could give her reliable news about Mike, it would be a comfort. She remembered her friends in the King Faisal Hospital, but Lily could not trust them. Contacting them might only lead to other problems. She knew some of them were not faithful to their partners. Other friends were good at denying the reality of their spousal problems. Besides, Lily had had a bad experience with them. Their unsolicited advice had not been morally palatable for her.

The night was long for Lily. The following day, she had dates with both Ana and Ellen. The two ladies satisfied Lily's longing for companionship.

People were swarming the food court at the Sunridge Mall, the venue of their meeting. The three women talked over lunch. Two hours was not long enough for them to share their stories with each other.

They observed right away that Lily was having a hard time. The start of their chat was not as lively and full of laughter as some of their others had been.

"Got any problem, Mare?" said Ana.

"A misunderstanding with Mike?" seconded Ellen.

"I've been here for almost three years and only last night did he tell me about his plan," Lily said. "He didn't even mention whether or not he wants to move here. I have to wait for a week to know exactly what his is plan for the two of us."

"You're kidding!" Ana said.

In the back of Lily's mind, her intuition was trying to tell her something. She could not pin it down exactly.

From nowhere, Ana said, "That's not good news. I may be wrong, but it seems like the chances of him coming are very slim. I'm not a betting woman, but based on what you shared to us, I would say Mike is being taken care of by someone else there."

They were supposed to be enjoying the food and the upbeat atmosphere of the mall, but Lily suddenly felt very sad. It only took a few seconds before a tear ran down her cheek. Ana quickly handed her a tissue and Ellen moved her chair closer. She wrapped her arms around her crying friend.

"We're very sorry," Ellen said.

While they were in this serious situation, people around were busy stuffing themselves with all kinds of food. A trendy group of young teens was secretly glancing towards their table, curious enough to tone down their once lively talk. Two tables away was a Pinoy family. The baby was about a year old and her brother was about to graduate from being a toddler.

The emotions coming out of Lily's eyes were no secret anymore. She was hurt, feeling neglected and abandoned.

"What shall I do?" she pleaded to her friends.

"A tooth for a tooth," blurted Ellen with conviction. "If another woman can do this thing to you, why can't you do the same? You remember that guy who introduced himself to us when we attended the church's fellowship last year?"

Glen had been a widower with two full-grown kids. He had been running a cleaning business as his livelihood. His business accounts included some of the big corporations and office buildings in the downtown core. Without pretension, Glen was looking for a serious relationship with a Filipina.

The events in Lily's life were unfolding too quickly. Mike's stolen and tender goodbye kiss when she had left him at Jeddah International Airport was still fresh in her memory. The time they'd been together from the Philippines to the Middle East had represented a major emotional investment. So many memories were at stake! What about their friends and families? What would they say if Lily ended it? The engagement ring Mike had given her during her graduation celebration was getting harder and harder to fit on her finger.

Her life was filled with uncertainty as the weekdays ahead loomed large. Mike would call her anytime to tell her of his plan. Blaming herself for moving to Canada would only compound her confusion. It would not help. She needed the support and encouragement from her most trusted friend and employer—Dana.

Dana's concern was sincere. Dana often told her that she was always included in her prayers, everyday. Her advice was to wait first for Mike's plan, then decide what to do. However,

Ana and Ellen were very eager to see Lily follow in their footsteps.

—

Her friendships had branched out to other nannies in the city. In the Middle East, women's movements were limited. In Canada, though, women could do anything they wanted, any time they wanted. They could be with whomever they liked for as long as they liked, as long as no laws were broken.

Mall, parks, and group excursions were the most common opportunities for making friends. As a member of Dana's family, Lily was always mentioned or included in the invitations she and Rudy received.

Going around and making friends, and experiencing the tastes of some of her favorite foods, was something she would treasure forever. Simply knowing the experiences of other nannies also gave her the wisdom to face whatever realities were awaiting her in the future. Learning from the mistakes of others and avoiding them would surely spare her from unnecessary headaches.

As the saying went, "A wise person learns from his own mistakes. But a smart person learns his lesson from the mistakes of others."

Chapter 14

"A friend of mine invited me to their group's scheduled distribution of phone directories in Chestermere," Lily said to Dana as she prepared Junior's breakfast one Saturday morning.

"When?" responded Dana.

"Cora will pick me up at 7:30 next Saturday morning."

"What is the distribution for?"

"It's a fundraising drive for their church group."

"What do you mean?" Dana asked.

"They call themselves 'Filipians,' and they've been financially helping out Christian churches in the Philippines. The money being raised is sent to deserving ministry needs."

"How many people will be involved in the distribution?"

"Their best guess is roughly fifty people."

"Chestermere is a small town, but it's well-known to be the pot capital of Alberta," Dana pointed.

"What do you mean, the pot capital?"

"Haven't you been reading the news? There are more

marijuana grow-ops in Chestermere than in any other muni-cipality in the province. So just be careful when approaching the houses."

Junior's favorite breakfast cereal was Corn Pops. He fin-ished his first bowl in five minutes. Lily poured him some more milk for his second bowl. Lily wanted him to have a ba-nana with his cereal, but he didn't like bananas; it would be a fight to force him. For the adults, a grilled cheese sandwich and a cup of hot coffee was enough to last for the day. In the back of their minds, they were making lists of items they were going to look for in that day's garage sales.

Their destination was Douglas Dale, a community just to the west of them across Deerfoot Trail. Douglas Dale was known for its affluent families, and the community garage sale was open from 8:00 in the morning until 6:00 that evening.

The weather was a cooperative twenty-five degrees. Ex-cept for Junior, they were all wearing shorts, slippers, and plain t-shirts. The forecast for the day was beautiful. The sun would be up all day—it was an outdoor shopper's paradise. They were all smiles as they left the house, their car loaded with every-thing they would need for the day. The traffic along Deerfoot Trail was getting busier in both directions.

Rudy parked the van just across from the Catholic School along Douglasdale Boulevard. The first garage sale along the street was already packed with people. There were old cassette recorders, faded curtains, a soiled couch, distorted utensils, and a lot of other good-for-nothing stuff. The other people were out simply looking for antiques, paintings, and drawings, among other things.

The couple ahead of them was loaded down with a fishing rod, six golf clubs, and a 1950 edition of stories from Readers' Digest. Junior was busy playing with some of the plastic toy animals scattered around the floor. Other kids joined Junior in playing and they wrecked whatever toys they grabbed from the toy bin. Dana's focus was on the cutlery, which was laid out on top of a table.

Lily's eyes were on an old digital camera and a not-so-old umbrella, which together would only cost five dollars. Rudy, as usual, was busy scouring for tools. Though he was not a handyman, he was better with tools than most of his friends. He purchased a small pair of pliers and cable jumpers.

"We better be going," Rudy said. "There's more stuff waiting for us at the next house."

In total, they spent twenty-five dollars at the first house. There was still plenty of room left at the back of the van. Junior's attention on his newest toy, a plastic Albertasaurus, only lasted five minutes. He was looking forward to more toys, as promised by both Dana and Lily. A couple of blocks away, Rudy turned right, following a sign taking them to the next house. The street curbs were already cramped with cars and people crisscrossing from one house to another. Rudy parked the van and his troop walked straight into a garage full of exactly the same stuff as the first house.

"Let's check the next house," Dana said. "There's not much of anything interesting here." She was pointed to a third house up the street, where there looked to be more stuff on display.

Lily was very curious. This was her first venture into a community garage sale. Aside from this annual summer event, there were lots of other places to buy used goods, such as Value Village and a host of other thrift stores around the city. Newcomers to the city could pick up almost everything they needed from these inexpensive shops.

Lily was thrilled as they wandered from one house sale to another. It occurred to her that today was the perfect time to buy. She thought of cooking utensils, cutlery, and other kitch-en-related needs. There was a toaster oven in need of fixing for only two bucks. There was a wardrobe and bookcase also looked good, though they were not her highest priority. She was looking for small items that she could store for a while and use later.

They found a microwave model that was as big as a seven-teen-inch television, but it would not be good in terms of power consumption. An electric can opener and a set of knives for five bucks were other good buys. She was now carrying around a box already half filled with stuff—books, curtains, and other small and ordinary items.

The line between the things she needed and wanted was becoming hazy. All the deals around her were so inviting. Be-sides, she was thinking of her closet. Fifty percent of what was in there had not been used or touched in at least a year.

Rudy drove them back home at 3:15. They had filled four medium-sized boxes, all filled to the brim, and all for just seventy-five dollars. Once unloaded, their purchases occupied a sizeable space in the living room. Rudy's newfound treasures or toys were taken straight to the garage. It took the rest of the afternoon for him to inspect and enjoy the look and feel of the tools he had bought. Junior spent about five minutes with each new toy before discarding it. He had a short attention span.

Both the laundry machine and dishwasher were running. Dana was making sure that the stuff she bought was clean and ready for use. Downstairs, Lily was excited to try on a blouse she had bought. As planned, the garage sale and all the excite-ment afterward took up their whole Saturday.

But the feelings of satisfaction over the good deals only lasted for a week. The thrill was soon gone and their desire for more stuff came back. The enticement of these feelings crept up on Lily very subtly. The attraction of buying new things grew stronger and more justifiable with each passing day.

Was buying used stuff a norm or habit in this part of the world? To what extent did the majority of people have to stop buying things? These questions kept running through the back of Lily's head.

For a week after that bout with the garage sale, Lily was both encouraged and challenged to evaluate her priorities in terms of material things. It was important for her to know the difference between wanting things and needing them. This became her measuring stick with respect to managing her resources. Her room was only so big, and there wasn't much space available in the garage, either. The garage was already ninety percent full of various items, of which less than a quarter was used regularly. For this reason, she restrained herself from buying more stuff in the future. She also noticed that electronics and computer items become obsolete in no time anyway, so there was no sense in buying them, even if they were in good, working order.

Chapter 15

She had just finished off the last bite of her waffle when her cell rang.

"I'll be out in three minutes," Lily said, answering the phone.

The family was still enjoying their sleep-in. It was Saturday, and the day before had been hectic and stressful, as usual. Junior, with his never-ending quest for whatever interested him next, made him like an adult in a kid's body. He was tired and irritated the whole day long. Dana's job and her mandate for keeping her household up and running, day in and day out, had made for a long and burdensome week. A week filled with overtime had rendered Rudy as useful as a vegetable. Everyone agreed to sleep in until at least 11:00 in the morning.

Lily didn't even bother to wake the family when she left for her scheduled date with friends. Still fresh in her mind was the day's upcoming phone directory distribution. She pulled two frozen bottles of water from the freezer and put them in side a plastic lunchbox with her sandwich and three servings of fruit. She was aware that calories would be burned.

She only had one more item to look after and then she would be ready to go. From the top of the closet, Lily pulled out a cap. The forecast was calling for a twenty-degree high, so she also applied sunblock. She looked younger with her new sunglass, which she had bought the previous weekend at the garage sale.

She had a sparkle of excitement in her eyes. What was this distribution all about? It would require lots of walking around the neighbourhood of Chestermere, the newest sprawling community east of Calgary along the Trans-Canada Highway. Known for its lake and the golf course that snaked between the streets, Chestermere was roughly fifteen kilometers from the city. The number of immigrants who lived there was also increasing.

Her friend Cora's smile greeted her when she arrived. They had to wait five minutes for the other two volunteers to show up.

"So, shall we go?" Cora asked while adjusting the rear-view mirror.

"Why not?" chorused Lily and the other women.

"The place is about fifteen minutes from here."

"What time are we supposed to be there?" asked one of the ladies at the back."Between 8:00 and 8:30."

"We're on time," Lily said after checking her wristwatch.

The group was expected to distribute four thousand directories to this new community. With the beautiful weather, everyone was excited to be part of this first ever fundraising event. The goal was not only to bring directories to every doorstep, though; they were also going to raise money and awareness for the Filipians.

When they reached the spot where the fifty-three-foot trailer truck was parked, in a Safeway parking lot, people were already waiting for them. Some of the volunteers had already gone into store to buy water and other snack items. It was agreed that after the distribution they would have a picnic just across the parking lot along the edge of the lake.

After ten minutes of waiting, the guy in charge of the truck arrived. He handed out additional instructions. Taking into consideration the size of the group—around fifty people, with seven vans and two trucks—the distribution was estimated to take four to five hours. The men and the boys were assigned to do the legwork while all women's responsibility was preparing the food for the picnic afterward. The truck was opened and people got in line to load the books into the waiting vans.

For a while, Lily and her group were expecting to be part of the action. However, it was soon made clear to them that their role was to help prepare the site for the picnic. With the searing heat and lack of wind, the women were convinced that food preparation was really the best they could do.

By around noon, the groups started to arrive back at the picnic site. Each group had their own stories to tell. An unleashed dog was the scariest one. It was a good thing no one had been hurt! One house had refused to take a copy of directory, since they were about to move to another community.

The picnic table was all set up and the coolers were open, ready for dry throats. After a brief prayer, the younger volunteers were the first to attack the food. There were no worries about running out of food. Each family had brought enough.

Just before the food was brought out into the open, gophers came up out of the ground. They were attracted by the younger kids, who were playing around. The parents noticed that their young children were playing Hide and Seek with the tiny critters. The gophers were feasting on crumbs and the unfinished chunks of leftover food. A number of scared toddlers started to throw rocks at them. Young as they were, they were thrilled to see gophers flipped over once struck by a rock.

The kids' fun was cut short when, from nowhere, two young ladies approached the group and boldly reprimanded the nasty kids. The group was even told to pack up and leave the place if they were going to let their kids throw rocks at the small animals. The protection of animals was a big concern for the people who were manning the park. It became clear to the group that they had no other choice but to follow the municipal laws related to the park's animal life.

There were still over a hundred directories to distribute, so after a sumptuous lunch they decided to finish the job before heading home.

The day had been exciting and eventful for the young ones. It had been their first time walking around and exploring the ins and outs of this community. The group had earned eight hundred dollars, which made the effort a worthwhile one—and one they would be certain to repeat the following year. It was this initiative that showed Lily the importance of teamwork and cooperation. Each volunteer had shared not only their time, but also their energy. Each of them felt a sense of being needed and appreciated. Lily was happy to have been part of the endeavor.

The women, satisfied with what they had prepared, were quick to pack up the food containers and clear off the table. Their consolation was that all the food had been consumed, meaning their cooking skills had once again proven excellent.

Lily, on their way back home, started the conversation with a question. "Those women in the park, why were they so concerned about the gophers?"

"They love those critters," Cora said. "They keep the ecological balance of the park intact. That's why you can't even touch the animal holes in the ground."

"Yes, I heard that from the ladies, but did you see the guy who was limping?" Lily asked, bouncing back the question to the rest.

The guy had stepped in a gopher hole right along the edge of the pathway. Whether by neglect or misfortune, the guy had torn a ligament in his ankle. Who was to be blamed for that? Was it the gophers' unplanned housing project, or the man for being careless? It was hard for Lily to understand why so much more concern was given to these animals than to the safety of people.

Worrying too much about this newly discovery aspect of Western values was a waste of her time and energy, though. She just shrugged her shoulder and closed her eyes for a short nap while their car trekked along the highway back to Calgary.

Chapter 16

Lily's network of friends was getting bigger and more diverse. Almost every time she went out someplace, she developed one or two new friendships. This brought her lots of opportunities to expose herself to various aspects of relationships, values, and other cultures. Her outlook on life was greatly impacted by her network of friends and the unusual experiences she had with them.

This included a very unusual situation involving a male nanny. On her way to the grocery story one Saturday afternoon, Lily encountered Cora. As they chatted together, snaking around the aisles of Superstore with their carts half full, there was so much to talk about—the way their employers treated them, their neighbourhoods, celebrities, families, and other caregivers they knew. They were never bored.

Aside from communicating on the phone and through texts, everyone was learning new ways of staying in touch with each other—like email, Twitter, and Facebook. They were trying to stay current with the newest technological advances.

"Connie brought her brother Alex over from the Philippines to care for her husband, Rod, who is suffering from multiple sclerosis," Cora said. "His condition had been deteriorating and Connie was getting impatient taking care of him. She wasn't prepared to take care of him 24/7, so she brought Alex to help her."

"I suppose her work is being affected by all this," Lily surmised.

"Yes, but based on what I'm hearing from other people, there's more to it than that."

"What do you mean?"

"There's another man in the picture!" Cora declared.

"Really?"

"Of course. Think about it. If you were in your late forties and married to a disabled man who was stuck in a wheelchair, how would you handle your social, emotional, financial, and even sex life?"

"Oh, I see what you mean," Lily said.

"The sad thing is that the new man in Connie's life is a Caucasian widower in his mid-sixties. He has three grown children!"

"So?"

"The children are fighting for their share of the inheritance. They want the old man to divide his property and possessions among them so that they can continue the same lifestyles they're already enjoying."

"Is it a wasteful lifestyle?" Lily asked.

"You said it, not me."

"Why did Connie entertain this man in the first place?"

For six years, Connie had been working in a senior care center in Forest Lawn. Her job included helping seniors who were still able to move around. Connie's caring qualities had endeared her to an eighty-year-old woman who was living at the center. Their caregiver-patient relationship had turned into a real friendship. Connie even cooked for this old lady, and in return Connie received gifts from time to time from her family—perfume, dresses, and the like. Just like with all care-givers, these gifts were accepted without a second thought.

When the old lady celebrated her eighty-fourth birthday, all of her three kids came to visit. Paul was the eldest, and he lived just thirty minutes away from the nursing home. He was the one entrusted to decide and act on his mom's behalf. He brought with him a cake for the celebration. It was then that Connie and Paul got to know each other. Connie was not sur-prised to learn that Paul was a widower. His mom had already told her about it. Paul's wife had succumbed to breast cancer after a two-year battle. His only consolation was their children, who were all settled now and had families of their own.

The frequency of Paul's visits doubled with each passing week, which meant that he and Connie saw each other much more often. A year ago, Paul had asked Connie to go on a date with him. Paul was aware that Connie was married, but he wanted to have someone to listen to his story. Connie was at-tracted to Paul's sense of humor and responsibility.

"It's been months since I heard the latest news about them," Cora said, finishing the story. "They moved to Ontario and I heard that Connie left Rod with her brother."

"So Connie moved in with Paul?" asked Lily.

"I'm not sure about it, but… well, there's a twist to the story. A relationship developed between Connie's brother and Rod," Cora said with a sigh.

Connie had only recently discovered that her brother Alex was gay. Connie had left the Philippines when Alex was only three. Due to the necessity of Rod's situation, the mutually beneficial relationship had finally been made public. Rod needed somebody to take care of him and he had money. Alex needed this arrangement to live with a bit more ease and comfort, and he needed money.

It occurred to Lily that the bottom line of their moving to Ontario had been to avoid shame and humiliation. An affair with a widower, her brother's relationship with her husband, and her husband's succumbing to the situation... well, it was altogether too much to carry around. Connie and Paul had to move on.

Cora and Lily parted ways. Lily was still reeling from what she had heard. She seemed to learn of such unusual twists every time she met with a friend these days.

Chapter 17

Maria and Tony had been living together for fifteen years. She was Tony's third wife and he was Maria's first husband. The couple had a twelve-year-old girl and another five grown children from Tony's previous marriages. They lived in the city of Brampton, Ontario. Known to many caregivers, the couple had been a source of courage and inspiration—and also jewelry. Their wealth and generosity drew caregivers from as far away as Scarborough for weekend visits.

Tony's eldest son, Willy, had an amazing story. He was in his thirties, married to an Irish woman, and was a popular singer in the community. He was very good-looking and had a cultured voice that sounded like Elvis; he had once won an Elvis impersonator contest in New York in 2006. For all the preparation and discipline Tony imposed on his son, Willy grew up to become a symbol and source of pride in his community. He was also the reason why so many caregivers circled around the family.

"But Calgary is so far away from here!" Willy said one day.

Tony responded, "It is the hottest place in Canada. Aside from being the energy capital of the country, it has the highest per capita income of all the major cities."

"Meaning?"

"You can launch your singing career there and be a success story to our community."

"I have to talk to my wife about it."

"Can you not decide for yourself?" Tony asked. "You always ask for her approval."

"She made it possible for me to compete in New York and win that contest."

"I think she will be okay with the plan."

A group of nannies in Alberta made a plan to invite Willy to perform in Calgary. The group was very much aware that his talent would be noticed and patronized by the ever-growing population of Filipinos. Though he was born and raised in Canada, Willy's knowledge of other metropolitan areas, like Calgary, was limited. Still, he was his father's son.

Willy's love for music had started when he was ten. His dad's fascination with Elvis had been intense. All of Elvis' records and movies were piled up in a secured corner of the house. Willy had no means of knowing about this "King of Rock," as Elvis had died when he just a child. But the popularity of the King's music lasted for generations. Willy was like a dry sponge, eager to soak in the music of Elvis. He learned to love both Elvis and his songs.

Tony's prodding gave birth to a passion in Willy's heart. His height, complexion, and voice even resembled a young version of Elvis. All he had to do was grow sideburns!

"When is the planned performance?" asked Willy.

"September or early August," Tony said.

"I have to talk to my boss and find out if he can give me a week off."

One of the reasons they were feeling bit hesitant was the fact that they had no friends in the West. Their only contact was through a friend who owned a Filipino community paper in Toronto called Taliba.

Taliba released its first issue in 2001. Managed by a respectable man named Relly, the paper originally ranked third in terms of circulation and readership, but as its quality and content expanded, especially the joke corner, Taliba became the most sought-after paper in the Filipino community. Relly's paper even reached Calgary in 2003.

Willy was featured in the January 2007 issue of Taliba, advertising his summer performance in one of Scarborough's music halls. Tickets were selling briskly at thirty-five dollars per head. One thing was certain—caregivers familiar with Tony and Maria were ecstatic at the opportunity to watch and listen to their idol, Willy the King.

When the news reached Calgary that a Filipino had won an Elvis lookalike contest in New York, many were excited at the prospect of the show coming to Cowtown.

Posters were distributed to all Pinoy establishments, offices, and businesses. Tickets sold like hot cakes, at a reasonable price of forty dollars. As part of their marketing strategy, promoters and sponsors were doing their very best to attract more people from the neighbouring cities of Edmonton, Red Deer, and Lethbridge. Local talents were also included in the concert.

Jubilee Auditorium was booked for mid-August, weeks before the start of another school year. The concert was the talk of the community. Posters were visible in all Filipino stores and businesses.

"I got us tickets for Willy the King's concert," Dana said one day while unpacking her stuff from the office.

"You mean the guy from Toronto who won the Elvis lookalike contest in New York?" responded Lily.

"Rudy worked a lot of overtime last month, so we decided to go see this guy."

"Cool!"

The concert started at 7:00 and cars were already lining up for the parking lot at 5:30. Thirty minutes before the show, they finally parked in a spot far from the concert hall. Junior was excited to see so many other small kids in the crowd. The lobby was jammed pack when they entered the building. In the air, they heard the soft music of the King being played.

"I really feel at home," Lily said.

Dana smiled. "It even smells like home!"

Moving around in a crowded environment like this one reminded Lily of a scene in Divisoria. Divisoria was an overcrowded outdoor marketplace in Manila where people desperately did whatever they could to survive. Here, in the lobby of Jubilee Auditorium, immigrants wore the finest suits they could find for such an occasion. People had spent a lot of money to be included in this event.

Versace, Calvin Klein, Hugo Boss were among the many signature fragrances competing for their attention. High-heeled women in backless dresses were everywhere. The colour black was definitely the choice of the night. There were a few who dared to settle for a pair of jeans and a sweatshirt, but for the most part people were dressed up.

When they were five meters away from the door, Lily was startled to hear her name being called from somewhere behind them. Suddenly, a woman in a gray gown waved at her.

"Noemi?" Lily called, recognizing the woman.

"Yes!" Noemi called back. She approached.

"Meet my employers," Lily introduced. "This is Rudy, Dana, and Junior, my buddy."

"Hello, how are you?"

"Good, thanks."

Ten minutes was enough for Noemi to become acquainted with Dana and Rudy. Noemi's joy of running into Lily was cut short by the announcement that the show would start in five minutes. Each pulled out their tickets to make sure they found their way to the right seat. The auditorium was already almost full.

"So that's Noemi?" asked Dana. "I assume those other women with her are also regulars from the strip bar."

"You are correct," Lily answered.

When the show opened, Lily was amazed at how good Willy was. Indeed, it was like Elvis in Willy's body. The opening song was such a thrill to the audience. Throughout the show, they stood, clapped their hands, and stomped their feet to the music.

"I love you, Willy!" someone shouted from the balcony.

The hall was filled with loud laughter.

After the first ten songs, a ten-minute break was announced.

The hall was filled with laughter and tears. Lily's eyes were wet, but her lips were smiling. The concert made her think of Mike, who was a big fan of Elvis.

Chapter 18

Northern Luzon was ripe with political turmoil in early 2006. People were hard-pressed to remain silent and dared not talk about politics during the election that was going on. The political parties were trying to outsmart each other before the face of the electorate. Some candidates resorted to harassment, torture, and bullying to generate support. The one with the most money or ammunition usually ended up winning.

The region was only a small speck on the overall political landscape of the Philippines, but it was still intense for the people who lived there. The turmoil had become so common that most people simply tried to ignore it or just let it pass them by. What was the point in caring about problems if the government couldn't do anything about them? Complacency and neglect dominated the psychology of the people. Very few institutions were not affected by politics. Political appointees and politicians' names were everywhere on various buildings, schools, municipal murals, fences, and streets as the election approached.

The result was depressing to people who were serious about moving forward. Powerful people were either ignoring or fleeing from the influence of politicians by leaving the country during election seasons. Over the course of many years, they learned how to dance to the music of these elected public servants. They kept their distance from these politicians while keeping their reputation and livelihood intact.

They needed a strategy—work hard, save more, and get out of the country.

A nurse by profession, Cely and her husband Manny had a growing family. They decided to try their luck. The couple was invited by a friend to attend an orientation meeting hosted by a Calgary-based recruitment agency. The meeting was held in Munoz, Nueva Ecija. The town of Isabela, where they hailed from, was a three-hour drive away.

The couple took their five kids to Manny's parents' home just three blocks from the edge of town. Manny's parents were very much aware of the purpose of their visit to Nueva Ecija and saw this as the chance they had been waiting for so long. The kids were not that interested to know what was happening. As long as they were with their grandparents, everything was okay. Their grandparents, both retired high school teachers, spoiled them.

Cely and Manny arrived in Munoz at 6:00 in the afternoon. They wondered why it had taken them almost five hours to travel from Isbaela to Nueva Ecija. They had forgotten that bus drivers had to stop over for lunch along the way.

When they arrived, the couple went to the home of Mercy, one of Cely's dearest friends from university.

"Come in," Mercy said as she opened the door and led the couple into the living room.

Mercy had been Cely's classmate and close friend many years ago. Both had graduated with their Bachelors in Nursing from Isabela State University. After their graduation, Mercy had moved to Central Luzon and found employment at the Central Luzon State University Hospital as an attending nurse. She enjoyed the work atmosphere and camaraderie with her coworkers. She had met her own husband two years ago while at the university. She was proud of him for being the head coach of the university's varsity basketball team. They had three kids together. One was in junior high and the other two were still in elementary school.

The house they were renting from the university had three rooms and was spacious enough for guests. For two nights, the house would be packed like sardines. Cely and Manny occupied the room of one of Mercy's kids.

For Cely and Mercy, it was a sweet reunion. Their school days were full of memorable events—with their classmates, school requirements, and even boys. The little room at the back of the library was a source of giggles as they reminisced about the past. Manny and Ed, Mercy's husband, were busy trying to connect with each other. Manny had played basketball while he was in high school, and the sport held not a hint of interest for him now that he had a family. Ed thought that his basketball team's triumphant win the previous week seemed like the best way to trigger a good conversation with Manny, but it was to no avail. At the end of three minutes, both were able to connect though a series of complicated questions: What were the chances of Manny's family going abroad? Why did they have to leave the country? What life awaiting them overseas? What jobs could they expect there? Were there any contacts out there who could help them settle down someplace?

The day before, the recruiter had distributed brochures around the university about the opportunities that were open to successful applicants. Mercy had taken an extra copy of the brochure, and now showed it to Cely. The brochure was the focal point of their evening discussion. They noted and marked down all the possible questions to ask. It was late in the evening when they finally headed to their respected rooms. Both couples decided to get up earlier than their usual morning routines normally called for.

The university was roughly a ten-minute drive from the building where the meeting was taking place. From the parking lot, the couples witnessed the number of people in line for the registration. They still had ten minutes before the start of the orientation. They met a handful of their friends and classmates in the crowd. Some had become engineers, architects, managers, government employees, and even artists.

The lobby was cluttered with tables and exhibits covered with brochures and other informational materials. They were encouraged to pick up any of the materials displayed on the tables. Two receptionists handed out program pamphlets as the attendees walked by. Each participant was charged a registration fee of fifty pesos.

They spotted four vacant chairs three rows from the podium on the right side of the meeting room. In no time, the room was full. After making a preliminary introduction, the host started to discuss the opportunities available and the manner in which those opportunities could be accessed.

The presentation sounded too good to be true. The presenter reiterated to everyone in the room how Canada was in dire need of no less than one hundred thousand workers in the next five years. The list of eligible jobs under the recruitment program had swelled to more than twenty. Added to the list were janitorial workers, people in food services, cleaners, hotel service professionals, and fast food employees. Caregiving was still one of the occupations with the highest demand.

Caregiving was Mercy and Cely's goal for attending the orientation. Manny and Ed, finally, had found an interesting connection—furniture making. Both were handymen. They could build anything from scratch, especially if they had the necessary tools. The presentation was the most persuasive when the videotaped testimony of a recruit was shown to the group.

The recruiter ended the first half of the day with a challenge to the audience.

"Follow your heart. If you believe the Philippines is the best place to raise your family, there's no need for you to stay another hour. If Canada is what you see in your dreams, then stay and take that first step of faith with us." They were encouraging words as everyone emptied out of the session hall and headed for their lunch break.

The canteen was just meters away from the meeting room. The couples rushed in that direction and ordered big bowls of wanton soup. Some of the participants settled into one corner of the canteen and enjoyed their lunch.

"I'll try the caregiving program," said Mercy. She was halfway finished with her bowl of soup.

"I think that is the best and easiest way of going to Canada," added Cely.

"Manny and I will try furniture making," Ed said with confidence.

"What about food or hotel services?" snapped Cely.

Manny sighed. "Only if you want us to become obese or attracted to hotel receptionists."

"Never mind then," Mercy said with a smile on her face. "Just go and make furniture."

Their laughter was contagious.

When the time for the afternoon session was announced, a dozen people left the building feeling indifferent. Leaving the country and working as "slaves" did not appeal to them. They preferred to stay and enjoy their present lifestyle rather than brave the snow and be treated as a second-class people. It was their choice.

"Alberta is the most promising place to work," the host said once they took their seats. "It is the energy capital of Canada. The economy is strong and many companies are demanding that the government intervene in recruiting workers from around the world. The Philippines is a preferred place for recruitment because of our skills and command of the English language."

The biggest portion of the presentation was dedicated to the volume of labor demand, labor laws, and aspects of acculturation. What would it take for them to live as foreign workers?

The question and answer portion went thirty minutes beyond the scheduled time. Three associates were on hand to lend assistance to people who wanted to put in their names as applicants. Both couples were convinced and handed their prepared resumes to one of the associates. An application form was handed to each of them. Recruitment fees were not mentioned. The agency would shoulder it. The only thing they needed to do was prepare their documents and start saving as much money as possible. As promised, the recruitment agency would take care of their airfare and accommodations upon arrival.

The assistant clarified all their other questions. The people started to disperse one by one, many of them leaving with more questions than answers. For the two couples, their concern was where to get the money.

They left the room with many people still working on their papers and applications. The parking lot was half empty and many happy faces were still loitering and talking about the prospects and opportunities waiting for them in Canada.

Cely and Manny packed up their stuff at Mercy's place right away upon arrival from the meeting. They decided to head home that afternoon. It would still be early when they got back to Isabela. Their kids needed parental guidance now. Besides, the following day was Sunday. As a Christian family, they had to go to church, no matter what.

The return trip was a bit shorter, with less hassle.

They went straight to Manny's parents' place to pick up the kids. The kids didn't even ask about their parents' trip. Instead they focused on the gifts and other items that had been brought back for them. Manny's parents went to bed early. It was 1:00 in the morning when they finally lay down in their beds.

They woke up early the following morning and hurriedly proceeded to their own home, changed clothes, and headed out for the worship service. On their way to the church, five blocks away, the kids were suddenly excited to hear from their parents.

"When are we going abroad, Dad?" asked the oldest one.

"I like snow," the youngest insisted.

Before they could share the story, the church gate was in front of them. They promised the kids that they would talk all about it when they returned home later.

The kids proceeded to their respective Sunday school rooms. Manny and Cely joined the young couples' bible study group in one of the rooms behind the pulpit. For forty-five minutes, they studied the life of Joseph, learning about how God had turned it into triumph from despair. The idea of leaving one's homeland was reinforced for Manny and Cely. When the time came to get the list of prayer requests from the group, Cely didn't hesitate to share their experience from the recruitment meeting.

When the rest of the group heard about it, they became alive and excited. How come they had not been made aware of this opportunity? How could they contact the agency themselves? Many other questions were thrown to the couple. It was a good thing the time was up for their Bible study session. They promised the group to bring more information the following Sunday.

As a receptionist in one of the town's medical clinics, Cely was aware of some of the issues people faced—medically. She wanted one day to practice her profession as a registered nurse. Looking for that kind of job in another town, however, was not a good idea. Her kids were still young. Manny's job as salesman for a feed company was not very stable. His salary was dependent on the volume of sales he made. One of the positive things about their situation, however, was the presence of Cely's in-laws just a few minutes away from their house. Most of their financial gaps were covered by Manny's parents. Manny was the only son, and he had always been spoiled.

Everything was going fine when one day Cely received a phone call while at work. The clinic was not that busy when she answered the phone. Manny was in the hospital with a broken back. A freak accident had taken the life of Manny's officemate. They had been driving along a back road when his friend lost control of the car. The car ended up upside-down at the bottom of a ravine. The car following them had been helpful in getting them to the hospital, thirty kilometers away.

Manny's friend didn't make it.

The prognosis was not good. Based on the findings of the medical doctor looking after Manny, his chance of paralysis from his hips down was almost a certainty. There was severe damage to his spinal column. The nerves were ruptured and Manny's movements in that part of his body had been immobilized. Unless a miracle happened, he would never walk again.

It was a big blow to the family. After two months in hospital, and half their savings gone, Manny was discharged and sent home. The support they received from his parents was desperately needed. Their kids' education was affected. Cely had to look for a part-time job. The insurance would not release the compensation for Manny's hospitalization. Friends and the church could only pray for them. The kids were spending more and more days with their grandparents. Manny's rehabilitation program was expensive. Even the rental of his wheelchair was consuming some of the kids' allowance.

On the eighth birthday of their second oldest child, a letter reached their mailbox from the Canadian embassy. Cely's emotions were a mixture of excitement and anxiety. The couple cried after they found out that Cely's application had been accepted. She was advised to contact the Canadian embassy in thirty days for the processing of her application. Her employer in Calgary was expecting her to start working in the middle of summer.

The family had to make a big decision. Manny's life was tied to a wheelchair now, and the kids were still too young to be left behind. Though Manny's parents were still around, they could only do so much. The family was stuck and couldn't think of the right thing to do. Would she go ahead with the plan of working abroad or just stay and take care of the family? Cely was confused and full of anxiety. She didn't know what to do.

The following night, Cely phoned Mercy to find out if she had received the same notice and asked for advice regarding their situation. Half of their conversation was spent on the tragedy. The rest was focused on a mutual friend, Lily, who had moved to Canada. They needed to hear Lily's opinion before they decided to move to Canada to work as caregivers. But more importantly, the prospect of Cely's family future, given her husband's situation, generated a number of speculations.

—

As Dana and Lily winded up their time discussing the case of Cely and Manny, one of the Tim Horton's attendants gestured that in a short time they would be closing the store.

Cely's life had now been added to Lily's concern. She could not just ignore the plea for help from two of her most trusted friends still in the Philippines. What she would be doing about it was another story.

Chapter 19

"Just new to Canada?" asked Mely while working behind the check-out counter. There was a long line of customers waiting in her line. Full carts were common, especially on Tuesdays, when everything in the store was half-price until 9:00 in the evening.

It was Pat's first time shopping at Value Village. Her first few weeks in Canada had been spent with on-the-job training at her new job. She had also spent a lot of after-office hours familiarizing herself with the community.

As a contract worker for McDonald's, her first responsibility was to be acquainted with the store. Working in the kitchen had been her first assignment. The other women she had been with had been tasked to other stores around the city. They only saw each other at nighttime, and usually only on occasions like this one, taking advantage of sales offered in discount stores. Thrift stores were economical and practical alternatives for those newcomers to Canada who didn't have any relatives or friends who could spare to give away hand-me-down items.

"I arrived last month," Pat responded with a reserved smile.

"What's your worker status? Are you an independent, landed, sponsored, or foreign worker?"

"Foreign worker."

"Where do you work?" Mely was good at multitasking. She could do many tasks at the same time. This particular task, cashiering and talking to customers, was a piece of cake to her.

"McDonald's."

"From what province do you come from in the Philippines?"

"Ilocos Norte."

Mely totaled the price and loaded the purchases into a big plastic bag. The whole bag was only thirty dollars—a good deal. Pat was confident that all the items she had bought would take care of her for a year, unless a drastic change occurred with respect to her size and weight.

"I hope to see you again," Mely said as they parted. She got ready to serve the next customer, another Filipina.

"Thank you," Pat said while carefully carrying her bag towards the door.

Pat phoned and checked the scheduled arrival of Bus #73 at a station just a half-block away from the thrift store. She and many other people with their bargains made it to the station seconds before the bus stopped. She got on and found a seat. The bus started moved eastward as she tucked the big bag under the seat. She was comforted by the fact that most of the people riding the bus were like her—working people. Some of them still had their office uniforms on. Students were also visible, based on the stuff they were carrying. Many others were busy killing time by reading books or gossip magazines.

Pat had been able to master the skill of using her transit pass to find her way around the city. It had only taken her a week.

Boredom could sometimes make a person depressed. Newly arrived immigrants, especially foreign workers, were especially afflicted with this problem. The antidote was going out with friends for entertainment. Shopping together for great deals was even better!

After ten minutes of contemplation and a smooth ride, the bus suddenly came to a stop. Another Route #73 bus was ahead of them, only it wasn't moving. Its front tire was flat. Its passengers were pouring out of it and lining up to hop onto Pat's bus.

The first person to take an empty spot next to her was Lily. She was carrying two bags from the same Value Village store Pat had just left.

"Hi, *kabayan*," greeted Lily.

"Hi." Pat responded with smile. Now that Lily was with her, her time on the bus would be worthwhile.

All the seats were taken and many passengers were forced to stand. The bus started moving slowly, and the drivers waved to each other as they passed. Pat and Lily adjusted their bodies to a more comfortable position. Both were from the southeast corner of the city and needed extra sitting comfort.

"I just came from Value Village, too," Pat said.

Lily smiled. "I bought some stuff destined for the Philippines."

"Today was my first time shopping there."

"I go there all the time."

"So, what do you do for work?" Pat asked.

"I'm on my last year as a caregiver for a friend of mine."

Pat nodded. "I'm working at McDonald's in McKenzie Town Square."

"My employer is from that community, too," Lily said.

"Really?"

"Where do you stay?"

"McDonald's is renting a house for us."

"Where?"

"A block away from Wal-Mart," Pat said. "What about you?"

"I'm staying with my employers."

"Good for you!"

Lily looked at her friend. "What do you mean?"

"There are fifteen people living in my house," Pat explained. "My parents came from a big family, so I know how it feels to live in such a crowded environment."

"I know what you mean, but how come there are fifteen people in that house?"

"Do we have a choice? I don't have any relatives or friends here. I just arrived last month. We're all strangers in the house, and we're all just getting to know each other."

"How much do you pay for your rental?" Lily asked.

"$350 per month, with salary deductions."

"How's your cooking, cleaning, and laundry arrangement?"

Pat shrugged. "That's one of the problems we're facing. We don't have a leader to look to for direction. Everybody wants to be the boss of everybody."

The conversation was getting too in-depth and personal. Lily's curiosity had led to other issues she hadn't anticipated. Both her status and Pat's were the same—they were contract workers. Both of them worked under the same rules, and yet they had different living arrangements. Her life with Dana and Rudy was far more comfortable than Pat's situation. In the northeast side of the city, it was more common to find up to four families staying under one roof, but not in the southeast!

"One of the good things about my situation is the work schedule," Pat continued. "A third of us are working the night shift, another third is on the day shift, and the rest work in the afternoon."

"Your employer must be smart."

"Or an opportunist."

"Both, probably," said Lily.

To change the subject, Pat pointedly threw out a very personal question to Lily. "Are you married?"

"No, but I have a boyfriend."

"Is your boyfriend in Calgary, too?"

"He's in the Middle East."

"So you've been away from each other almost three years?"

"It's hard! But what can I do about it?"

"I know," Pat said. "My boyfriend actually doesn't want me to work abroad. However, due to our circumstances, I don't have a choice."

Pat related her story to Lily. She was the only child in her family, which was descended from a wealthy family in Ilocos. She had finished her business administration degree in one of the private schools in Manila. Through her father's family and business connections, she had landed a managerial job at Jollibee, one of the most popular fast food franchises in the Philippines. Her first few months as a manager had not been bad. She had what it took to be a person of influence in the company. Her education, natural talent, and people skills were all utilized as part of the job.

The store she handled had been along Maharlika Highway, thirty minutes west of Manila. Since it was one of the busiest stores, thirty people reported to her. The sales were good and the place was well-known to many.

While she was working there, one of the cooks caught her attention. Ray was a native of Cagayan. Both Pat and Ray spoke their native dialect—Ilocano. He was a university dropout and frustrated civil engineer. To find his place in the world, Ray had left his family and ended up at Jollibee. The training he'd gotten from his mom in cooking and other household chores had been good enough for him to get a decent job. He'd been in the store for almost three years, more than a year longer than Pat.

Ray knew his stuff. Commercial cooking like this was not that difficult. Once he mastered the restaurant's standard procedures, everything was easy.

After several months of working together, Ray and Pat developed an informal friendship. Pat's break from work usually ended in the kitchen, where extra crumbs of food were always available. She needed to laugh and somebody to listen to her story. At first, Ray had not been that interested in exchanging words with his supervisor. He was pretty aware that Pat was well-known to the company's executives. It was not proper for a cook and a manager to be talking in the kitchen during breaks. The only way for him to avoid this habit-forming situation was to bring a book and read, or to just pretend to be busy around the kitchen when Pat came around. Ray loaded hundreds of songs onto his iPod. Sometimes he was not even aware that Pat was secretly watching him as he nodded his head to the tune of the music.

His work paid well and allowed him to save money for his studies. He planned to work in the store just three years, after which he would continue his engineering degree in Manila. In fact, he was aiming for the Middle East after graduation. It was no secret that the Middle East could make you a rich man if you were an engineer. Certainly he could earn enough money to build his own house, start a business, have a family, and even retire early.

The qualities that attracted people to Ray included him being well-mannered, having a sharp mind with a unique sense of humor, and living responsibly. It was a common sight for other young women at work to circle around him during break time, too. Others were not hesitant to ask him out for dates.

Pat was aware of what was going on in the store. Her curiosity grew and she wanted to know why these young women were so excited talking about Ray. There was something about him that attracted other people's attention.

Being a subordinate, Ray had no choice but to report to the boss. Being the supervisor, Pat had every reason to summon Ray to her office whenever she wanted. The frequency of their meetings resulted in smiles between them. They got to know each other on a very personal level

Ray was a year older than Pat. Both were fond of outside activities, like hiking, going for picnics, and strolling in the park. *Adobo* was Ray's favorite Filipino delicacy, while *letchon* was Pat's. Their subordinate-supervisor friendship was being broken down into a more comfortable relationship. It only took a few months before the other employees knew their secret.

They were seeing each other.

Their weekends were spent on friends, movies, shopping, and church. Pat's scheduled visits to her family in Ilocos were becoming rare. For Ray, visiting family wasn't a concern. He had already been away from his family for a long time. He only communicated with them through letters and phone calls. His family had no idea where he was, anyway.

Then one Monday afternoon, coming from a business meeting in Manila, Pat's dad dropped by at the store unexpectedly. Pat, Ray, and a couple of the store associates were having their break at the back of the store when her dad appeared at the door. It was too late to hide Pat's casual mingling and interaction with her subordinates. Her dad even observed how close she was to Ray. This was her dad's first visit to the store and his first time seeing his daughter sitting so close to a guy. His smile was forced and calculated. Pat pretty well knew her dad and all his accompanying gestures. She knew he was good at reading situations and that he had caught something from that first encounter with Ray.

He had come to inform her that the following Sunday the family would be attending a special birthday celebration. The son of a close family friend was celebrating his twenty-fourth birthday. Their presence, especially Pat's, was the main gift for the celebrant.

It was still a custom in their hometown that parents betrothed their children to one another as future husband and wife. Pat was brought up this way. Her mom and dad were products of an arranged marriage.

The coming Sunday's birthday celebration was being planned secretly by both Pat's parents and the guy's parents. It was the time to inform Pat and the guy about their future together. Her throat felt like choking when her dad insisted that she attend. She grabbed her dad's hand and off they went to her office.

From the very start of their meeting, Pat's dad was pretty sure that she was keeping a secret from him. The guy, Ray, had been leaning too close to her when he saw them—no doubt that was the reason for her reluctance to go with the family. It became clear to him that Pat had committed to attend another event that Sunday. After minutes of controlled and silent discussion, he left the room with a sad face and headed straight to his car. The driver was still napping when he arrived and smacked the window. Seconds later, the car sped away.

Pat did not move from her chair after her dad left. She stared out the window with tears falling from her eyes. It was obvious that her relationship with her dad was strained. She couldn't attend the birthday celebration. Sunday was Ray's baptism in one of the small churches in San Eldifonso, Bulacan. Their friends knew about it and some of their trusted staff in the store would be coming with them.

The day after her dad's visit, Pat's mom was on the phone pleading her to consider her dad's request. In that conversation, Pat poured out her mind and heart. She thanked her parents for all the things they had done for her—for her schooling, care, and love throughout the years. Even if the career she was in had not been her choice, she would be always thankful for it. During that phone call, she managed to reveal her relationship with Ray to her mom.

Ray—a lowly cook, school dropout, and stowaway—was not the kind of man her parents desired for her to be with. As a respected family and well-known clan in the province, the only way out of this surefire embarrassment was a compromise. Pat cut off her relationship with Ray and went abroad for a year to consider all the possible options for her future. With her father's vast network of business connections, it was relatively simple for her to go to Canada as a foreign worker.

A week after Pat left the country, Ray resigned from his job and moved away. Nobody knew where he went. The only thing that kept Pat hoping was a promise left by Ray right after his baptismal. As long as they were committed to each other, no distance, time, or person would ever separate them. He would look for her wherever she might be, even if it was on the other side of the world.

Before Pat could continue telling Lily her story, Lily cut her off subtly. She turned the table and started to throw questions to Pat.

"So what do you do at McDonalds?" Lily asked.

"I'm assigned to do the food prep."

"I suppose you have experience with that."

"Actually, I have experience managing one of the biggest Jollibee franchisees in the Philippines."

"The one in Makati, along Buendia Avenue?" Lily asked. "I've been there many times."

"No," Pat corrected. "Do you know the one along Maharlika Highway in Bulacan?"

"Yes. In fact, that's the very spot where my boyfriend gave me this engagement ring." Lily held up her hand to show off the ring. "That was also the last place where we ate out before he went back to his work in the Middle East. But just look at us now! Here we both are, sweating about our boyfriends, and we don't even know what they're up to."

"I'm not worried about Ray," Pat said. "He is a Christian and I know he'll keep his promise. My concern is that he has not sent a note, called, texted, or emailed me since I left the Philippines a month ago."

"Maybe he's still feeling the pain of being away from you. Give him another week or two. Who knows? Maybe you'll be so busy you won't even have time to worry about notes and texts."

"I hope so. I feel lonely here."

"You're not alone," Lily assured her. "Many of us feel the same way."

Their conversation was cut short when the bus stopped at the Chinook Bus terminal. Lily and Pat stood up and both walked towards the door. Walking down from the second level of the terminal, they saw a crowd of people at the waiting platform of the train station. Rush hour was really becoming busy, and not only in the street. People of all walks of life were cramming into the train station—on both sides of the tracks. There were more Filipinos in the crowd than any other ethnic group.

As the two mingled in the midst of the commuting populace, they were able to exchange notes and phone numbers.

Lily boarded her bus and her mind started to work. She tried to digest the encounter she'd had with Pat. Why in the world had two lovers been cut off from each other because of the whim and preference of their parents? Was there a chance for them to be together again? Who would be the most gravely affected if they did—Pat, her parents, or Ray?

Weeks went by and Lily craved a burger. She knew where to go. Pat's store was only a minute's bus ride from her place. With excitement in her eyes, she stepped off from the bus and headed straight to McDonald's. The line of people was not that long. While waiting for her turn, Lily's eyes scanned the people working at the other side of the counter. The three women manning the counter, all Filipinas, were each new. There was a smile on the face of the woman at the third till.

"What is your order, ma'am?" she asked Lily.

Lily placed her order, and then asked, "Do you know Pat?" She handed $5.25 to the woman, paying for her meal.

"Pat left the store two weeks ago."

"Where did she go? Is she still with McDonald's?"

"I think her dad was here to take her back to the Philippines, but she didn't go with him. I think she went to Edmonton. The last time we heard from her, she was employed as a caregiver in the Wildwood area north of the city."

Lily was puzzled. Pat's family was wealthy, but her parents couldn't just dictate what was good for her. Having the freedom to seek and live her life alone was better than submitting to the whims of her parents. Besides, Pat was no longer a minor.

Lily found a vacant table just east of the store facing the street. More cars were lining up for the drive thru. There were five kids playing in the kiddy corner. Lily was reminded of Junior and her own longing for a child. As she ate, she couldn't get Pat out of her mind.

Pat's situation was unique. She was running away from her dad, finding herself in the midst of an uncertain career, and at the same time hoping for her boyfriend's promise to come true. Would this one be another story of joy or sadness?

Crumbs of her sandwich clung to her shirt as she left the store.

Chapter 20

"I'm begging you to wait another seven months," Tina said on the other end of the line.

"Seven months is way too far away. I really miss you. Can't you just move here and live with me? There's lot of work around here," responded Terry. This was the third time Terry had asked Tina to come and live with him in Fort McMurray.

It was in the early 1980s when Tina's family moved from the Ilocos Region in the Philippines to an island southwest of Manila, four hours away by boat. The island, Palawan, was known for the many opportunities it afforded its residents. Palawan was one of the most sought-after islands in the archipelago and was known for its environmental beauty and abundant natural resources. Population wise, the island had the lowest inhabitant-to-land ratio. People from as far as the southern tip of Mindanao to Batanes lived there.

Agriculture, forestry, fishing, and mining were the major sources of economic activities and livelihood of the populace. Puerto Princesa, capital of the island province, was well known for its beautiful young ladies. The local government, to up the ante of development, offered tax and relocation incentives to hard working and entrepreneurial people moving into the province. These were the very reasons Tina's family had decided to migrate there.

The family settled in the east corner of the capital. The distribution of agricultural land and forestry was administered by the Agrarian Reform Department. Tina's dad was fortunate to acquire a five-hectare parcel of land. From the savings the family had, her dad was able to purchase the basic necessities of life. He fixed up a rundown house on the land purchased a water buffalo for farm work, along with other farm implements. Seeds were available from multinational agricultural corporations, distributed free to farmers as a promotion and introduction to the new variety of crops in the region.

Palay was the main crop, and it was planted three times a year. Other crops, like banana and different kinds of fruit trees, were planted around the house. The five siblings, three girls and two boys, were the main source of labor for all chores in and out of the house. Tina was in the middle. All the kids were eager to go back to school. They hated the work required in the early weeks of moving to a new place and environment. There was so much work to be done.

Months passed and they adjusted to their new lives. Before long it was time for school to start again. The kids were happy and excited to make new friends, but they still missed their friends back in Ilocos.

Tina's school was just a ten-minute walk from their place. She eventually graduated high school with flying colours. Just an ordinary girl with an ordinary dream for the future, she enrolled in one of the colleges in the capital. One of the most sought-after careers for young high school grads was being an accountant. Banks, department stores, and the government were among the top employers for accounting graduates.

Her third year of college was not easy. The influence of friends and their hormones were hard to resist. Radio, television, and magazines clouded her focus in life. Churchgoing, which the family used to do every Sunday, was minimized to once per month. Tina and her parents were on a collision course. Her desire to live independently and the problem associated with the identity crises of adolescence were the major causes of conflict at home.

Tina's only refuge was her friends. Her parents, sisters, and brothers were not that concerned about the conflict going on in the family. They had their own stuff to attend to. She started trying many new things to the detriment of her schooling, such as going to parties and skipping classes. Her parents feared to see her slacking off. But the work on the farm was yielding positive results. Financially, the family was better off than ever.

Parental guidance had been minimal in the family. Her college education was pushed back behind the list of her goals and priorities in life. It was mid-semester of her fourth year in college when she found out she was pregnant. It was a big blow to the family. The father of the baby was a young police officer named Bobby. She had been attracted to the way he looked in uniform. Suddenly, her baby was more important than working on her requirements for graduation. She thought she could pursue her degree once the baby was born.

The couple rented a house close to Tina's family. Being involved in a very risky job, Bobby had no time to even talk about getting married. He was always working in the street, part of the police crew that took care of traffic in the capital's busy districts.

The family's disgust with Tina was eased when a beautiful baby girl was born, who they named Ashley. It was a time for reconciliation, for the sake of the newest member of the family. The grandparents were more than willing to take care of Ashley so that Tina could go back to school.

She instead opted to work in one of the local banks as a teller. Her first few months working there were nice and easy. Tina's easy and outgoing personality attracted many clients. Management was pleased to have her on board. She was promoted and received a raise in salary after a very short time. Smart as she was, Tina started to save money without Bobby knowing about it.

Their relationship was going smoothly when one day, while Ashley was with her grandparents, Tina discovered a condom in Bobby's pocket. She knew they had never used one before. Her intuition was right. The bastard was a womanizer.

Her own agony led her to run away from that shameful relationship. She decided to work abroad. Hong Kong was the most logical place to go. She was confident that her parents would take care of the baby.

She presented the plan to her boyfriend, hiding the real reason for her wanting to leave. Being a person that didn't care, Bobby took no time saying yes to the plan. It would be easier for him to chase girls around with her out of the picture. With all her savings, and a connection to the recruitment agency, Tina left Philippines with a heavy heart.

Her employer in Hong Kong was a retired couple. It took her months before she figured out the basics of the Cantonese language.

The flow of communication between Palawan and Hong Kong was good. Talk of Ashley dominated her conversations with her parents and Bobby. In one of the phone calls Bobby made, he presented a plan to start up their own business. He was aware that Tina was doing fine in terms of her income. In her attempt to help the guy straighten up his act as a family man, Tina agreed to the plan.

Being in the police force for five years, Bobby's dream of establishing a security agency finally materialized. Much of the money in putting this business came from Tina in Hong Kong. It took almost two years before the business took off with financial ease. The flourishing of the business, however, didn't change one iota in Bobby himself. Girls had been, and always would be, his weakness. Left and right, he was chasing women in bars without shame. He even targeted secretaries in his department.

Hong Kong was only a three-hour flight away from Manila. The pain and frustration she felt with Bobby were so great that she decided to travel even further away. Without Bobby knowing, she was determined to seek a better place to start anew—never mind her career or education. As long as her parents could take care of Ashley, everything would be all right.

On her daughter's eighth birthday, Tina finally made it to Canada. In 2006, Canada experienced one of its most promising economic turns. The boom in Alberta's gas and oil industries attracted all kinds of work. With Tina's experience in caregiving, she easily found employment by a young couple in Calgary; both the husband and wife were working in the oil patch, and they had two young boys. Tina had previously cared for two seniors, and she thought caring for two preschool kids would be the same. In reality, it was entirely different.

The pay was better than what she had been getting in Hong Kong. When her boyfriend found out where she was, she only heard a congratulatory note—nothing less, nothing more.

Their security agency was booming, and so was Bobby's passion for skirt chasing. Ashley had a new stepsister from one of Bobby's mistresses. One of the hardest experiences a mother could have was to see her own daughter take care of a baby who was not her own.

In three years' time, Tina was fully aware that Ashley was about to become a full-blown teenager. Her plan, therefore, was to bring Ashley to Canada and leave Bobby for good. She was convinced that there was no future for her or her daughter with Bobby. She could sacrifice and forego the business and get on with their life together in Canada.

Bringing Ashley to Canada was not too difficult a task. Her only problem was the inconsistency in her daughter's name. The birth certificate indicated a different last name. The certificate bore her father's last name while her baptismal and school records bore Tina's last name. Tina was aware how difficult this kind of trouble could be, especially in Canada. The government was very strict in making sure the person coming in was the right person according to the documentation they carried. She had no option but to rectify the discrepancy.

She had to go home.

She arranged for some holiday time to make it right and talk to Bobby about the possibility of her taking her share from the business. She was also aware that it would take time to process the application for Ashley's immigration papers. While waiting for the application's approval in the Philippines, she also wanted to take her daughter out of Palawan and bring her to Manila. That way, Bobby would have no way of finding her.

Tina's work permit would expire in eight months, so time was not on her side. She needed to act swiftly. Her open visa would be arriving in the upcoming year, and there remained many issues to consider in the short time available to her.

Spending the nights alone in her employers' basement suite led to boredom and depression.

She needed to be careful in executing her plan. She called her aunt in Manila. It was her aunt's wish to see them settle peacefully in a foreign land away from Bobby. Tina's aunt agreed to be part of the plan. They would move Ashley to Manila, and only the two of them would know where. Ashley would study there and, after months of processing her immigration papers, she would join her in Canada. Her aunt had no problem with this arrangement. She got together the money needed to execute plan, and her aunt agreed to act as her daughter's trustee.

In March 2008, Tina returned to the Philippines for a visit. Together with her aunt, they found a place in Manila to rent.

The trip was exhausting. It was thirteen hours from Vancouver to Manila, and another four hours by ship from Manila to Palawan. Another two hours passed as she traveled to their place from the seaport. The rented car stopped in front of her parents' house well into the night.

Everyone in the house was shocked by Tina's appearance at the front door. Her mom and dad couldn't believe what in the world their daughter was planning to do. She hadn't even bothered to inform them of her plans to come home. Her daughter suddenly came out from a room adjacent to the kitchen. They hadn't seen each other in five years. Ashley finally came to her senses when she stared closer at the woman standing between her grandparents. The family's joy was so great that nobody went to bed until 5:00 in the morning.

It was 1:00 the next afternoon when Tina and Ashley got up for the sumptuous lunch her mom had prepared. She enjoyed the food. The *adobo*, steamed peanut with boiled tomatoes, brought back memories of her younger years. Her dad was busy dressing the turkey for dinner. Ashley was very much attached to Tina and the stuff she had brought for her from Canada.

As the family was having lunch, Tina laid out the plan. Ashley would move to Manila and continue her last year of high school there, living with Tina's aunt. Nobody in town would know where Ashley was, especially her dad. Tina would talk to Bobby once and for all regarding their properties and other investments. Tina would also fix the discrepancy of her daughter's name as it appeared on her legal documents.

Though it was hard for Ashley to understand the true reason for this plan, the lure of studying in Manila was hard to pass up. It was a great opportunity for her, as a young woman, to feel, hear, and see what Manila was all about.

The plan would be known only to them.

On the third day of the trip, Tina contacted Bobby. The surprise on his face lasted only a few minutes when they met in a restaurant in the city's downtown core. Tina was aware that Bobby was having affairs everywhere. Right then, he was living with a woman and their year-old baby girl.

Tina ordered *halo-halo* and *monay*, her favorite refreshment from her high school years. Bobby settled for a cup of coffee. She couldn't waste time and Bobby wanted to hear the news right away. Tina was very careful sharing her idea. She'd been rehearsing the lines ever since leaving Canada. Though Bobby knew what was coming from Tina, he kept himself calm and patiently listened to her. Tina was a bit surprised by Bobby's attitude this time. There had been remarkable change, she thought. Hopefully, he was changing for the sake of their daughter.

It was very clear to Bobby that almost all the money invested into the business had come from Tina. What Tina was after, however, was the original amount she had invested. She cared less for the interest or income from the time she had left for Hong Kong. Bobby paused for a few minutes, trying to absorb the request. He was aware that the business had branched out to other cities in the past two years. The amount being requested would not affect his operations. He could manage to return her investment at any time. He assured Tina of her share, that it would be given back the following Monday after she signed a release form. The release form would keep Tina from other assets of the company.

The agreement was a relief for Tina.

Tina also indicated that Ashley would continue to stay with her parents. Bobby didn't comment about that. In fact, he agreed to the plan. Anyway, that had been how it was ever since she left the Philippines.

Their talk only lasted forty-five minutes. Being a busy businessman and policeman, Bobby landed a peck on Tina's cheek, indicating his care and best wishes for her. When Bobby was out the door, tears fell from Tina's eyes. She was overwhelmed with relief and consolation that the plan was going just as expected.

The next day, Tina and her aunt boarded a rented car and went straight to the pier for their early trip to Manila. Ashley would live with Tina's aunt in an apartment somewhere in the Novaliches district of Quezon City. The landlord knew that they were coming to discuss the arrangement.

Along the way, Tina opened up to her about her life in Canada. The four-hour trip was long enough for her aunt to learn all that was happening in her life.

Tina's caregiving role wasn't as hard as the job she'd had in Hong Kong. It was a blessing that her job was in Canada. There was plenty of opportunity there for a family to make a decent living. Tina didn't hesitate to bring out personal and intimate matters about her life in Calgary. Her aunt was a bit surprised to know that she was engaged to a man named Terry—a Caucasian.

Terry was originally from Ontario. He moved to Edmonton in his early twenties to finish his degree in engineering, then found a job and settled in. He was a man of adventure. He spent lots of time and money skiing in the winter along the slopes of the foothills. In the summertime, he loved to go hiking. He didn't get serious about his life until he was almost thirty, when he met a woman in an Edmonton. His stature—he was more than six feet tall with wide, bulky shoulders—attracted lots of young ladies. One young lady at the time, Cindy, was a bank teller in the north end of the city. After a series of dates, Cindy got pregnant.

Terry didn't want to get married, so the couple lived together as common law husband and wife. Prior to the final month of Cindy's pregnancy, Terry was assigned to work in Fort McMurray as the lead engineer in one of his company's new projects. The challenge of the opportunity enticed him to move. Still at the age of irresponsibility, Terry didn't even discuss how they were going to get on with their life and the baby.

In the first few weeks of working in Fort McMurray, he spoke with Cindy on the phone almost every day. He took three days off and visited Cindy when she gave birth to a beautiful baby girl. His visits to Cindy and his baby girl, Samantha, however, were getting few and far between, especially when the project he was leading ran into some operational problems.

To deal with his boredom in the middle of the oil sands, Terry started to go to bars and mingled with different kinds of workers. The pressures and demands of the company had to be relieved for a while. Wine and music were effective, but only for a time. His hormones were telling him to pursue a woman. He was very much aware of his physical needs.

Scott has been with the company as long as Terry. They knew each other, but they were not that close. Both were in their late twenties and experiencing the same dilemma working in the oil patch—boredom. Having the same interests, their friendship deepened. Soon, they were like brothers to each other. They talked about family, friends, work, and entertainment. Scott was still single while Terry was contemplating going back to his girlfriend and baby in Edmonton. He desired companionship—Cindy and their daughter—but he was not prepared to have a family. Though he could afford to support them, he was not emotionally ready for those responsibilities.

After months of working together, Scott revealed to Terry his plan for settling down. Scott had met a young lady at a wedding party he had attended in Grande Prairie. Clarita was a tall, slender, smart, and pretty Filipina caregiver. She had finished her Bachelor of Nursing in the Philippines in 2001. A year ago, she had received her open visa and passed her nursing exam. It was not hard for Clarita to transfer her job from Grande Prairie to Fort McMurray.

Seven months later, Scott married Clarita. The couple was generous to their friends and coworkers. Their hospitality was a well-known fact among the people working under Terry and Scott.

Clarita was not only a nurse, but she also was a great cook. It was no wonder Scott gained five pounds. At their house, their guests were able to experience all different kinds of Asian delicacies.

The progress in the couple's life was obvious, and this fact didn't escape Terry's notice. One summer night, Scott invited Terry to their place for a night of barbeque. It was also the night when Terry and Tina met for the first time. Tina had been Clarita's best friend back in Hong Kong and they hadn't lost contact since they both moved to Canada as caregivers. Tina had been able to arrange to take a break from work and fly to Fort McMurray to be with her friend. It was a reunion of sorts.

The turkey was perfect and the rest of the meal was excellent. Tina's areas of expertise were oriental noodles and barbeque. Terry was not only attracted to the food; he was attracted to Tina's energetic and caring personality. The dining room was cozy with only the four of them. They talked about life and reminisced about the past. It became apparent that Tina and Terry were interested in each other. Their closeness and familiarity went beyond friendship. By the end of the conversation, they had each discovered some intimate and personal secrets about the other.

Terry was directed to take the couch for the night, while Tina occupied the guest room.

The following morning, Scott and Clarita wanted to go to church and attend a worship service together. The couple loved to share their life, home, and faith with no string attached. As Christians, it was their duty to share the good news of God's provision for salvation and the joy that accompanied it.

Tina and Terry's friendship didn't end at Fort McMurray. Weeks after their first encounter, Terry found himself knocking at Tina's place in Calgary. The visit was followed by many more visits, until Tina accepted his marriage proposal.

Now on her way back to Canada, Tina found the time to list all the major elements of her planned wedding. Her only major concern was Terry's responsibilities to Cindy and Samantha. Would Terry be willing to leave them? What would happen to her daughter, Ashley, all the way back in the Philippines? And what if Bobby found out about her plan? These questions nagged at her during the trip.

Tina wasted no time when she got back to Calgary. Every weekend after her arrival she toured the shopping malls. She wanted all the items on her list taken care of right away.

One weekend in one of the malls, with her shopping cart full, Tina headed towards the food court. She felt a craving for pizza, so she ordered one. The table she sat at faced south. She parked the cart to one side and looked out the window, through which she could see that the nearby Macleod Trail was empty of traffic.

At lunchtime during weekends, the food court was packed with people. So when Lily walked into the food court, she immediately picked out the empty seat to Tina's left. Even though Lily didn't know Tina, her comfort level was high; after all, they were both Filipinas.

They established an easy connection, since they had ordered the same food.

"It looks like you're getting ready for a wedding," Lily said, referring to the cart full of wedding items.

"I'm shopping for my wedding," Tina answered with enthusiasm. "What about you? Are shopping for your family in the Philippines? How many kids do you have?"

Their talk led to a casual friendship. By the time their conversation ended, they had shared some serious life issues they were each facing. The two parted with their minds full of challenges and opportunities.

Lily was smiling deep down inside. Tina had thought the items in her shopping cart were meant for her family. How she longed to have one…

Chapter 21

"I made it. I passed!" Lily was exhilarated.

"How many mistakes did you make?" the woman behind the counter asked. She stood and bent over to reach for Lily's answer sheet.

"Just two," Lily answered.

"Let me see it." The woman looked over Lily's answers. "Sorry, lady. You pushed the end button too quickly and consequently didn't finish the last question. You only answered nineteen questions out of twenty. Yes, you got two wrong, but one answer is missing, so you actually failed."

Lily, still feeling foolish, left the driver's license office short of ten bucks and full of frustration. Her dream of taking an in-car driving lesson was cut short by her failure to pass the licensing exam. Her only consolation was that it was only her first time taking the test. She promised herself to be aware of the mistake the next time. And there would definitely be a next time. She exited the testing office and headed toward the bus station.

The bus stopped in front of her. It was a Saturday morning in May and it was neither hot nor cold. She was the only one boarding the bus heading downtown. There weren't many people inside the bus, either. She took a seat at the back. It was her habit to sit on the backseat, so that she could watch the other passengers board the bus. Lily leaned her head against the window and once again thought about her failure. She managed to hide her frustration by closing her eyes and enjoying the first few minutes of the ride.

The sudden stop of the bus awakened her. In front of the bus was a small Corolla with a sign on top that read, "Your Driving School." If it hadn't been for the bus driver's quick reflexes, there would have been an accident at the four-way stop. The driving instructor opened his window and flashed his middle finger for the bus driver to see. The driver responded by pressing down on his long, loud horn. What a scary moment that was for everyone on board.

Just a few weeks ago, she had witnessed a scuffle inside a bus. And now she'd experienced a close call with a student driver. As the bus inched its way from the scene, her heart rate subsided to normal.

When the bus entered downtown, Lily stood up and rushed to the front. She grabbed the transfer ticket handed to her by the driver. She got off the bus and found herself at the rail station. She pushed the door button of the waiting train and stepped onto it with anticipation. The three-coach car line was heading to Sundridge Mall, Lily's destination. Old and new friends, she was hoping, would be waiting for her in one corner of the mall's food court. She already knew what she was going to have for lunch. She was in the mood for chicken curry. It had been four years since the last time she'd had that, in Saudi Arabia.

The train stopped at Whitehorn Station at 12:30. The loading platform was filled with families. Saturday was a day for families to spend time and money in the malls. Shoppers often paid a visit to the movie theatre after a long day of shopping to catch the newest film openings.

As expected, Lily was last to arrive at the meeting place. Two of the women were already half-finished their lunch. One of them, Gina, had just taken her first three bites.

Gina was from Tarlac, and she was a full-blooded Ilocana. She had come to Canada in 1996 under the foreign caregiver program. She was one of the many young people seeking opportunity in North America. She had earned her nursing degree from the oldest school in the Philippines, University of St. Tomas. For three years after graduation, she worked with the Distress and Trauma unit of the university hospital. She was gifted with a sharp mind, agility, and orderliness in almost all aspects of her work. The head nurse was very impressed with her performance. Every year, Gina got a promotion.

Gina was the hope of her family. Her parents were not young anymore. The other five children following her had not been responsible enough to live on their own. They needed their parents and Gina to look after them.

Her job at the hospital might have been great if it hadn't been for a young laboratory technician named Roger. He was not only good-looking, but also good at calibrating medical instruments. His friendliness caught Gina by surprise. Their proximity at the workplace was the main reason for their very short-lived courtship.

Their five-month engagement was not a healthy one. Though Gina knew about birth control, her religious beliefs prevented her from using it. That had been a mistake, for she soon became pregnant. She was only in her mid-twenties, and she wasn't ready to have a family of her own yet. Her family in Tarlac was still her priority. Roger wanted her to have an abortion, but she couldn't go through with it. It was a wedge that kept them apart.

Gina left her job with a heavy heart and stayed with her family until the baby was born. Her town's health center helped the family survive over the last eight months of her pregnancy. As one of the community nurses, Gina's situation was obvious to everyone. She had to face the reality of being a single mother-to-be. It was the right option for her and the family. When her younger brothers and sisters found out that Gina was not able to continue her responsibilities to them, they realized their need to become responsible people in their own right. They had no option but to face life head-on. They were not children anymore.

The plan was for the family to take care of her baby while she ventured abroad. Her first priority was to update her list of contacts overseas. An assistant nurse she knew from her previous job at the hospital had moved away from the Philippines three years before and was now working in Calgary, Alberta, at Foothills General Hospital. One of her classmates had also immigrated to Canada and was working in Montreal. In a letter from Montreal, Gina vividly remembered that it was vital for people working in public service to speak a second language, such as French. It had taken her friend five months to master basic French greetings and enough vocabulary to get by. She ruled out Montreal as a destination. Considering her age and all the family concerns that still rested on her shoulders, she couldn't be bothered to learn French.

After three attempts, Gina finally got in touch with her friend from Calgary. With the ever-increasing demand for health care professionals in Alberta, especially nurses, Gina was encouraged to apply as an independent immigrant. Based on other people's experiences, this route would take at least two years of waiting. The best and most efficient way to get to Canada was to apply as a foreign caregiver. That would only take her three months.

One of the medical doctors in the hospital where her friend was working was looking for a nanny to take care of her first baby. Gina was recommended and her papers were processed in less than five weeks. As planned, Gina's application papers were processed, approved, and she was advised to be in Canada by the fall of 2004.

Gina now carried the load of single motherhood, but the baby she was taking care of was not her own. She spent almost every weekend with friends to distract herself from the longing she felt for her baby daughter back home in the Philippines. Every day she and her friends went strolling in a mall, she bought one new item for the baby in Tarlac. Every other month, she sent them a box full of toys, dresses, and canned food.

"What made you late today?" the woman to Gina's left asked Lily.

"It's Saturday, and the buses don't run as often. Besides, we almost got into an accident."

"No rush," Gina said. "We still have forty-five minutes before the next show starts." From the sounds of it, they were going to see a movie after lunch.

Lily put down her stuff on an adjacent table and went to order her food. She didn't even have to wait in line. The aroma and taste of the curry chicken was unmistakable.

"I'd like iced tea with that," she told the woman behind the counter. Her face was half-covered by a scarf.

The order was steaming hot. She proceeded to the group with her tray full of food. Gina was about to finish her sub sandwich and the other women were already finished eating. They were now topping up their lipstick.

"While you were ordering," Gina said, gesturing to Lily, "we talked about what movie we want to see."

"I'll go with whatever you all decide."

The people lining up for Spider-Man 3 extended up to the front door of the theatre. It was ten minutes to show time and still the friends were at the tail end of the line.

"How many?" asked the teller when they got to the front of the line.

"Three for Spider-Man 3," Gina said.

Just two minutes before the movie, with cola and bags full of popcorn, the three women groped their way up the steps to the back row. They were the last ones to sit down. As usual, there were ten minutes of ads and announcements before the movie started.

The sun was still up when they emerged from the theatre. People were expressing all sorts of different reactions to the movie. Some older folks were not that impressed. Others, especially the younger ones, had been taken away with the story. They seemed to be able to repeat the best lines perfectly. As they left the theatre, they saw the next group of movie-goers waiting in line to get in. Lily noticed that more than half of the immigrants waiting in that line were from the Philippines. She guessed that most of them were just like her—nannies.

Once out of the building, the three women started talking about the film.

"That was a nice camera trick," Gina said, referring to one particular special effect she had enjoyed.

"It's all camera tricks," Lily pointed out, wiping her strained eyes.

It was Lily's third time watching a movie with her friends. It was becoming very clear to her that life in Western society was somewhat patterned on the plot and stories of movies. It was no wonder the majority of immigrants, even those who came from conservative countries, were enticed by and very subtly copied the ways and dictates of the entertainment world.

Her struggle was not on the issue of *if* she would be influenced but *when* and *how great* the influence to her moral fiber would be. Would she be part of the crowd or the one who tried to make a difference in the lives of people around her?

Chapter 22

The van was ready for the one and half hour drive to Red Deer. One of their friends' kids was being christened there at 3:00 in the afternoon. Red Deer was north of Calgary, and there were more than two thousand Pinoys residing in the city. Known for their barbeque on Canada Day, the Filipinos in the small city were a bit closer and united than their compatriots in Calgary, Edmonton, or Winnipeg. The growing number of Pinoy families was phenomenal. So many of them had come to Canada to be caregivers, but they were now advancing their careers through night classes and online schooling to become active registered nurses.

The house was packed with friends. It was interesting for Lily to listen to the stories being shared—the joys and pains of being caregivers. Lily easily fit into this group. Her ears were wide as she picked out the stories being talked about. Mostly, the topics revolved around relationships.

"I was dating a guy—yes, a filthy rich old white guy," said one of the ladies. She was wearing far too much makeup.

"What have you done with the other one you were seeing, the one from Innisfail?" asked a voice from the back of the group.

"He was good for nothing. He had bad breath and I didn't know how to fix his wig."

"So this guy you're dating now is the fifth in two years?"

"I'm hoping to get lucky with this one."

While they were enjoying their desserts, Lily walked elsewhere and heard as Thelma, an older woman, shared about her recent experience with her employer.

The Dollar Store was one of the most popular destinations for people who enjoyed shopping at discounted rates. The phenomenon had even swept to the small towns outside the city. Thelma's employer owned one such store in Red Deer. Part of their mutual understanding was that she could work part-time hours at the store every evening from 5:00 to 9:00, after she finished her caregiving workload. At first, it was easy and beneficial, and the extra money was a welcome relief. And of course, the cheap buys made her feel good. Her room was full of stuff, and she couldn't remember the reason for having bought at least half of it. One of her friends had suggested that she arrange her room like a Wal-Mart, given the volume of items scattered around every corner.

Her dilemma began when some of her fellow community members learned of her arrangement. At the time, she was still under the government's caregiving program, which meant that having another job was against the law. Out of envy and jealousy, the case was brought before the proper authority. It took her employer almost three months to clear up the mess.

"Here's the moral of the story," Thelma boastfully proclaimed to all those present. "Don't ever, ever trust people—

even our *kababayan* with your situation—unless you *fully* trust them."

"So, you still need one more year and an open visa before you can look for another job?" Lily asked

Thelma nodded. "That's right. In fact, one of my friends in Saskatchewan was deported for a similar breach of contract."

Lily had heard of plenty of other nannies who had similar stories. Many of them couldn't wait to get second jobs, perhaps because they desperately needed the money and were too impatient to follow the rules of their contract. It was very unfortunate that some of them were reported and deported. Others simply jumped quickly from one employer to the next, just to get away from the law. In some instances, Pinoy workers crossed the border down south and stayed with their friends or relatives as illegal aliens. Some of them simply disappeared into the sea of people roaming around the United States of America.

If Lily was ever thrown that kind of curve ball, her ability to make the right choice would be tested. It was important to gather the wisdom of people around her.

As the evening came to an end, the guests started getting ready to head out. Others simply went straight into the kitchen, where leftover foods called to them. Plastic containers filled with food were ready. The woman hosting the party was more than happy to share the leftovers.

They hit the road back to Calgary after midnight.

"Even if they know the laws regarding the foreign caregivers program, many simply ignore them and do their own thing," Dana said in a sad voice as they drove home.

"Do you know of any others in Calgary who break the law?" Lily asked.

"It's not just caregivers, Lily. A few years back, a placement agency in Red Deer was busted by the police for operating unscrupulously. To add insult to injury, it was a Filipino couple who was behind the scam."

"And that was big news to the community?"

"What do you think?" Dana asked. "In the late nineties, a Filipino geologist was responsible for bringing down a gold mining company into bankruptcy. He ended up committing suicide by jumping out of a helicopter somewhere in the middle of the Indonesian jungle."

"Oh, yeah. That guy!"

"He's gone now, and so is the company. It was a really big blow to our community."

The Calgary city limit sign was lit up as they passed it. There were very few vehicles on the road. Everybody in the car was awakened when the van arrived home and stopped in front of the garage.

It was the end of another long day for the family.

Lily was getting used to the busy life, and she had to love it—free rides, travel, food, and new friends. What else did she need?

Mike!

Chapter 23

Lily boarded the bus one Saturday morning and headed to Anderson Train Station. She got on the train and went north. There were only a handful of other people comfortably enjoying the ride. Others still had their eyes closed, probably fresh from a graveyard shift. The woman three chairs away from Lily was applying her makeup.

The morning wind was so refreshing. Once again Lily observed the beauty and cleanliness of the city. It was green everywhere. Both industrial and residential lawns were perfectly manicured. A number of RVs were cruising down Deerfoot Trail in both directions.

When Lily reached the station, she had to wait another ten minutes before the northbound train arrived.

The early summer morning breeze was warm and humid. Outside, the city was coming to life. People from the night shift were piling up at the Olympic Plaza station. Lily got off the train and walked straight across the platform. The electronic signboard indicated that the next train was heading to

Whitehorn, the last train station on the north side of the city. She still had twenty-five minutes left to reach her destination. When she got off her last bus, she had to walk double time to be on time for her daylong CPR course at the St. John Ambulance Training Centre (SJATC).

Her contract with Dana and Rudy required her to receive regular CPR upgrades. CPR training was mandatory for almost all occupations in the province. This was because the ever-increasing demand of the workplace occasionally rendered workers vulnerable to fatigue, stress, and breakdown, resulting in work site accidents. Companies were being sued on account of health and safety negligence. Operations were affected, resulting in shutdowns and slowdowns.

The room where the class was being taught held twenty-five adult students. First aid mannequins and other props were arranged properly along one side of the room. A seventeen-inch television was strategically positioned at the top corner of the blackboard, facing the class. The instructor was seated, enjoying her cup of Tim Horton's coffee as she waited for the class to begin. Training syllabuses were distributed, three to each table. Evaluation sheets were tucked at the back of the material.

There was one other Filipino participant, Lily noted. The instructor had been facilitating this course for the last five years. She had been with the Emergency Management System (EMS) of the Calgary Health Department for three years, and teaching CPR was part of her job. Dealing with students energized her. The session would be delivered through discussion, practical application, and a video.

Lily hadn't received any training like this in the Philippines. It reminded her of a tragedy years ago in her senior year of college, when the janitor of their boarding house had fallen after cleaning the windows. People below jumped in and tried to help, but their assistance only made the victim get worse. Nobody there had been aware of the EMS of first aid. His neck was broken when he was lifted up without support. He had ended up in a vegetative state.

Another memory she couldn't forget was from her time in Saudi Arabia, when Karen, her friend and roommate, had fainted. Without the supervision of the first aid personnel of the hospital, Lily and the rest would have made the situation even worse. Karen had been two months pregnant. It was a traumatic experience.

The video presentation was very informative. The facts were made more interesting through the clear and concise way they were presented. She couldn't remember if she'd learned it before, but the video said that the average breathing rate for a healthy adult at rest was in the range of ten to twenty breaths per minute. The facilitator discussed the different conditions that warranted AR (artificial resuscitation) after watching the video.

The group was asked to proceed to the other side of the room, where clean mats were laid out. There were rubberized dummies on each mat. Participants were familiarized on the steps needed for AR. Sterilized swabs were provided, which they used to wipe the dummies' mouths. At first it was a bit awkward to kneel and take the position needed to compress her dummy's chest. The mouth-to-mouth artificial respiration evoked smiles from all the students.

Lily's profession was delivering babies, so when the facilitator discussed the other method of AR, the mouth-to-nose method, her eyebrows arched. The technique became clear to her as she watched the demonstration. First she tilted the head back and lifted the chin, then she closed the dummy's mouth with her thumb. She covered the dummy's nose with her mouth to provide ventilation and watched as the chest rose.

"Every other year I have to enroll in this lesson," said a black lady during the lunch break. She had a sandwich and a pop, and was sitting behind Lily.

"Our company is very concerned about health and safety," said a Chinese woman next to her. She was eating noodles out of a Tupperware container.

"Where do you work?"

"Bow Valley Daycare Centre, located downtown. What about you?"

"At the Cargill meat processing plant in High River."

The discussions all around them revolved around various safety scenarios in the workplace. Lily was serious about her lunch—a tuna sandwich, cookies, and bottled water.

"Hi, I'm Joey. Where are you from in the Philippines?" asked the other Filipina sitting just a chair away from her.

"Nueva Ecija." Lily answered with a smile.

"What do you do?"

"I'm the caregiver for a two-year-old boy in the McKenzie area. I was a midwife for ten years before getting this job. It's a bit of a career change."

"How long have you been here?" Joey asked.

Why in the world was she asking so many questions? Lily was getting irritated. "Almost three."

They still had fifteen minutes before the afternoon session. Why not widen her horizon and make a new friend? "Where do you work, and where are you from?" Lily asked with a smile.

"I work at Cargill, too, and I'm from Mindanao. Have you been to Cagayan De Oro City?"

Lily recalled that her best friend in university worked there. "My friend Nora is working there as a social worker. She moved there about three years ago." Lily wiped sandwich crumbs from her lips. "I don't suppose you know her, do you?"

"I've heard about her. If she's the one I'm thinking of, she's advocating for the equal treatment of workers in Dole's pineapple plantation."

"What happened there?"

Before Joey could answer, people around them started getting up for the afternoon session. They stood, picked up their leftover food, and placed it back in their lunch bags before proceeding to the classroom.

Lily scored eighty-five percent on the exam given after the session. Joey, her new friend, was not that concerned about her score. All she needed was a certificate to submit to her human resource manager. Her company just needed to know she had attended the class. It was easier for them to spend money to have their employees trained in CPR than to pay thousands of dollars for negligence later on; the worst thing that could happen was for an injured employee to sue them. The government was also very concerned about CPR training. Health issues played a vital role for all levels of government as well as private corporations.

They left the building with much relief. Another challenging day was over, and they were now fully certified in first aid.

When they arrived at the train station together, they had to wait fifteen minutes for their train to roll in. The transit system was very efficient, so it arrived right on time. They got on the train and sat down.

Making friends was not hard for Lily. Her long years as a midwife gave her the skills she needed to establish rapport and goodwill with others, especially other women. They eventually got off the train and walked to the nearest bus stop.

Joey pulled out a small plastic bag from her backpack and offered Lily some candy. "This has been my favorite candy since I was in elementary school," Joey revealed.

Lily grabbed one, unwrapped it, and put it straight into her dry mouth. She was a bit surprised to discover that these candies, popular in the Philippines, were available in this part of the world.

"I was thinking about your friend, Nora," Joey said while trying to fish her bus ticket out of her backpack pocket. "She was hailed as a hero by the community.""Where are you headed for? Straight to work, or somewhere else?" asked Lily.

In the distance, they saw the bus coming. The other people waiting crowded closer, forming a line leading to the door of the bus.

"I'm going to Chinook Mall," Joey said as they boarded the bus. "I'm going to meet my friends and see a movie. If you're not doing anything, you should come with us."

"That's a good idea. Anyway, Chinook is on my way back." They sat together by a window. "How many other Filipinos are working at Cargill?"

"Around six hundred, I think," answered Joey.

Cargill Foods was one the largest meat processing plants in Canada. Roughly five thousand heads of cattle were butchered and processed there every day. Many newly-arrived immigrants found work at the plant. The staff turnover was high, though, so the company was constantly recruiting new employees. Even people from other provinces were coming to Cargill as their stepping stone to settling down in Calgary.

"How does it feel working for Cargill?"

"I've been working there almost three years now," Joey said. "If you have any other place to work, it would be better. However, if your family is young and you need money, Cargill is a relatively secure place."

"How are your relationships among the other workers?"

"Good and bad. Good because you make lots of friends, multicultural ones. The bad part is that, especially in our community, I find that many of my coworkers are having affairs with each other."

Joey told her about one of the ground supervisors, who'd had at least two affairs in the last four years. Not only was his family in shambles, but he eventually had to sell his house to facilitate the end of his marriage. Boredom, familiarity, and closeness with each other at work often sparked interest in experimentation and exploration. For those who were working in the same unit day in day out for many years, attractions could be intense.

Joey's story was cut short when the train reached the station platform.

The two got off at the mall. The next movie screening was still an hour and a half away, so they had enough time to walk around the mall and have a snack. As expected, Joey's friends were excited to meet them in the food court. Joey introduced Lily to Carmen and Ester. As they were waiting in the line, Lily brought out her cell and dialed the house.

"Dana, I'll be late tonight. I met a friend who invited me to a movie here in Chinook Mall."

"Okay," Dana said. "Enjoy. Take care and I'll see you later then."

Carmen had been in Canada for three years now as the nanny for a three-year-old boy with autism. She really needed break times like this to maintain her sanity. Too many frustrations, demands, and pressures from the kid made her life very stressful. Going to watch a movie with friends was one of her outlets. Looking at her bank account provided some relief, though, as her employers both worked in the oil patch. She made two thousand dollars per month, plus free lodging. She was single and still waiting for her fiancé to arrive from the Philippines. Carmen was good at managing her resources. Just last month, she had gotten her driver's license. She was now driving one of her employers' cars, an Intrepid, except on the weekends.

"Autism? What are the symptoms of the disease?" asked Lily.

"It's more about the kid's cognitive and motor faculties. They are not functioning normally."

Before completing her answer, the teller handed them their movie tickets.

It was 7:00 when the four left the theatre together. Outside, the sun was still up, as it always was late in the northern summer evenings. They still had time to roam around, but instead they each decided to head home. From Chinook Station, Joey and Carmen boarded the northbound train, and a few minutes later Ester and Lily took the southbound.

As the train started to move, Ester asked Lily, "How long have you known Joey?"

"We just met this morning at first aid training."

"Joey and I came from Taiwan four years ago," Ester said.

"Both of you as caregivers?"

"She was. I was practicing my nursing degree. Joey was the first to come. Then, after a year, she told me to apply for my working visa. Her employer's family friend then was looking for a nanny to take care of their month-old baby girl. She recommended me, and in less than six months I arrived from Taiwan."

Moving to Canada had brought great relief to Ester. The pay was good and her work conditions were much improved. Her only regret was that, after three years of working, her employers had failed to tell her about their kid's ADHD illness. At that age, without Ritalin, the kid brought chaos everywhere he went. Ester was slim and short, and Lily couldn't resist imagining how she handled him.

Her bus arrived earlier than expected and Lily proceeded to the back seat. Ester boarded another bus heading north. They waved to each other as the buses began to move.

After just three stops, Lily's bus was packed. Everyone was in a hurry. Sweat and perspiration dominated the bus. As usual, Lily covered her nose and mouth with her handkerchief, pretending to be asleep. Her eyes were closed, but her ears were wide open to all kinds of noise and gossip swirling around the bus. More than once, Lily could not control her giggles; the things she heard or observed from people around her, especially the conversation of two nearby seniors, one from Ilocos and the other one from Ilo-ilo, which was quite funny. They talked about in-laws, their employers, and their youth.

The driver, with his colourful turban, never stopped smiling to people getting into the bus, especially to those who were also wearing turbans. There were so many languages being spoken. Who cared about Canada's bilingual laws? Once you were inside the bus, you were like a lost passenger on Noah's Ark. Speaking in tongues was the norm.

Two more stops and Lily would be home. At the center of the bus was a drunk, cranky man. He was very irritating. People's response was to ignore him. Looking for added attention, the guy started to push and shove people around him. A shouting match soon ensued, however. The driver stopped the bus and called for help from the city's transportation security. The conflict became verbal, which led to a physical alteration. Dumb as he was, the drunk underestimated his opponent, an off-duty RCMP officer who was tall and bulky. The driver opened the bus doors and people started to get off the bus. While the drunk and RCMP officer were struggling and wrestling, Lily just stayed put, watching the two men fighting each other. As expected, the drunken man was overpowered and banged his head into one of the metal railings. Blood began oozing from his head wound and he lost consciousness.

A few minutes later, police cars and transit security forces encircled the bus. The off-duty officer flashed his badge to the approaching police and led them to the guy, who was slumped on the floor. Lily's face now showed relief. The drunken man was groaning in pain, and blood continued to ooze from his left temple. The paramedics were a minute behind the police officers. They unfolded their stretcher and placed it just in front of the bus door. Why not just carry the man onto the ambulance right away? What was the point of circling around the victim and not doing anything?

The mess was cleared away and the man was rushed to the hospital. The off-duty officer gave his statement and the passengers got back to their respective spots. The responsive driver, with his turban tilted a little to the left, looked relieved. A minute later, the bus was inching its way back onto the road.

It finally occurred to Lily why the paramedics had circled the man. They had been applying the first principle of first aid—emergency scene management. The paramedics were professionals and Lily was thankful to have witnessed firsthand how they applied the principles she had learned just a few hours ago. In third-world countries, more often than not people acted out of instinct and adrenalin rush. They reacted swiftly without concern for the implications of their actions.

Rudy and Junior were watching the hockey game when she got home. The Detroit Red Wings and Calgary Flames were in the fourth game of their playoff series. Dana was in the kitchen, busily cooking dinner. Ten more minutes and the table would be ready.

From her room downstairs, Lily emerged fresh and ready to help Dana with the meal. Plates were laid on the table. Spoons and forks were positioned on the right side of the plates. Napkins and glasses of water were also in place.

"The food is ready," Dana's loud voice called. The kitchen windows were open. As expected, Rudy was in a hurry to eat. The hockey period ended, and there was a ten-minute break. Commentaries and play-by-play analyses played in the background as they sat down. Rudy was listening to it carefully. The projections were in favor of the Flames.

After saying grace, Rudy and Junior enjoyed the hot *adobo*. The women, on the other hand, tested the food to see whether or not it was too salty. From Lily's experience, both the women's tastes had become identical.

"How was your first aid training?" asked Dana.

"I learned so many important things," Lily said. "Employers here are very much concerned about health and safety. Even small business employees take the training."

The score was 2–1, with Calgary leading in the third period. Rudy and Junior were like kids whose joy could not be contained.

"In fact, I was a witness today to how the principles of first aid are applied."

"What was that?" probed Dana.

Lily related the incident on the bus.

Calgary won the game, which meant their series was tied. Their next game was scheduled for Detroit. This playoff series would determine which team made it to the western conference finals. The men on the couch were so jovial about Calgary's win. Junior was a diehard fan of Miikka Kiprusoff. He wanted to be like the goalie, with that scary mask and his moves like a human yoyo.

"Is the table ready for dessert?" Rudy's asked. His voice was louder than Junior's.

"Five more minutes," shouted back Dana.

"I already had my sweets today, with new friends at Chinook Mall," advanced Lily.

"You have more new friends?" Dana asked.

"Their names are Carmen, Joey, and Ester. I met Joey at the first aid class. Carmen and Ester are Joey's friends. She invited me to see a movie with them. We also had a light dessert."

"Good, I'm glad you're making new friends," Dana said. "Nevertheless, be careful with them. You really don't know their past, personalities, or what they're up to."

Some people were good at looking nice on the outside, all the while hiding their true selves. Most were naturally good people, but there were a few who could care less about other people. Friendship is the best way for someone to get what they want in a relationship. Caregivers and other immigrants tend to easily people who exhibit care and concern for them. Friendships were cemented by an occasional eat-out, going to a movie on the weekend, attending group parties and related social gatherings. Emotional bonding bred even deeper trust. Sometimes this was followed with economic partnerships, such as buying a condo or a townhouse as a joint investment. Then at the end, people could fall victim to opportunistic *kababayan*. It was too bad.

"What do you mean, Dana?"

"Some people are opportunists, meaning they will make friends with you to gain your trust and confidence. Then, later on, they might ask you for favors—even money."

"Then what happens?"

"They're gone. You never see them again."

"Have you encountered one?"

"Yes! There was this young nanny we thought was nice and trustworthy. She knew many friends of ours, so we trusted her. One time, she borrowed five hundred dollars for her apartment's damage deposit. She promised to pay us two weeks later, and we're still waiting for the payment. That was three years ago." Dana had to cut the story short.

"Is she still in the city?" Lily asked.

"A friend of ours said yes."

"Are you not planning to contact her?"

"She has been known to fool many other people, too. That's why she's always on the run. The money she owed us will not make her rich. We believe her life is just in a mess, and we hope that the money we lent might help her find herself."

Dana's head tilted towards the direction of the living room, where Rudy and Junior were still glued to the play-by-play account of the game.

For Lily, the day had been very meaningful, insightful, and nerve-wracking. Making friends demanded caution and discernment. Being aware of what was going on around you, especially if you were by yourself traveling, was very important. Who knew what was going to happen?

Lily proceeded down to her room to rest and settle down from the day's many happenings.

Chapter 24

"In the past, I've had difficulty understanding why people shop so early for Christmas," Lily said. "But now I understand."

It was a week before Christmas, and the malls and other shopping strips around the city were bulging with people. Chinook Centre was the prime destination. Christmas carols and the smell of cinnamon lingered around food courts. That scent seemed to go hand in hand with tired and exhausted shoppers. The decorations put up in stores and lobbies were so inviting that people had no option but to go in and examine the merchandise that was there waiting for them—toys for the kids, kitchen stuff for moms, and electronics for men topped the list of things to buy.

A long line of moms and their kids waited impatiently for their turn to take pictures with Santa Claus in the middle of the mall, making foot traffic congested in all directions.

Teenagers were busy inspecting their prized purchases. Jeans from Old Navy, sweatshirts from Lulu Lemon… fashion was the heart's desire of this young generation. Gadgets like Wii, Playstation, Game Boy, and multi-functional phones were the perfect gift for imperfect and easily-bored young people.

The appeal of materialism was becoming so intense that people's lives were revolving around material possessions. Shopping carts were full to the rim. Courtesy clerks were busy loading boxes and bags into parked cars. Store delivery cars were catching up with delivery schedules. Widescreen, high-definition televisions were common items on the lists of struggling new immigrants. Many believed it was becoming a status symbol, especially for those who hailed from third-world countries. Watching the Filipino Channel (TFC) in a widescreen television was not only for entertainment; it was becoming the norm, almost a necessity.

The latest models of electronics and computers were the dominant force pulling baby boomers. Even if they were aware that better models would flood the market in six months' time, they would still buy them.

In a very subtle way, Dana was carried away by this phenomenon. She bought a two-gigabyte Nano for $125.

"It is very helpful during my laundry time," she jokingly advanced while trying to figure out how to make the gadget work.

"I'll just stick to my ten-dollar AM/FM radio I bought from Value Village," said Lily, laughing out loud.

"You better change that radio. The day after Christmas, we'll go to Market Mall and take advantage of the low prices of electronics."

"Isn't that Boxing Day?"

"Yes!"

Boxing Day in Canada was one of the holidays people looked forward to with much enthusiasm. The day after

Christmas, many people flocked to malls and shopping centers and spent all their savings. Vendors offered up to seventy-five percent discounts on almost anything on display. This was the best time of the year to add clutter to North American houses. It was not uncommon to see people lined up the night before for the opening of a store. People were camping outside the gate of big electronic stores the night before Boxing Day; they didn't seem to care that it was freezing outside! It was as if the only thing that mattered in life was getting hold of the new craze.

In the last three years, the average expenses incurred by Calgarians on Boxing Day ranged from $275–$350. With the favorable exchange rate with the American dollar, some simply drove south of the border to do their shopping, including people hunting for their dream car from American dealers.

Dana's Christmas list had fifteen items on it. Lily's priority was Junior, but tucked in her jeans pocket was also another list of gift ideas for her family. The only thing she needed right at that moment, however, was something to put into her mouth. They had been at the mall for quite some time and needed some rest and refreshments.

Dana's shopping cart was half full when they felt their legs begging for a little stop. Two hours of standing and walking was not an ordinary task for Dana. For Lily and Junior, standing for two hours was nothing. The three decided to take a break at the food court. Lily got a combo of Chinese food, while Junior was satisfied with his fries and a cheeseburger.

A few meters from their table was a group of Filipinas scouting for a vacant table. Two of the five women were wearing backpacks. The other three were able to secure a table at the end of the hall, near the washrooms. From the look of the group, they were there Christmas shopping as well. While enjoying their meal, a woman in a red jacket pulled out a receipt from a backpack full of stuff. The expression on her face was twofold—first a smile of contentment, and then a frown.

"Have they not observed anything about this season?" Dana said after adjusting her chair facing the glass window with Macleod Trail clearly in sight.

"About what?" Lily asked.

"Look around. Look outside. What do you see?"

It took a while before Lily picked up on Dana's point. After licking her fingers Lily said, "I got it."

Yes, the spirit of Christmas had been diminishing. The buildings across the street featured colourful greeting signage, but those decorations were more about the *look* of the season and not the *reason* for the season. "Happy Holidays" and "Season's Greetings" were void of the meaning of Christ's birth.

Outward displays of faith and belief were the victims as diversity and multiculturalism gained more attention across the Canadian landscape. One radical school of thought advocated for the removal of all faith-based celebration—and Christmas in particular! Some people argued that the celebration of Christmas was contrary to human rights. They contended that it was a form of discrimination against distinct minority groups, especially those coming from the Middle East. To appease and appeal to all sectors of society, businesses took the safe road by modifying their celebration greetings by getting rid of the word "Christmas."

Lily was silent and had nothing to say. Dana's observation was valid, though, and Lily's only response was to nod her head in agreement. A bit of Lily's spiritual side was awakened.

The rest lasted about forty-five minutes.

"This is the most practical and convenient time for gift shopping." Dana pointed out as they got up to continue.

Indeed, for the last two Christmas seasons, Lily had been the victim of stressful shopping. She still harbored memories of the previous year, when two weeks before Christmas she had spent five hours roaming around the malls and ended up buying only half of what she needed. By waiting so late, a lot of the stuff was gone and substitute products were not as good.

Once the food sank in and their eyelids were heavy, Dana and Lily packed up, getting ready to head out. However, they found out that Junior's silence was literally the result of a deep sleep. They decided to stay put for a while and wait until Junior was awake.

Their temporary silence was interrupted when one of the Filipina women from the nearby table started to laugh loudly. Based on their chitchatting, they were from different places in the Philippines—one from Pampanga, two from Ilocos, and the rest from Visayas. Their talk revolved around the issue of what volume of stuff they would be sending back home. A bagful of toothpaste, soap, deodorant, and many other toiletries were the focus of their laughter. Dental floss and mouthwash, too.

They were all singles. There was no mention of toys or kids' dresses. They were buying items for their fiancés. One of the women had bought musky cologne and a pack of underwear for her boyfriend, who was working for a steel company in Manila. Another had bought shoes, a sweatshirt, and a digital camera. The remaining women contended that their stuff would only be sent to parents, sisters, brothers, and other relatives. Other items like toiletries, soap, toothpaste, antiperspirant, towels, hand cream, and lotions made good Christmas gifts.

They seemed to have plenty of money to send substantial gifts, too. That was one of the advantages of working as caregivers in North America. Their salaries were far more generous than anywhere else in the world.

Shortly, the women decided to move off. Dana and Lily waited another ten minutes, staying put so that Junior could finish his nap.

"On Boxing Day, we'll go out and find cheap deals so that we can send gifts home to your family," Dana suggested to Lily.

"Where's the best place to do that?"

"A friend of mine told me the newly renovated Market Mall is the best place to shop."

"Isn't that far from our place?"

"That's why we'll take the car."

"What time do we need to be there?" Lily asked.

"Ideally, around 8:00. That way, we won't have any problems with parking."

Finally Junior's eyes were wide open and ready for more action. The pace of their exit from the mall was hindered by the heavy traffic created by hundreds of souls going in and out of the doors.

Dana tapped the door of the van. Rudy adjusted his reclined sit and greeted them with a good smile. He was satisfied with his rest while waiting for them to finish shopping. They left the parking lot early enough to get other things done at home.

As promised, they all got up early the next Saturday. In less than thirty minutes, everyone in the house was ready to hit the road. Their destination was Market Mall in the Northwest. The mall was separated from the University of Calgary by Shaganapi Trail. Cars were cruising down the street leading to the mall. It was early enough that traffic was not yet too heavy.

The mall's parking lot was packed and it took them time finding a spot. Even the boulevards separating the street from the mall were packed with SUVs and trucks. They should have come earlier, they thought as they waited for a car to exit from a spot a long way from the mall door. The weather was messy. They'd had two nights in a row of heavy snowfall.

Once inside, they easily blended into the sea of people. There were lots of immigrants everywhere they looked. A chorus of different dialects and languages dominated the place. The music playing over the speakers was no match for the volume of peoples' happy discussions.

Lily and Dana were amazed by the sheer number of people in the building. Chinook Mall was bigger, and yet this one was more crowded. People were packed in like sardines. Shoppers had to wait in long lines just to make it to the check-out counters. Sales associates were in great physical shape, and though the temperatures outside were below zero, many sales-ladies were revealing skin to attract male shoppers. There were sales of up to 70% off, which enticed bargain hunters. Boxing Day really was something!

After just forty-five minutes of walking, they finally headed to the food court. Coincidentally Junior awoke just then from his early nap. Dana and Lily secured a table after minutes of roaming around the court. Junior asked Lily for a burger while the two of them ordered sub sandwiches.

"This place is crazy!" said Dana.

"I was hoping to get a new blouse at the GAP store," Lily said.

Dana nodded. "I'm not sure what I want for myself, but for Junior I'd love to get some new clothes for New Year's."

"I like Nintendo, Mommy," shouted Junior while still working on his fries.

"We'll look around and find out where to buy one. Finish your food and we'll get back to shopping."

Lily's previous Boxing Day experiences had not been as exciting as this one. There had been fewer people, and most merchandise was mostly made in North America. This time, almost all the stuff people were crazy about were made in China and other Asian countries. Still, sales for these items were hot.

Chapter 25

"I was moved by that preacher. It hit me right in the core of my being," said Lily.

Dana put on the buckle of Junior's car seat. "How's that?"

"I think I'm living my life far away from God. The root of my worries is my own selfishness. I only think about myself and Mike, and very little time about others."

"We are all prone to that."

"What do you mean, Dana?"

"In one way or another, we all commit sin, right?"

"You're right."

"That's the very reason why God gave his son Jesus to die on the cross, so that you and I, all of us sinners, can find peace with God and find salvation through Jesus. Unless a person has a personal relationship with Jesus, life will be troubling."

"I'm getting interested with this religious stuff," Lily said. "Can we talk again about it when you have time?"

"I'll be more than happy to share my walk and journey with you," Dana said with a bright smile on her face.

They were at the German Baptist Church near the corner of Memorial and Deerfoot Trail. The parking lot was only two-thirds full. It was camping season, and it was the practice of many people to spend their summers on the road. Church attendance was greatly affected, and so was the offering.

What surprised her was the fact that almost half of the parishioners were Filipinos. It was early September, so it was cold for the Filipinos to go camping. In fact, they seldom went camping. Instead, they were excited by birthday celebrations and church fellowship.

One Sunday morning after the worship service, Dana and Lily heard that a group was heading for the community of Sommerset. One of the guys was celebrating his fiftieth birthday. The rumor was that it was a surprise party. The celebrant had no idea what was going on. However, more often than not the info was leaked early, in which case it was more a matter of just pretending not to know about it.

It occurred to Lily that birthday surprises were common to this group, old and young alike. Though they had been invited by the wife of the celebrant, they decided to stick to their original plan and stay home.

"Are you aware that Leony had her placement agency already?" Rudy asked as they drove home.

"Is she the one who moved from Saskatchewan last year?" Dana said.

"Yes."

"Isn't she a nanny?"

"When she got her open visa, she changed jobs. She's now working for a senior living alone in the Mount Royal area. She's a companion nanny."

Mount Royal was a community for Calgary's millionaires. There were more millionaires living there than in any other city west of Toronto. As usual, oil and gas were the reasons why the people in this community had prospered.

Leony's employer, Mrs. Buckley, was a retired medical doctor whose late husband had been the CEO of a big oil company. The old woman's kids were all grown up and successful in their chosen fields. The oldest was chairman of another oil company, and the youngest was the head surgeon of Baker Cancer Hospital at the University of Calgary.

As a companion nanny, Leony drove Mrs. Buckley to all her appointments—to her monthly visit to her daughter, the beauty salon, shopping, and to an exclusive seniors' bingo night far to the north of the city.

Mrs. Buckley had also been instrumental in helping Leony's sister come to Canada as a caregiver, too. Months of personal interaction with Mrs. Buckley had led to an idea—recruiting caregivers. Now she was actively pursuing this business with the help and encouragement of Mrs. Buckley. Weekends were her precious time. She even traveled to far-flung communities in Saskatchewan, luring seniors to hire foreign caregivers. It was no wonder she wasn't able to attend church very often.

At last count, Leony had five sure clients looking for nannies from the Philippines.

Unfortunately, according to a vast network of gossipers in both Manila and Canada, certain bureaucratic delays were preventing Filipino applicants from being granted working visas under the foreign live-in caregiver program at the Canadian embassy in Makati. These delays were costing potential employers a lot of time and resources, including Leony's clients. Some manufacturing companies' production lines were suffering, affecting productivity. Their orders were not met, resulting in delivery delays. These companies needed foreign workers very badly.

The problem first became noticeable through the efforts of a cleaning company in Calgary—owned and operated by Dana and Rudy's friend—to hire Filipino workers. Interviews were scheduled at the Canadian embassy in Manila and only a few papers were said to be required for the applicants to make their final travel arrangements. Suddenly, a letter from a government office in Manila then arrived which added a complication to the process. According to the letter, the applicants were required to submit a certificate proving that they had attended a janitorial training school. The letter also listed the names of the schools where the applicants could study cleaning and other janitorial services.

The same issue not only related to potential janitors, but also to some other trades, like cooking and food preparation. Even some of the recruitment agencies based in Manila were following this new prerequisite. They required applicants to produce a school or trade certificate, and they also suggested what schools to attend.

Leony was furious. She didn't want to break her promise to her clients. Her company's integrity hinged on the timely arrival of new workers from the Philippines. She contacted her business partner in the Philippines and figured out how to get around this rule. It came to her knowledge that the required certificate was, in fact, a requirement from Manila and not from Labor and Immigration Canada. Based on her investigation, the whole issue was a racket, a way of extorting money from the applicants. The leading recruitment agency and the trade schools in question were owned by a group of people with a very good connection inside the government office in Manila that oversaw the country's overseas employment programs.

Knowing this, Leony changed her strategy. She shifted her focus to recruiting workers from the Middle East.

"I have a friend in Mindanao. Her name is Nora. Can I give Leony's email address to my friend?" Lily asked, taking out her pen and a piece of paper from her purse.

"What is she doing there?" asked Dana.

"She's a counselor at a government-run orphanage for displaced children."

Lily was aware that the government of Alberta had increased funding to child care services and that new spaces would soon be opened. This initiative was one of the city's top priorities for the next ten years. The only problem was that the people who would be hired had to be childcare educators. Where would the government hire those people? There weren't enough in Canada.

Lily looked out the window as the scenery in the car window passed. They were halfway home and she was having a good day. She had something to give Nora some hope that someday they would see each other again.

Chapter 26

In less than a year, Lily was free to apply for an open visa. This was one of the most important transitions in the life of a working visa holder. It was second only to taking on mortgages and paying bills. Having an open visa opened the gate of opportunities, giving them privilege to go back to school and upgrade their education. Their dreams of buying apartments or houses of their own became real possibilities.

Lily placed a long distance call to her parents, telling them about her present predicament and how it would put a big strain on her savings. After all, the applications cost $500 each, and she would be required to leave the country for a time while the visas were processed. Her folks needed to know what was going on. Her age insisted that she could decide for herself what was good and right for her. She had to move on, whatever Mike's decision.

Her letter, six pages long, was ready for mailing a day after a scheduled call with Mike. In it, she detailed her working conditions, the places she visited, her trusted friends, the skills she had learned in caring for a Pinoy family, and Mike's uncertainty over being with her.

It was 8:00 in the evening. Right after he gave Junior a bath, her phone rang. With her hand shaking and throat getting dry, she picked up the phone.

"I promised to let you know my decision last time, but due to the nature of my job, I was not able to get back to you. I'm very sorry, but lately I discussed my plan with my family in the Philippines and came up with a more sensible plan for our future," Mike said by way of introduction. Lily learned that Mike's employer was stuck with a five-year contract so big that Mike's presence was very much needed. Mike would be getting a promotion and increase in salary and benefits in just one month's time. He also said that there was another matter he had to settle. What was this other matter all about?

They talked for over twenty minutes, but it was neither warm nor exciting. They spoke casually about their own priorities and said nothing of their future together. She sensed hopelessness from Mike. His tone of voice was very cautious and calculated. Was Mike the same man she had fallen in love with, or had he changed? She sensed he was keeping a secret from her.

Another week passed and, as usual, Lily headed to Chinook Mall with Ellen and Ana, whose husbands were busy working on their respective garages over the weekend. Together they had time to relax over a plate of tacos. They exchanged bits and pieces of gossip under the roof of the food court.

"So what do we get today?" said Ana hungrily. They settled for pizza. Without any introduction, after finishing off her iced tea, Lily told them about her last call with Mike. Ana and Ellen had no choice but to hurry up with the rest of the pizza.

"So what are you thinking now?" said Ellen.

"I don't know yet. Tomorrow I'll mail a letter to my parents and let them know what's happening to my relationship with Mike. I need to hear what they think of this situation before making a decision."

"Just take care of yourself and do what you think is best for you," Ana and Ellen said in unison. Their promise to help her out, no matter what happened, was a boost to Lily's self-confidence.

For dessert, they shared a banana split, which was gone in less than three minutes.

Then, from Ana's purse, came out an invitation for them to attend her friend's church's Good Friday celebration. Both Ellen and Ana were excited to go, which shifted their conversation to spiritual matters.

The death of Jesus on the cross was one of the most notable and celebrated Christian events. From generation to generation, the event was taught to be the climax of Christian faith. The death of a God-man, and the miracle of him being raised from the dead, was a symbol of how Jesus conquered death; it was the very substance of Christian faith that someday man would be with God for eternity through His son Jesus Christ. The only way for a man to experience this eternal presence with God, as it was taught in the holy book, was when a person put his trust in Jesus. Through Him alone the salvation of man was made possible, and when one came to accept this truth, one's life changed from sinfulness to righteousness. Lily had heard this teaching hundreds of times before. She'd attended church all her life. The doctrine was interesting, but her mind was still occupied with thoughts of Mike.

Nonetheless, all three women decided to attend the Good Friday service together. True to their words, they met at the church thirty minutes before the service was to begin. The service before the fellowship time was serene and graceful. Lily witnessed the power of the speaker when people started to respond to an altar invitation. People walked forward with tears in their eyes, acknowledging their need for a savior.

"Are they for real?" Lily whispered to Ana.

"I don't know," Ana responded, "but these born again Christians are good at presenting the good news and convincing people to decide for God."

After the doxology and saying grace over the food, the minister instructed the people to proceed to the gym for fellowship and food. That was exactly the reason why many had attended the event.

Ellen and Ana's husbands were sitting at one end of the long table. Both were busy chatting with each other about their jobs. Just like any other potluck, this one had variety and colour. It was also a time where Lily could expand her horizons and forget, for a while, the past week of confusion over Mike. Was this the right time to make new friends? In the back of her mind, she wondered if the time had come to explore the possibility of a friendship with another man.

On the table was three kilograms of *adobo* that Ellen had cooked the evening before. Ana brought *guinisang mungo* in a fifteen-litre pot. Chocolate pork (dinuguan) was not a hit with the majority of people present, and the puto and pansit were devoured faster than expected. 3F events like these—free food, friends, and fellowship—were few and far in between, so everyone was taking advantage of the opportunity by trying all the items on the table.

Lily's mouth was still full when a man in a gray suite stood in front of her across the table. His name was Glen. He had a smile on his face and two cups of iced tea in his hands. She almost choked when Glen asked if the spot in front of her was taken.

"No," she said, her voice a little nervous.

"I saw that you don't have a drink, so I brought one. Care for iced tea?" Then, he asked, *"Kumusta na?"* It was a slang term for "How are you?" and it was enough to make Lily smile.

"I'm good," was her reply. The seed of friendship was planted.

The soothing effect of tea and coffee was welcome to people of all ages. Deserts filled a table near the kitchen door. Everyone had plenty of stories to tell to anyone who was interested enough to listen.

Without her knowledge, Ana and Ellen intentionally stayed far away from Lily and Glen—far enough that they wouldn't be noticed. However, they eavesdropped on the conversation between the two, which was obviously light and inspiring.

After a while, Glen stood up and proceeded to the dessert table. He gathered two small paper plates of *puto* and a bottle of cola, then headed back in Lily's direction. Ana and Ellen, in no hurry to head home, continued to watch the encounter develop. They were taking this moment very seriously. They knew that this meeting could be the start of big changes in Lily's perspective about friendships and life in a foreign land. Having been in similar situations themselves, they were perfectly aware that it took courage and practicality to move ahead in life. This was the moment they had been waiting for.

Time passed and soon they were the only ones left in the hall. Ana and Ellen walked closer to the table where Lily and Glen were sitting. Glen tried to be polite and offered Lily a ride back home, but his insistence was met with indifference.

The girls left together at 10:15.

Halfway to Lily's place, Ellen shifted the discussion to Glen. She wanted to know how far their talk had gone. At first, Lily was hesitant. Ellen's husband had sharp hearing and could hear everything they were saying.

"We just talked about our likes and dislikes," Lily said. "About how life in Canada is for me. He wanted to know more about my family and my life back in Saudi. You know, stuff like that—"

"So what did you learn about him?" said Ellen's husband.

Before they could extract more info from her, they arrived at the front of Lily's place. It had been a long but interesting night for Lily. As she went to bed that night, her thoughts were consumed by Mike, Glen, and Jesus.

—

The mailman usually delivered mail late in the morning. When the mail arrived, Lily ran out to get it and gathered together all the junk mail and letters. Her heart started to pound when she opened her father's letter. The advice and admonitions he gave were, indeed, fatherly in nature. There was much they wanted to do to help, but the distance made it impossible. They could only pray for her. What was relieving was the thought that they would respect and honor whatever decision she made. It seemed just like yesterday when she had run to her dad for counsel every time a decision was needed. Now she had to decide for herself.

She couldn't hide her loss of appetite and bad moods from Dana.

One Friday evening, after Lily finished her daily chores, Dana invited her to go to Tim Horton's for a cup of coffee. Aside from Ana and Ellen, Dana was her most treasured confidante.

Dana knew all the intimate and delicate aspects of her life. It wasn't healthy to keep secrets from her. She had to share it for her own good. Dana's wisdom and care were genuine and she was well-known for her sincerity in helping others.

Lily ordered a large French vanilla cappuccino. Dana settled for just a regular double-double coffee.

"Here's my dilemma," Lily started. "Tatay said I should make my own decision. Mike's still unclear of his plan to be with me. But there's also another man in the picture—Glen. His intentions are very clear. I'll have an open visa by next year. What should I do?" Lily was somber while sharing her concern.

"In any decision, it's important to consider the signs and the timing," Dana said. "Listen carefully to your gut feeling. It will confirm to you the sign you are looking for. Also give yourself time to sink in and discern the meaning of the sign. Then, seek second opinions from your most trusted friends. From there, you can make your decision once and for all. Your future is at stake here. However, make your decision plain and clear to Mike. Remember, you are still engaged to him." Dana's admonition was clear and upfront. It was getting late. The two boys at home would soon be wondering where they were.

She thanked Dana for the coffee and the advice. They left the restaurant hoping that everything would be all right. When they returned home, the boys were slumbering on the couch.

Lily went straight to her room. Her mind was still working through what Dana had told her. She needed to look for some signs or confirmation related to what her guy was telling her. However, her eyes were getting heavy and exhaustion was pulling her down onto the bed. She didn't have a lot of time to make up her mind; tomorrow was her deadline for submitting her application for an open visa.

While sitting on the edge of the bed, her attention was caught by the Bible on top of the nightstand. She had not read it in ages. It had been a gift from the church where she had first met Glen. She grabbed it and pulled out the bookmark inserted in the middle of the book. She remembered that her last reading had been from the book of Proverbs, and written on the bookmark was one of the most famous verses in the book. The coincidence startled her; it was the very verse where she had stopped reading last time:

> "Trust in the Lord with all your heart and lean not on your own understanding; in all your ways acknowledge him, and he will make your paths straight." (Proverbs 3:5–6)

As she laid her body on the bed, the message of the preacher from that church came to her mind. With the confidence and hope promised by God, Lily had the soundest sleep ever that night.

———

"Where are we going today, Tita?" asked Junior while tying up his shoelace the next day.

He was at an age where curiosity started to surface on his face. They'd been together for a long time and it was no secret to Junior anymore when Lily was lonely or in a good mood. Lily had been Junior's second mom.

Today she would mail her open visa application. At the back of her head, she promised to decide on two things. If Mike indicated to her his decision to move to Canada before her open visa was granted, she would know she was meant to be with Mike. If she got the visa and Mike still wasn't on the horizon, she would open the gate of her heart to others—maybe to Glen. The application would take about three months to process, so this gave Mike some time.

Nonetheless, the sadness on her face was very evident.

"Why are you sad, Tita?" Junior asked.

It would be hard for Junior to understand what was going on in her life. As honestly as possible, Lily told Junior about how she missed her family and friends in the Philippines. Her closeness to Junior was one of her life's greatest joys—and he constantly reminded her of her longing to have a child of her own. What was the purpose of life if it was only spent on oneself?

Their trip to the post office was long enough for them to make a stop at the mall. As Junior got out of control, she realized that she needed to share her aspirations, dreams, and values with a family—a family of her own. This was the very essence of life's continuity from here to eternity. Lily had to be a part of it.

Chapter 27

Summer was one of the most interesting seasons in Canada. Calgary, known for its Chinook winds, was one the most popular tourist destinations for visitors from across the Pacific. Banff and Lake Louise also ranked high in the priority of places to visit. Wildlife frequently crisscrossed the long and winding Trans-Canada Highway, and so wildlife advocates had initiated the building of many animal bridges along the stretch of the highway.

The family was getting ready for an overnight trip to Jasper. The family's lunchbox was ready and everything they needed was packed. Rudy's van was warmed up and ready to roll. Dana and Lily were in their best travel outfits for their visit to the Rockies. Without making any side trips, the drive would take them six hours.

The visit had been planned since the previous winter when Dana decided to take the family to see one of her long-time friends, Amber. Amber was so excited for a reunion in this far-flung village.

Dana and Amber's friendship had blossomed when they were in their last years of university back in the Philippines. Their favorite subject was home economics, which they both really enjoyed. It was in this subject that their love for house making was founded. Amber, after graduating from school, went to Saudi Arabia to work as a caregiver.

She was now in her fifth year as nanny to a wealthy Canadian family. Her employer was a well-known politician and former Premier. Her stay with the family had been a long and unforgettable experience. She had a lot of responsibilities as the one in charge of the upkeep and maintenance of a mansion in a plush residential part of metro Calgary. She had no regrets being a nanny. The perks were good and the family took her along on many holidays to different parts of the continent. They also gave her numerous opportunities to take vacations back to the Philippines, to see her family.

Amber had planned the weekend visit well. While her employers were on holiday, she had invited all the Pinoys working around Jasper. Her employer had been generous enough to open their resort house to her friends, even those coming from as far as Calgary.

When the family reached Banff, the sun was nearly halfway up the east sky. The warm air was seeping into the van. A few minutes later, Rudy signaled to turn left into a parking lot filled with cars, SUVs, and RVs. Behind the cars was a visitor's center with the name of the spot—Crowfoot Glacier. The peak of the mountain was covered with a white thick glacier shaped like the claw of a crow. It was an amazing formation. Digital cameras were clicking everywhere. The family was even brave enough to mingle with a group of Korean tourists. They stayed for twenty-five minutes.

Their next stop was Payto Lake. Tourists there were trying to fit onto one of the observation decks. The family had to squeeze their way through the crowd. The lake was stunning and beautiful. More megabytes were used.

Their longest stopover was at the Columbia Icefield. Rudy secured a parking spot near the visitor's center. Hundreds of vehicles filled the north side of the parking lot. Inside the building, people of different colours, heights, and weights were lining up to buy ticket rides to the top of the icefield. The tickets, unfortunately, were prohibitively expensive, so Rudy and the family decided to just use the big binoculars stationed at one of the viewing decks; it only cost a dollar.

All the picnic tables scattered around the facility were taken, but there was one near the washrooms that was vacant. Rudy ran to secure the spot. In no time, they ate their lunch with great relief. Then they packed up and proceeded to their destination.

It was about 6:00 in the afternoon when Rudy passed under the sign reading "Welcome to Jasper." There was not much activity in the neighbourhood, but there were plenty of people in the wilderness of the national park. It was Lily's first trip to this beautiful mountain town. Her first impression was that it was fantastic. The place looked like Baguio in the early 70s. The mountains were majestic. Tourists were all around—mostly Chinese, Japanese, and Koreans.

From the map on his lap, Rudy located the address of Dana's friend. When they arrived, they found lots of other cars in the driveway, including an MVP Mazda, a 96 Caravan, and a 2004 Seina. Based on the smells and noises coming from the house, no doubt this place was the place to be, especially for hungry travelers like them; the only thing on their minds was food.

As the family approached the open door where Amber was standing, Dana ran up and hugged her friend with great excitement. She almost forgot about the family. After several minutes of introductions, hugging, and preliminaries they were all led into the living room. There were fifteen adults and ten kids of all ages waiting for whatever was going to come next.

Lily's wandering mind was interrupted when Amber took center stage and announced to her guests what they could expect from this gathering. Amber started to introduce the guests to each other. It took twenty minutes before Lily scratched the surface of everyone's background.

The last woman she met was from Guimba, and she looked familiar to Lily. She was positive she had met this woman somewhere way back in the Philippines. Without hesitation, Lily approached her and made the first move to introduce herself.

"I'm Lily, from Munoz. Have I met you before?"

The woman smiled. "I'm Gloria. I'm not sure, but you are also familiar to me. I graduated from Central Luzon State University in 1980."

Lily remembered her three-month service at the Guimba Health Center. She had delivered twins there, one of the most challenging deliveries she ever performed.

The introduction led the two into a deeper understanding of their past and present aspirations. Gloria had come to Canada first. Her life was not only colourful; it was also tragic. She had worked for her current employer for seven years, and their relationship was full of ups and downs. She was the third nanny for the couple. Her main responsibility was five-year-old Jessica, the youngest of three kids. Jessica was a paraplegic. Years ago, she had also been diagnosed with severe Attention Deficit and Hyperactive Deficit Syndrome (ADHD). Considering the wealth of the family, she couldn't figure out where in the world the kid had gotten the disease; the wife was a lawyer while the husband was a chartered psychologist. The older siblings were enjoying their preteen years with friends.

After working for the family for four months, Gloria began to notice certain signs. Her observations proved correct; the mother was not only addicted to smoking, she was also an alcoholic. She only stopped smoking three months before delivering Jessica, and her alcohol consumption was lessened from three bottles a day to just one. However, the residual poisons in her body had brought on considerable negative impact to both her health and her child's.

The couple's wealth was astonishing and impressive. Aside from their cabin at the foot of Mount Kidd in Kananaskis Country, their vacation house in Mexico was also the envy of their friends. Their house was filled with expensive furniture, imported items, and decorations. In spite of this affluence, the couple lived a meaningless life and seemed to run around in circles. In the Philippines, Gloria thought to her herself, one of the determinants of a couple's spousal relationship success was the abundance of their material possessions.

Gloria ended her story on a sad note. The couple's divorce papers were filed and currently under judicial review. Her continued employment was therefore a big concern. As Lily tried to grasp her new friend's concerns, she recalled a family in Calgary that was looking for nanny.

"I'll contact you when I get back to Calgary," Lily said, ending their conversation.

The party didn't end until early the following day. The guests from out of town got ready to explore the area after lunch. Rudy, Dana, Lily, and Junior got ready to hit the road. They were going to drive up to Malinge Lake, a popular destination to go walking, boating, or marveling the beauty of God's creation.

Their day was well-spent. They would forever remember the beauty and majesty of the mountains, rivers, lakes, and wildlife. The environment was so clean, fresh, and inviting.

Amber was more than happy to accommodate them for another night. Rudy had a good, long night's sleep while the ladies stayed up late. They knew Rudy needed to rest for another long day of driving. After chatting until all hours of the morning, the ladies finally went to bed.

They left Amber's place earlier than planned and decided not to make any more stopovers. They all wanted to get back home as soon as possible. Junior was sleeping steadily at the back of the van. After three hours of driving, Dana and Lily were talking about everything they had encountered in Jasper, including the lives of their new friends. It was made clear to Lily that wherever she went, everybody had a story to tell.

After two quick stops to eat and rest, Rudy was able to reach home at 8:00 in the evening. The ladies unpacked their stuff while Rudy and Junior went straight to bed. Dana and Lily, while unpacking, still had the stamina to talk late into the night.

The list of things to do the following day was hanging on the front of the refrigerator. After lunch, Dana and Lily finally left the house to go grocery shopping. In the fruits and vegetable section of Superstore, Lily was surprised to meet Lucy, one of the women she had met in a church fellowship they had attended a few months ago.

"How are you, Lily?" said Lucy.

"Good! How about you?"

It was apparent to Lily that a huge chunk of the time she spent at this store was spent sharing her stories and recent work experiences with friends. While Lucy and Lily talked, Dana and Junior continued shopping, having a mother-son bonding time.

Lucy shared a number of stories about her last employer, Bob, a divorced father of two who owned an autobody shop in the southwest corner of the city. The business enabled Bob to lend one of his cars, an '88 Volvo, to Lucy. As part of her job contract, Lucy had no choice but to drive, since the kids needed somebody to drive them to school, parks, and other appointments. She had to pay for the gas and insurance herself. Having a car of her own was a status symbol, heralding to other caregivers that her employer was wealthy.

One Sunday night, after returning to her employer's place, Lucy was surprised to see that the lights in the house were on. She was very much aware that the children's mother wouldn't be dropping them off until the morning, so her employer was usually home late at night. It was only 8:00 and her room's light was on. Silently, she unlocked the door and slinked like a cat down the hallway to her room in the basement. A few feet away from her door, she heard groaning. With her stomach churning and hand sweating, Lucy stepped back and walked straight to her car to catch a bit of fresh air. She turned on the switch and drove around the neighbourhood for about fifteen minutes, hoping the action would be over by then. Moments later, the garage door opened and Bob drove out with his secretary in the passenger seat. She knew it was his secretary because that woman had delivered something to Bob last month.

Lucy was so disgusted that Bob had used her bed for his infidelity. It was then that Lucy finally decided to scout for another employer. She had already received her open visa, so she could apply for any job she wanted. Her goal was to get a job at a big company in downtown Calgary, perhaps in one of the large hotels.

She finally got a job at the Marriott Hotel. The job was a major blessing. It was there that Lucy cultivated her passion for customer service. She was assigned to the kitchen. Her responsibility was to make sure that all the staff was well fed. The task was not hard. She made new friends there, and was also exposed to different types of personalities and cultural backgrounds.

Among the other kitchen workers was a former dentist from the Philippines, a bank manager, and a medical doctor from Pakistan who was now forced to wash dishes for a living.

Months later, Lucy took a vacation to the Philippines and wedded her fiancé. Her four-week holiday was spent getting to know her husband. She came back home feeling sad over leaving her spouse back in the Philippines. However, her patience paid off. After months of processing, her husband's papers finally arrived.

Hard work and perseverance enabled the couple to buy a house in Evanston. Lucy finished a management course from SAIT just a few months after they moved in. Her husband got a job at Hayworth, a cabinet-making company.

However, starting a family was still far from Lucy's mind. Though she was still young, her husband was excited to have a kid. It was very obvious that the couple was struggling to figure out what was best for them—her career, or a family. Even their close friends were divided on the issue.

The story reminded Lily of her desire for having a family of her own. But when would it happen?

Chapter 28

One Sunday morning, a hundred pews at church waited for people to sit down in them. At the north side of the building was a group of seniors and adults in their Sunday best, enjoying hot coffee served by volunteers. People were trickling by. Some of the ministers were busy walking around the foyer as if looking for some very important people lost in the crowd. The service would begin in one hour.

The German Baptist Church was situated on top of a hill overlooking the east side of the city. North of the building was Franklin Train Station. As one of the stations that connected the northeast corner of the city to downtown, the station shared its parking lot with the three hundred parking stalls owned by the church.

Lily stepped off the train at 10:15, just in time for the 10:30 service. Rudy, Dana, and Junior couldn't make it that Sunday. Both Dana and Rudy had worked a lot of that week and needed to rest. Junior just wanted to stay with his parents.

Walking next to Lily was Carmen, the friend she had made after the first aid class almost a year ago. The bond they had formed was instant and had proven beneficial to both of them. Carmen's husband was still in the Philippines. In Lily's observation, Carmen was a woman of character, integrity, and faithfulness. Her wisdom related to spousal relationships was very insightful. Carmen engendered many qualities she had been looking for in a friend. Carmen's principles in life were very similar to Dana's.

Roughly four hundred and fifty people were enjoying the warm and cozy environment of the sanctuary. At exactly 10:30, the worship band started to crank up their instruments and played very contemporary music. Carmen was a good singer. Though Lily didn't know the words to the songs, she found them quite pleasant to listen to. She tapped her fingers on the back of the pew in front of her. Though she didn't sing as loudly as Carmen, Lily sang along to the main melody.

A new song and new environment, she thought. Not bad.

They were sitting on the south side of the sanctuary, third row from the back. One of the things Lily observed was the number of black-haired immigrants attending the church. It made Lily feel at home. Almost a third of the attendees were Pinoys. There were also people from Africa, the Middle East, and China.

The sermon, which focused on man's relationship with the true God, was delivered in thirty minutes. She had heard the same message at another church once before. A blue-suited man in his early sixties recited the benediction. The membership called him "Pastor Willy."

After the service, the foyer filled up with parishioners. Chitchat of all sorts was one of the ways for people to connect with each other. One group of people discussed their work.

Another group, made up of retired people, talked about holidays and investments. The north end of the lobby was filled with Pinoys. At one corner, a group of mothers was talking about five different things at the same time. The men were busy comparing their accomplishments from the past week. The youth, on the other hand, were excited to talk about their retreat the day before to a campsite two hours north of the city.

From nowhere, a young lady rushed over to them.

"Hi, Carmen!" she waved in their direction. It was Ester.

"Ester, how are you?" answered Carmen with a big smile on her face. The two friends hadn't seen each other in quite some time.

Ester was just months away from getting her open visa. Her employers were willing to release her. The kid under her care were now attending school only a few blocks away from her employers' place, so most of her services now revolved around taking care of the house and kitchen. She had more spare time than ever before. It was no wonder she had been able to secure a part-time job, in partnership with her two sisters.

"So, how are you doing now?" asked Carmen.

"Not bad. I'm busy with my new part-time job. My sisters and I are partners in a nanny recruiting agency."

Carmen smiled. "Good for you… but how do you manage your time?"

"My older sister is responsible for looking for potential employers, and my younger sister is responsible for recruiting nannies in the Philippines, and other countries from the Middle East."

"And what about you?" Carmen asked excitedly. "What do you do for the business?"

"I'm the one in charge of talking to the government and making sure our operation runs smoothly."

"How do you find the time?"

"With my laptop and Blackberry, I can manage my time."

"What about your employers? They don't mind you taking this part-time job?"

"Why not? As a matter of fact, they encouraged me to do so."

With the province's hot economy and the great demand for foreign workers, Ester was one of many Filipinos who offered her services by recruiting other workers from the Philippines.

Ester turned to Lily. "How are you doing, Lily?" They hadn't seen each other since the day they first met, at Chinook Mall.

"I'm doing well, but I'm hoping to change careers when my fiancé arrives."

"When is he coming?"

"I'm not sure," Lily acknowledged.

Lily was amazed to hear about Ester's part-time job. Caregivers didn't have much time for other jobs, and the foreign live-in caregiver program prevented it in most cases. Therefore most part-time jobs were under-the-table arrangements.

The most common part-time jobs for caregivers involved cleaning houses and buildings. Some Filipino families subcontracted cleaning jobs to nannies who were struggling to earn more money. A silent and active network had formed over the years. For the most part, it was underground and ignored by the authorities.

There was also a group of medical doctors in the city who employed nannies to clean their houses. Filipino nannies were known for their reliability and honesty. These employers usually felt confident referring caregivers to their friends. The caregivers, for their part, were willing and able to do whatever was asked of them.

This had been Carmen's experience, too. She had been in Canada for five years and her string of employers had included medical doctors, lawyers, and an oil and gas executive. She worked sixteen hours every day, five days a week, and all her employers were satisfied with the work she did. The best part of this arrangement came during Christmas. For three years in a row, her employers had given her unique, expensive, high-quality gifts.

She had smiled broadly one time while dusting off a couple's closet. Boxes of Viagra and Cialis were neatly placed in one of the corners of the second drawer. In another house, it had been customary for the husband, a defense lawyer, to leave notes and court briefings on top of his office table at home. Transcripts, memos, and rulings were scattered around. Names of clients and corporations were visibly legible from a distance. Carmen's job was to dust the table and not move anything away from their original locations. Even the position of the pens had to stay put. Her employer was very keen and methodical not only in the court of law but also in his little court at home.

At her last job, maps and graphs around the office had made Carmen a learned student of oil and gas. Drilled wells were all marked on a big, colour-coded map just left of her employer's table. On the other side was a graph indicating the trend of oil's price per barrel. 2006 had set a record of eighty dollars per barrel. The high price of oil translated into her boss' take-home pay and consequently Carmen received a raise in her hourly rate.

Trust had been established between Carmen and her employers. Both parties benefitted from her work. Over time, she even came to learn the very intimate secrets of her employers' spouses. In these cases, it was only a matter of time before the truth came out.

When they finished talking, Lily wondered what kind of part-time job she might be able to get. Would she even be allowed to take a part-time job? If she got a job, could it jeopardize her application for an open visa? What would her other friends say?

Their talk was over when they realized they were the only group left in the church. They promised to see each other again the next Sunday. Without hesitation, Carmen and Lily accepted Ester's invitation to drive them to Chinook Mall, where the two intended to go after the service.

It was a nice and pleasant Sunday for Lily.

Chapter 29

Starting in 2005, the problem of labor shortage in most sectors of the economy in Canada—and Alberta in particular—was the focus of long discussions in all levels of government. Companies were doing their very best to attract workers from other provinces. Others even pirated workers from competing companies. Recruitment and placement agencies were having difficulty supplying labor to their clients.

For some Filipino recruiters, this situation became a great business opportunity, especially as it related to the number of caregivers coming into Canada. Roughly eighty-five percent of nannies were single women. The loneliness they felt, especially in wintertime, was so strong that looking for a companion back home was a must. Online matchmaking sprouted.

One of their ways to keep their minds and bodies busy and entertained was to attend different kinds of concerts. Gabby, Pops, Florante, Eagies, and many other Filipino entertainers were finding it easy to perform in Calgary. The Filipino community was growing rapidly and this translated into a growing market. As expected, about one-fourth of the ticketholders to these concerts were caregivers. They wanted to reconnect with their memories of home. Watching a popular entertainer fresh from the Philippines was like warm air crossing the Pacific in the midst of winter. Original Filipino love songs ignited passion and memories that people cherished for many years. The night was a venue for them to express their true Filipino feelings of being in love.

On one particular evening, the Jubilee Auditorium was half full. Others saw it as half empty. It was cold and windy in late September, so the people outside were in a hurry to get into the building. The first week of fall was at hand. In a few weeks' time, snow and Old Man Winter would be knocking at the doors of Canadians.

Sharon Pineda, one of the success stories of the Philippines' entertainment industry, was onstage. It was said that she had the biggest entourage among all the entertainers who visited Calgary. According to gossip, it took five hotel rooms just to hold them all.

The show began with little fanfare. After the Canadian national anthem, the Philippines' national anthem was sung even louder, with energy from the audience.

The first three songs were a hit to people born during the 50s. Her belly-cracking poise while singing added appeal to her songs. Young and old alike became hysterical and nostalgic. They sang with her at the top of their lungs.

Lily, Carmen, and Dana occupied the third row of the balcony. Lily sang along timidly while Carmen and Dana, both carried by the crowd, were singing and dancing at the same time.

It was really a night to remember and enjoy those ballads and love songs of yesterday. Sharon's voice was terrific and enigmatic. It was sheer entertainment for those who had come.

"I can't believe it," said Dana when Sharon appeared onstage for the third time.

"How many kids does she have?" asked Carmen.

The sheer size of the lady was a shock for them. The last time they had seen the singer had been fifteen years ago, in the Philippines. They had heard from people who got their information from the Filipino Channel and other weekly entertainment papers beaming in from Manila that Sharon had put on a lot of weight in recent years. Carmen, Dana, and Lily had no access to these sources of information. They were tempted to catch all the gossip, but what good would it do them? This made them the exceptions to the rule, since more than forty-five percent of Filipino families in Calgary subscribed to TFC.

From a local talent in Calgary, another entertainer named Jenny was introduced to the crowd while Sharon changed outfits backstage. After taking a closer look at the local talent, Carmen said, "I know her. She's one of the entertainers in the Barrio Fiesta karaoke bar."

Barrio Fiesta was a Filipino restaurant and bar at the corner of Memorial and Highway 68. Many local talents were being discovered and promoted at restaurants like Barrio Fiesta. Lots of contract workers and nannies met there to satisfy their need for social interactions, companions, and sometimes even illicit unions.

Jenny's performance was like that of a professional singer. She had a beautiful voice, perfect diction, and poise in front of the audience. She was a great-looking young lady who had what it took to pursue a career in singing. There were many other talented young singers known in the community, but tonight was Jenny's chance to prove herself.

"Is that Jenny?" Dana asked in surprise. "She's the Seriakas' niece."

The Seriaka family was one of the prominent families of the Cavite, Laguna, and Bukidnon Association in Calgary. The husband was working for the city and the wife was with Enerflax, a big oil and gas company. Jenny was the live-in caregiver to the couple's four-year-old daughter. Jenny, who had only been in Canada less than a year, was doing well with her singing hobby, and it was paying off tonight.

"If she's only been in Canada eleven months, how can she be so successful already?" Lily asked.

"It's a complicated situation," answered Dana.

"What do you mean?" interjected Carmen.

"The Seriakas, according to reliable sources, hired Jenny as their nanny last year," Dana said. "The sad thing is that they pay her very little. Her stay with them is terrible, according to her friends."

The arrangement with Jenny was full of problems. Family friends commended the Seriakas for bringing Jenny over to stay with them, but just like many other arrangements, this one was full of inconsistencies. The family had needed someone to take care of their young children, and Jenny's ardent desire to get out of the Philippines made her the perfect candidate. She didn't care what happened next, as long as she got out of the country. Though there were many cases of families taking advantage of their own family members, her resolve to go abroad was very strong. If others could do it, why couldn't she? She had an opportunity, so she seized it, even though it meant leaving her boyfriend Danny behind. Dedication, courage, and hope kept her going.

It took two years to process her application, but finally she arrived in Vancouver. It was a joyous moment when she and the Seriaka family met each other again after so many years apart. The family now had somebody to take care of the baby, freeing them up to go back to their normal way of life as working couples. And yet there was still a problem.

"In what sense?" Lily asked.

"All her movements outside the house are closely monitored by the couple," Dana explained. "Her telephone bills are combed over and there is no clear understanding about overtime and the extra work load of cleaning the house. So she's singing to different Pinoy groups for a fee."

That was Jenny's way of supplementing her income. She had a family in the Philippines to support. Her salary from the Seriakas was not enough to cover even her own basic needs; her salary was only sufficient to buy quarter-pound hamburgers and a monthly bus pass.

The freedom given other caregivers was nothing but a dream to her. She felt like a prisoner, not even having the freedom to enjoy her friends on the weekends. She even had to take care of her cousin's friends sometimes. Though this meant making additional money, she still didn't have the opportunity to make friends of her own. She deserved rest and entertainment. According to her few friends, she would rather work for other employees than for her own relatives, who took advantage of her.

It was a sad but true reality that many nannies suffered the same fate.

Moreover, her boyfriend was expecting support for his college studies in the Philippines. To make matters worse, her parents' little store back home was on the brink of bankruptcy. Their customers were not that serious about paying their debts. This attitude was anchored to the fact that they thought her parents were doing well—after all, their daughter was in Canada.

It was one thing to work hard and be responsible for oneself, but she had a boyfriend, a family, and great expectations back home. Jenny was living in one of the most liberated and free countries in the world, and yet her life was stuck in a sea of control and manipulation.

She would have liked to report the Seriakas, but she couldn't. She had signed a contract and was under an obligation to follow it. She was also constrained from divulging her present arrangement to other caregivers. Very few people were aware of what was happening to her. The only ones in the know were those who had experienced the same fate or could smell out the situation.

Her only consolation from this chapter of her life was the joy she felt from getting to sing. If there was ever an opportunity to perform, she took it, singing with other Filipino groups in the city. For several months prior to the concert, Jenny had started performing regularly with a band which was looking for a new soloist. It was hard for the band to showcase and compete with the existing local Filipino bands without a singer of Jenny's caliber.

"Jenny is not the only caregiver who can sing," said Carmen.

"Yes, others are good at dancing, too," Dana pointed out. "There's a dancing group every Saturday night in one of the restaurants in the northeast."

"I suppose many others are expressing their talents through cooking, sewing, and other craft-related activities." responded Lily.

Dana nodded. "You are correct."

"So what kind of talent are you willing to offer our community?" Carmen asked Lily with a smile on her face.

"Call me next time you deliver a baby," Lily jokingly answered.

Sharon's songs recharged their spirits and their inert talents were challenged by Jenny's story. They left the concert with joy and gladness and were looking forward to the next bout of concerts by entertainers coming from Manila.

Chapter 30

With the passage of time, Lily and Cely's friendship blossomed and grew closer every time they met and fellowshipped with one another.

It was the third week of January 2008 when the Filipino community was shocked by the news that the body of a hardworking Filipino woman's body was found at the back alley between a big church and the Franklin light rail transit station. It was the fourth murder of the year. Another woman was on her way to work, around 5:30 in the morning, when she saw the body. She ran into the train station for a telephone to report the body to the police.

Police officers were dispatched to the area and in no time the church's parking lot was cordoned off with police tape. Police cars were scattered around two blocks away from the church. Media outlets braved the elements to set up their news coverage of the crime.

It was reported by the earliest morning newscast that the victim had been murdered between 10:00 p.m. Friday and very early Thursday morning.

"Hello, Cely. Have you heard the news?" Lily asked over the phone.

"It's six in the morning! What did you say?" Cely's voice sounded groggy. It was thirty minutes before her alarm clock was set to go off.

"There was a body found meters away from Franklin LRT Station this morning. The news said she's most likely a Filipina."

"You're not kidding, are you?"

"Why would I? Turn on your TV and watch the news."

The news spread across the city like a wildfire in summer time. Speculation ran rampant, with everybody offering opposing theories to explain the tragedy. It was reported that the police officers handling the case had encountered difficulty identifying the body. The victim's face was severely battered, and her purse and one of her boots were missing. However, it was soon discovered that the victim had placed a call to a friend just before she died; she had been asking for help. She was being raped. This allowed the police to finally identify her. In fact, the other people living in the house she was staying in had been out looking for her all night long. They had been about to report a missing person when the news flashed on TV.

While the authorities could not provide the name of the victim, the Filipino community already knew who it was. Her name was Celia. A bullet train was no match for the rumor mill.

"Did you know her?" asked Cely.

"No, but Dana said she attended a church in downtown Calgary. She worked in one of the printing companies in the southwest. She worked the night shift."

"What province in the Philippines did she hail from?"

"Up north. Isabella."

"How long has she been here?"

"Four years."

They hung up the phone.

Everyone who found out about the murder was asking the same questions; knowing the answers gave one a sense of connection. Once the connection was established, emotion kicked in. The community felt sorry for Celia, and even the need for vengeance. Others who worked late and took the same trains felt fear and anxiety.

Front and center in almost all the daily newspapers and tabloids was the story of Celia's fate. The news conducted a series of interviews and fact-finding initiatives in the name of getting the word out. In the aftermath of the tragedy, the city council passed a review and safety audit of all bus and rail transit systems in the city. People were clamoring for immediate deployment of additional police officers to all the train stations. Community associations and various citizens' advocacy groups were demanding better policing and effective safety education to the public.

Filipino associations and religious sectors were busy coordinating various initiatives to help the community cope with the tragedy.

A few days later, an announcement was made that a memorial service would be held in the downtown church the victim had attended. Preparations were made, people were contacted, and the Filipino Consul General based in Calgary hosted Celia's family, who had to be flown in from Quebec. The community was mobilized and the media was ready and eager, as always, to cover the memorial.

The church, with a capacity of seven hundred people, was located in the southwest corner of downtown Calgary. The church parking lot could only accommodate seventy-five cars, but it was estimated that there would be a lot more people than that. The memorial would start at 7:00, followed by a solemn time to console the grieving family.

"We need to be there around 6:30. The parking lot for that church is very limited," announced Dana to the rest of her family, including Lily. The whole family was getting ready for this important event. They wanted to witness and share their condolences with the family of the murdered woman. One of the somber experiences of a caregiver was to attend this kind of gathering, to pay respect to the deceased.

As a neighbour and new friend to Lily, Cely went with them to the memorial that night. When they arrived at the church, the media was already there with hardware related to setting up a live broadcast of the memorial. Rudy parked the car a block away, because the parking lot was already full. Streams of people were headed toward the door, visible in spite of the foggy, snowy weather.

It was 6:40 when they entered the building. The lobby was already full of people—mostly Filipinos, as expected. Inside the sanctuary, the closed coffin was placed in the middle of the stage. Opposite the hall was the reception room that could seat at least two hundred and fifty people.

They found their way down the right side of the sanctuary, three pews away from the casket. Ushers were busy accompanying guests to vacant seats. A group of musicians took the stage and started to play their instruments. The music filled the hall and people started to tone down their voices.

Flags hung down both of the sanctuary's side walls, proclaiming the different countries represented by the church's membership and indicating how diverse the congregation was. This diversity was reflected by the composition of people playing in the worship band and singing in the church choir.

In no time, the pews were filled with people. Many more souls were seated in the aisles. After the last piece of instrumental music, the crowd was asked to stand. From backstage came out a procession of people—two sisters and the brother of the slain woman were trailing behind two well-suited gentlemen. Once they occupied their respective spots, the worship band started to play "Amazing Grace." There was total silence after the song. One of the gentlemen went up to the podium, grabbed the mike, and shared his thoughts about the night's event before uttering a touching and powerful prayer.

The prayer touched on three subjects. The first was the reality that given our society's indifference to God, evil deeds often prevail. Second, Christians allow society to take God out of our schools and other institutions. Third, prayer has been under attack and many other faith-based activities are ridiculed and banned. The minister emphasized the supremacy of God and that He is in control. Finally, he emphasized that the body in the casket was not the real person the crowd had known. Indeed, Celia and the angels were now worshipping God.

There were no dry eyes when people who were close to Celia spoke and gave their final tributes and respects to the deceased.

Celia had been a member of a small Filipino group in the church. She had moved to Canada four years ago from Hong Kong to work as a caregiver. She had left behind a husband and five boys in the Philippines. A shy and reserved lady, her only priority in life had been to bring the boys over to Calgary. She had been a hard-working woman and a firm believer in God. She had dedicated her life to her family and friends, exemplifying simplicity and generosity to others.

Seldom did she talk or share thoughts during group bible study. However, when it was her turn, she bared her soul to them. She was a dear friend of many. At the age of forty-one, she epitomized dedication, hard work, and perseverance. Her two sisters and brother, all living in Montreal, were her immediate source of hope and encouragement in Canada.

The memorial service lasted for an hour. It took around twenty minutes before the sanctuary was emptied. People headed to the reception room west of the building for refreshments. Scattered around the room were tables of various finger foods and beverages. At the center of the stage was a table reserved for the grieving family. The church's senior pastor led them to the table for a sit and a rest. At his cue, guests and visitors started to line up to extend their condolences to the family.

Evident at the memorial was the presence of various Filipino community leaders. Some were standing just meters away from the family. The media was also around the table, trying to capture newsworthy shots of the event. The Consul General of the Philippines and his wife were busy attending to questions about the family. The local Member of the Legislative Assembly also mingled in the midst of the immigrants. A third of the people had their digital cameras ready. A particularly active woman in the community, who had indicated her interest in running for provincial politics, was there trying to ante up her profile.

As the memorial went on, it was heard that another prominent member of the Filipino community was also eyeing a seat in the provincial legislature. Both of the potential candidates belonged to opposing political parties. It was no wonder nasty remarks and name-calling was observed inside the room. Both wanted to outsmart each other in front of potential voters. That night, Filipino politics exhibited its cruelest form.

Once the crowd was settled down, the senior pastor requested everyone's attention. He indicated to the two police officers leading the investigation, who asked the family if they could address the crowd. All ears were tuned in as one of the officers, a woman, began to speak. People sitting at the far end corner of the room started to trickle down to the front, where the grieving family was seated. All others congregated to form a semicircle enclosing the family and the officers.

"This week has been very hard, hectic, and difficult for us," the officer began.

She related how the investigation had met difficulty. The missing boot and purse were still out there. The first few days had yielded no leads. The ground had been covered with snow, making it impossible to connect footprints to the crime scene. The area had been closed off to pedestrians for days, making sure the police could search the entire scene for any leads. Other police officers assigned to the case wasted no time talking to people who might have been at the station between the hours of 10:00 p.m. of and 5:00 a.m. the following day.

"Just a few hours ago, we made progress in our investigation," she finally announced. "An arrest was made. The suspect will be charged tomorrow, exactly a week after the murder. Hopefully, the case will be closed and the family will find justice and rest."

Upon hearing the announcement, the crowd jumped with jubilation. The family's teary eyes were no longer due to sadness. Tears fell as justice prevailed.

Before half the people left the room, another announcement was made. A vigil and healing service would be held. A group of concerned citizens planned to host this event. The crowd was told that the vigil would start at the Franklin Train Station Wednesday afternoon the following week. The procession would then proceed to the site where Celia's body was found—to lay down candles and a wreath of flowers. After that, they would proceed to the church for prayers and healing.

The family extended their gratitude to all who shared their loneliness and grief and had braved the weather to show their condolences. One by one, people left the church.

Dana, Rudy, Cely, and Lily boarded the car, one of the very few vehicles left in the vicinity, and after minutes of warming up the van, they headed home.

"That was very tragic for the family," were the first words out of Dana's mouth as they snaked out of the city core.

It was also tragic because they had found out that Celia had been so new to the city. She didn't have life insurance and had just received her open visa weeks before her death.

They dropped off Cely at her apartment, which was a block north of their place.

When they reached home, the driveway was covered with four inches of snow. It was no match for Rudy's driving skill. The warm and cozy atmosphere of the house welcomed them. After unwrapping their winter jackets, Dana and Lily decided to take a cup of herbal tea and come to terms with their day. Rudy and Junior went straight to their bedrooms and fell asleep within a few minutes.

Dana and Lily spoke more about the impact of the memorial service.

"There are things you need to know about and prepare for," started Dana.

"I got my life insurance last month and my RRSP is already in place. What else do I need to have?" asked Lily.

"Rudy and I have our wills and last testaments. We know that if anything happens to us, Junior will be taken care of properly."

"How do I get a will?"

"You can contact our lawyer and ask for an appointment."

After a few more minutes of contemplating the day, and the experience gained from attending the memorial, the two said goodnight and went straight to their respective rooms.

As Lily was lying in bed, her mind was dominated by the clear messages of the pastor and the music. The people's faces were still fresh in her memory. She remembered the agonizing moment when the family had entered the sanctuary. The bitter irony of Celia having been given her open visa only to have her life cut short by tragedy made her toss and turn.

It was 1:00 in the morning when she finally started snoring.

Chapter 31

In her years with Dana's family, Lily was able to hone her computer skills, especially when it came to emailing friends. Instant messaging and Facebook was getting popular not only for students, but also for her own friends. She was spending more time every week chatting with her friends on the internet. It was through such a chat that she finally traced Nora, her long lost social worker friend in Mindanao. They had a good time chatting together. Her life then became an open book to Nora. True to herself and to their friendship, Nora once again showed her deep concern for her friend.

Chatting online, her newfound vice, was confined only to Ellen, Ana, and Nora. She was never more than ten decibels away from Dana, so there was no need for Dana to be one of her online contacts. Besides, Dana only knew how to turn the computer on and off, and nothing more.

Texting over the phone was how Lily and Mike communicated with each other. At first, Lily was hesitant to tell Mike about chatting online. Nevertheless, one night she tried to send an instant message to Mike, just to say hi and find out if it was possible to chat with someone in the Middle East.

Not wanting to give herself away, she changed her online contact name to Lia. To her surprise, Mike responded, wanting to know if Lia knew of a nanny in Calgary with the name of Lily. In the spur of the moment, Lily didn't know how to reply. She didn't want to keep secrets from Mike; that was not her way of nurturing a relationship. However, she found it more interesting to maintain her identity as Lia. This way, she could figure out what was on Mike's mind.

The game was on.

As time passed, she spent lots of time chatting with Mike. Mike was so discreet in his chats. After just a few weeks of chatting, Lily was able to discern what Mike was after. Mike had told "Lia" that his girlfriend lived in Calgary as a caregiver, and their distance was making Mike's life lonely. He truly wanted to move to Canada, but due to the nature of his job, it was impossible for him to move right away. In the course of their exchanges, Lily sensed that Mike was somewhat hesitant to divulge his plan upfront. Lily felt relieved upon knowing that Mike still cared for her. But why was he flirting with Lia?

"Lia" promised Mike to look around for Lily. On one occasion, she mentioned to Mike that there was a Filipino caregiver association in Calgary and that she would try to attend their meeting, hoping to meet Lily. That was good news for Mike.

Their friendship, as Lily intended it to be, was blooming. Some secrets were coming out of the closet. Where she came from in the Philippines, her career, work experience, and other related info were all fabricated, but Mike took it all at face value. Lily once even wrote to Mike, telling him that she was desperate to have a boyfriend. She told him that her boyfriend, who worked in the Middle East, had ceased communicating with her for almost four years now. Their relationship was becoming hopeless. She also indicated that a Caucasian guy was courting her, but that she preferred a Filipino. At least that much was true.

She was having second thoughts and was still hoping that someday she would find the right person. The chatting was becoming serious, which went according to Lily's plan. But it was also becoming too personal. Lily was good at catching the real meaning behind Mike's responses. For the time being, Lily was quite comfortable being Lia, one of Mike's friends in Canada. Their exchanges became a weekly habit and the depth of their friendship led the relationship to deepen.

Lily's morning break time on weekdays was spent opening letters in the mail. She didn't spend much time on junk mail, but her heart began beating rapidly when she found two letters, one from the immigration office and the other from Jeddah. She didn't know which one to open first. The immigration letter pertained to her long stay in Canada, while Jeddah's letter pertained to her future with Mike. She had no option but to open both. Her open visa document was enclosed in the letter. Joy overflowed in her. She made such a racket that Junior was disturbed in his sleep. Momentarily, he went back to his nap.

Lily's mind started to think through some of her plans now that she had received the visa—plans to continue her schooling, change careers, and take driving lessons, among other things.

The second letter was surprising. It was Mike's first letter in years, and yet it was only one short page long.

Dear Darling Lily,

I miss you so much. How I longed to touch your face when we had our last phone call. Showering you with kisses and taking you into my arms is all that I dream about. Your thoughtfulness, gentleness, and love are far more treasured than my life here in Saudi Arabia.

You asked me last time about my plan for moving to Canada. I requested my company to give me a month-long holiday in the Philippines to figure out what my long-term options are with respect to my life, career, and future. Most likely, I'll be in the Philippines in July. Is there a way you can ask your employer for a holiday at the same time? I know it's only four months away. I think one month is long enough for us to really sit down and finalize our plans. Besides, I really miss you. Remember the time when we went on a field trip to Baguio?

I'll be working for a month in another province, 120 miles away from Jeddah. We are not allowed to carry cell phones or be near a computer. That's why this letter is being sent to you in advance. By the time this letter reaches you, I'll already be gone. Our deployment there was so fast that we didn't have enough time to prepare. We'll be back on March 14, so call, email, or text me on March 15. I need to know your response regarding being in the Philippines.

Missing and loving you so much,
Mike

P.S. Months ago, while I was online, the name "Lia" appeared on my contact list. She's from your city, Calgary. I asked her to locate you, but lately I haven't heard from her. Are you a member of Calgary Filipina Nanny Association? I hope you will meet her.

Without any hesitation, Lily showed the letter to Dana.

"It won't be a problem for you to take your holiday in July," Dana said. "Actually, we are planning to take a month-long holiday, too, in Cebu. I'll talk to Rudy about it."

The excitement and joy in her face were contagious. Even Junior, young as he was, was happy to see his Tita not only smiling, but most of the time singing.

The first order of business was for her to make a list of things to bring home for this holiday. A few inches had been added to her size, so certain dresses, shoes, and other articles of clothing no longer fit.

Ellen and Ana were happy to know that a plan was shaping up. They were looking forward to seeing their friend refreshed and focused on what was best for her life.

Her holiday to the Philippines was not a secret to Glen. In fact, Glen was looking forward to seeing her go and coming back early. This way, he could validate Lily's interest in him. Whether it was incidental or intentional, Ellen, Ana, and Dana were all not available to drive her to airport when the day of her flight arrived. By natural selection, Glen was more than willing to drive Lily to the airport. It was the only option.

Her departure time was 4:30 p.m. Lily's two large travel bags were nicely tucked at the back of Glen's 2000 Sienna. Junior was aware of what was going on and his eyes were getting wet knowing that Lily was leaving him. She assured him that they would be together again in a few weeks' time. Hard as it was, Lily took Junior on her lap and sang their song—Bah-Bah Black Sheep. The song comforted Junior, but her heart was having difficulty saying goodbye.

Glen's patience was remarkable. He'd been waiting in the van for almost forty-five minutes. Her final check to make sure she hadn't forgotten anything, along with all her never-ending goodbyes, took a large bite of her time. Dana and Rudy were excited that she would have a good time at home. They were also happy at the prospect of her making one of the most important decisions of her life—to entertain Glen or to wait for Mike.

There weren't many people in line at the check-in booth at the airport. After five minutes of waiting, Lily was able to secure her boarding pass. Glen had thirty more minutes to talk to Lily before boarding. He was very respectful of whatever Lily's decision would be. He was willing to wait and do whatever it took for her to accept him as he was.

Lily stopped at the door of the departure terminal gate and faced Glen. He got the clue and Lily welcomed his hug warmly. The way Glen gave her a peck on the cheek reminded her of Mike's gesture the last time they had been together.

"Thank you very much for driving me over here," Lily said with misty eyes.

"I'll do anything you want," Glen said. "Just let me know. Take care of yourself. I love you, Lily." He wore a half-smile, but the other half of his face was sad.

Glen stood outside the gate and watched as Lily lost herself in the midst of the crowd. It was a meeting full of confusion and uncertainty.

Details of this holiday had been made known to Mike ahead of time, but Mike didn't even tell her his detailed plan. What Lily knew was that both she and Mike would be arriving on the same day, and they would leave Philippines on the same day, too.

Mike was so elusive, but he was also honest, caring, and thoughtful. The lambing Filipino side of Mike was what she longed for, but on the other hand, Glen's presence was comforting. Her mind was juggling between Mike and Glen when she was distracted by the shaking and trembling of the plane taking off along the runway. It was a warm day outside, and green grass surrounded the airport. She marveled at the beauty of the city as it disappeared over the horizon. She lay down her head, put on the headset, and watched the onboard movie.

Vancouver International Airport was big. The hardest part of traveling was making sure she knew where she was going and what gate her next flight was departing from. If one was a slow walker, it could take ten to fifteen minutes to walk from the domestic terminal to the international flights terminal. Lily's walk was calculated. She had to wait two hours for her 5:30 flight.

The gate leading to the ticket booth was already crowded with people. Boxes secured by coloured string were everywhere. There were even a few pieces of luggage wrapped with strips of blue denim. Small kids were busy playing tag. Dialects from various parts of the Philippines were heard from all corners.

A sense of relief settled over Lily when she found out that almost every corner of the departure lobby was filled with Filipinos. The food court was located nearby, just on the south side of the Philippine Airline check-in counter. Facing west of the food stalls were couches, located at the base of a wooden sculpture. Those couches were so inviting that Lily, with a can of pop and bag of potato chips, sank her tired body down into one. The comfort of warm leather combined with the calming effect of her snack, made Lily fell asleep. She didn't care about anything that was going on around her. The place was so comfortable that many people were just slumbering, and others were already snoring.

The squeaking sound of luggage being pulled around by passengers in a hurry awakened her. The time on the wall indicated that she had to get up and rush to the line of people checking in. It took a while for her to collect and compose herself. She was relieved knowing that the plane was not fully booked. This implied that people would be free to roam around and sleep in any position they were comfortable with.

She located her seat and comfortably placed her carry-on bag in the overhead compartment. It took thirty minutes for everybody to get settled in. Lily's mind was again working through the details of the decision she would soon have to make. Glen's thoughtfulness and proximity to her were the most appealing factors about him, and they always stuck out in her mind. On the other hand, Mike's gentleness was just as persistent. She simply couldn't ignore these traits.

The plane taxied down the runway, waiting to take off. Seated alone next to the window, Lily sank down comfortably in the softness of the plane seat. In a few minutes, the plane took off without her knowing it. She was very tired and, more than anything else, her body needed sleep.

Dinner was served two hours after the plane left Vancouver. It was a nice feeling having Filipino delicacies on board. She was reminded of her old place in the Philippines. The aroma that filled the plane reminded her of her parents' house. She settled for a warm green tea. She kept one of the desserts in a sealed plastic container. The movie was not that interesting.

The blanket given to her earlier by the stewardess was warm and soothing. Once her food tray was cleaned up, Lily stood up and headed for the washroom. In the last row was a strange-looking man whom she couldn't help but look at. His hat covered his face. Though the plane light was dim, he had his sunglass on. Something about him was suspicious. His mustache and beard were unkempt and his hair stuck out in all directions.

Lily entered the washroom and stayed there longer than she needed to. When she heard somebody outside waiting to use the cubicle, she exited with relief and a smile on her face. Without glancing around, especially in the direction of the strange-looking man, she went straight to her seat. She pulled up the blanket from the empty seat at her left and covered herself for another snooze.

Just as she was about to close her eyes, a white envelope caught her attention. It was sitting on top of her bag. She couldn't remember pulling out any paper—or letter, for that matter—from her carry-on bag. Out of curiosity, Lily opened the unsealed envelope with the name "Lia" printed on it. Her heart started to beat faster and blood rose to her head. Sweating in an air-conditioned plane was unusual. The plane had logged five hours in the air and the other passengers were either watching the movie or snoring.

Flight attendants at the back were taking their break. Lily could hear their gossiping session. She was tempted to read the letter, but she hesitated to do it. Instead, she stood up and walked toward the attendants happily talking at the back. The guy was snoring and covered with the blanket.

Good for him, thought Lily. She asked the attendants about the letter.

"No, madam," the youngest-looking one said. "We don't know who placed that letter beside your seat."

Without any further discussion, she went back to her seat. The letter was probably from a previous passenger and had been left there unknowingly. But the letter was not sealed, and there was no return address—just the name "Lia." Indeed, she supposed that might have referred to her. Still curious, she pulled out the paper and spread it over her lap. Her sleepy eyes opened wide and all her being was awakened by what was written on the paper. Was it a joke or something deliberately planned?

The letter read:

Dear Lia,

You might be wondering about this letter. A friend of mine, Mark, from Edmonton, is also flying home for his wedding. I emailed this letter and requested him to deliver it to you on the plane. I told him about your flight plan and coincidentally he was on the same flight as you. Mark and his fiancée will be married in Boracay in the fourth week of July. A week after the wedding, the couple will fly back to Canada. From Edmonton they will move to Fort McMurray, where Mark's new assignment is located.

He will surely be looking for you on the plane and invite you to his wedding. He's a very clean-cut, nice guy. His seat is somewhere in the back rows. He knows your seat number. One thing is for sure, he will look for you. I'm just hoping he will not forget you. He's one of my trusted coworkers and friends who visited me last year here in the Middle East.

I just want you to know how much I long to meet and see my girlfriend in Calgary. Unfortunately, you seem to have been unable to locate her. Don't feel badly about it. Someday, I am hoping to meet her for good.

I hope you have the most unforgettable holiday in the Philippines.

Mike

P.S. Once you're back in Calgary, remember your promise to look for Lily, okay?

She was sweating and nervous. Mark was somewhere in the back rows of the plane?

Lily stood up and pretended to go to the washroom. This time, the strange-looking man was not there. His stuff was scattered around his seat, though.

Though the plane's lights were dim, Lily could see that the other passengers in the area were mostly seniors and women. Nowhere was there a clean-cut man that matched Mark's description.

The washroom door was locked. She waited with her back facing the door of the cubicle. Suddenly, the washroom door opened and the strange-looking man rushed out in a hurry. He was too quick for Lily to get a good look at his face.

There were goose bumps on her arms and her heart was thumping in her chest, all at the scent of the strange-looking man. She couldn't remember why that scent was so familiar to her. Just as she expected, the strange-looking man took his seat, opened the paper, and in no time was snoring again.

Lily stepped into the washroom, locked the door, and once again read the letter. When she finished, she folded the letter and started to wash her hands. Then she noticed the messy sink. The strange-looking man had shaved his mustache and beard and hadn't even bothered to clean up the sink properly.

"What an irresponsible person," she whispered to herself.

But wait, how was the messy sink related to the guy in the letter? Lily's mind was in a tailspin. She straightened up, made sure her appearance looked impressive, and then rushed out to where the strange-looking man was sitting. His ball cap and sunglass were still on, but he no longer had a beard or mustache.

He was clean-cut, indeed!

For sure, he has to be Mark, she said to herself.

"Excuse me!" said Lily. "I'm looking for Mark."

His head stayed down, but his hands were moving. Lily was certain the man was awake.

"Pardon me?" was his response. He came to life, then cleared the seat next to him. He offered for her to sit down. Without hesitation, Lily took a leap of faith and sat beside him. They needed light to have a good talk and see each other.

"I'm Mark. And you are Lia?" he asked.

"Yes, I'm Lia." Her legs were shaking and more goose bumps appeared.

Mark switched on the reading light and took off his ball cap and sunglass while Lily spread out the letter on her lap. When their eyes met, Lily let out a cry of joy. Two flight attendants heard her and rushed to where they were sitting. Lily's voice of joy had been heard all the way up in the front rows. People started to panic, but they were quickly calmed down by the rest of the crew.

"I know that scent!" she said, remembering where she'd smelled it before. He was clean-cut, a nice guy... "How could you ever do this thing to me?" Lily blurted out as she made eye contact with Mike.

Mike gave her his best smile. "I'm inviting you to my wedding in Boracay, and to Fort McMurray. Are you coming?"

Tears of joy flowed down Lily's reddened cheeks. They shared a passionate kiss.

The plane was still in the air for more than three hours before landing. In the remaining time, Lily was able to use Mike's laptop to send emails to Ana, Ellen, Dana, and Nora. She felt badly for Glen, but she was also pretty sure that Nora would be happy to meet him, when the time came. She could imagine how pleased and surprised Dana would be to hear the story. She also sent an email to Pastor Willy. Lily made up her mind to follow Christ into the waters of baptism. Her encounter with God the last time she had attended church was one worth remembering. For the first time in her life, she entrusted her faith into a person and not to a religion. God's faithfulness to her had always been there, even in the midst of uncertainties.

"Sir, madam, the plane landed thirty minutes ago," the flight attendant said, standing next to them. "You're the only two left aboard."

"Oops!" they said in unison. As a couple, they shared a good, hearty laugh.